18 x 1/21

Mail Order Ninja Vol. 1
written by Joshua Elder
illustrated by Erich Owen

Retouch and Lettering - Alyson Stetz
Production Artist - Alyson Stetz
Cover Design - Chris Tjaslma

Editor - Rob Valois
Digital Imaging Manager - Chris Buford
Pre-Production Supervisor - Lucas Rivera
Art Director - Anne Marie Horne
Managing Editor - Lindsey Johnston
Editorial Directior - Jeremy Ross
Production Manager - Elisabeth Brizzi
VP of Production - Ron Klamert
Editor-in-Chief - Rob Tokar
Publisher - Mike Kiley
President and C.O.O. - John Parker
C.E.O. and Chief Creative Officer - Stuart Levy

A **TOKYOPOP** Manga

TOKYOPOP Inc.
5900 Wilshire Blvd. Suite 2000
Los Angeles, CA 90036

E-mail: info@TOKYOPOP.com
Come visit us online at www.TOKYOPOP.com

ISBN: 978-1-59816-728-6

First TOKYOPOP printing: July 2006
10 9 8 7 6 5 4 3 2
Printed in the USA

MAIL ORDER NINJA

VOL. 1

WRITTEN BY JOSHUA ELDER
ILLUSTRATED BY ERICH OWEN

HAMBURG // LONDON // LOS ANGELES // TOKYO

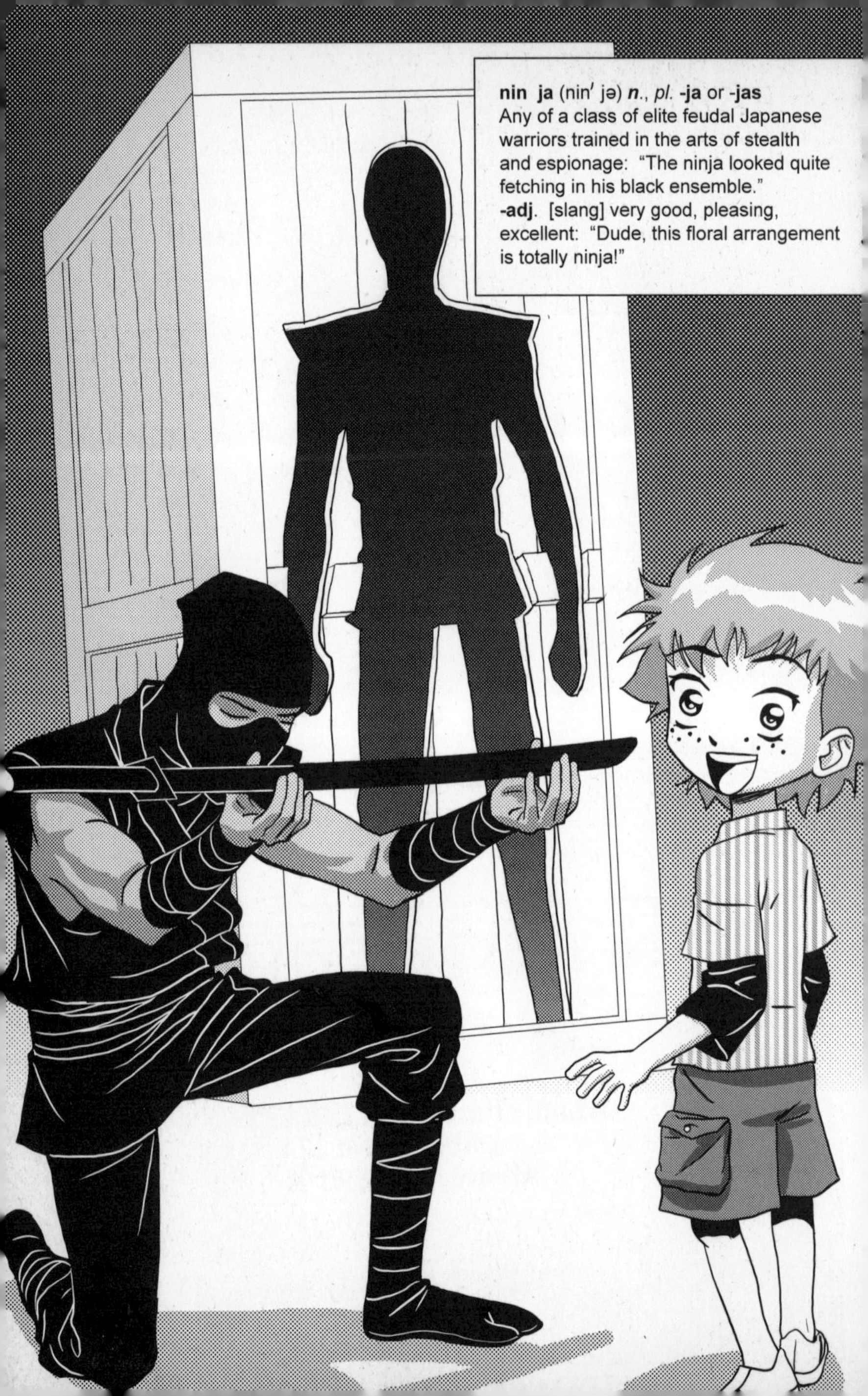
nin ja (nin′ jə) n., pl. -ja or -jas
Any of a class of elite feudal Japanese warriors trained in the arts of stealth and espionage: "The ninja looked quite fetching in his black ensemble."
-adj. [slang] very good, pleasing, excellent: "Dude, this floral arrangement is totally ninja!"

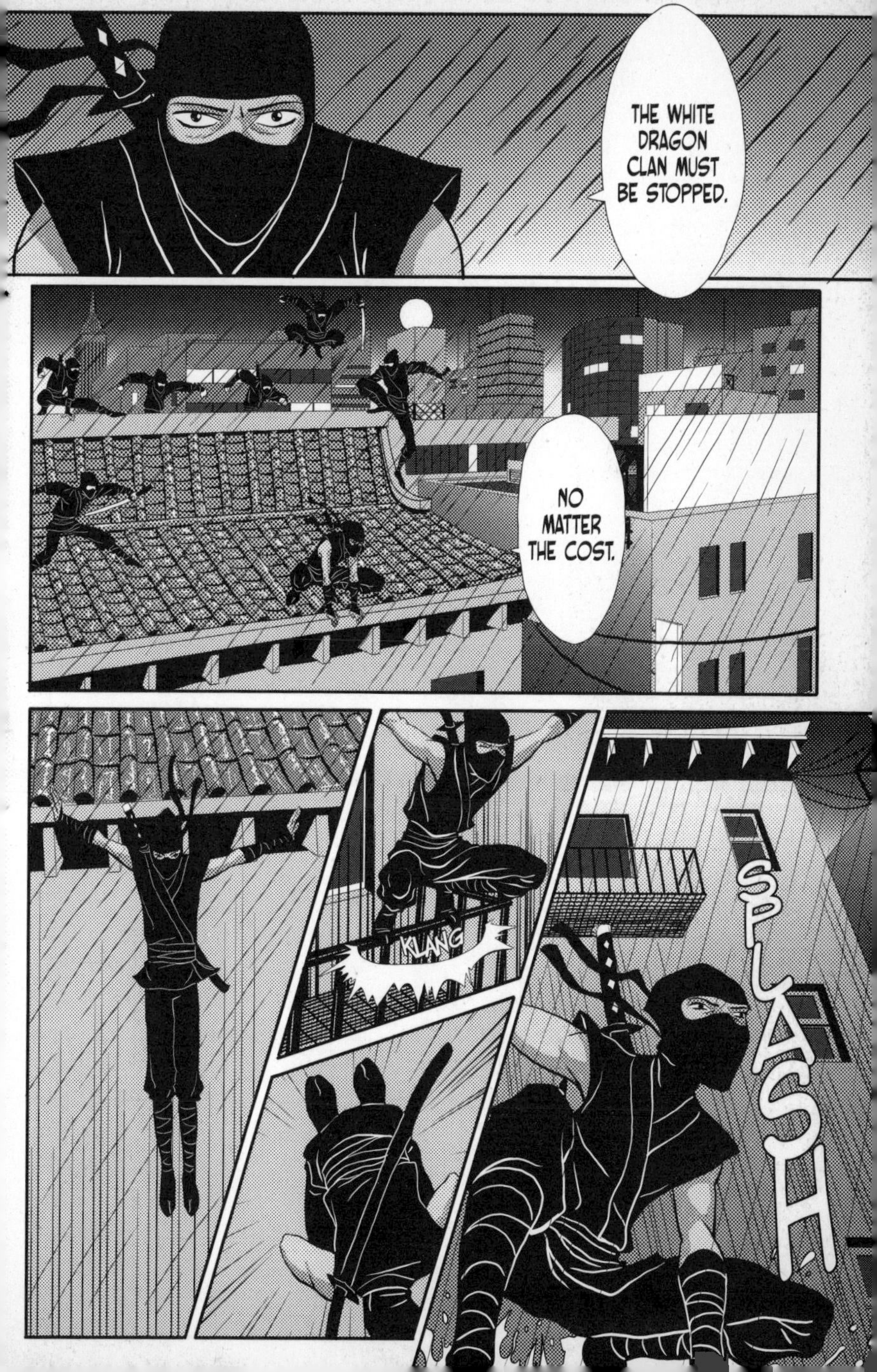
THE WHITE DRAGON CLAN MUST BE STOPPED.
NO MATTER THE COST.
KLANG
SPLASH

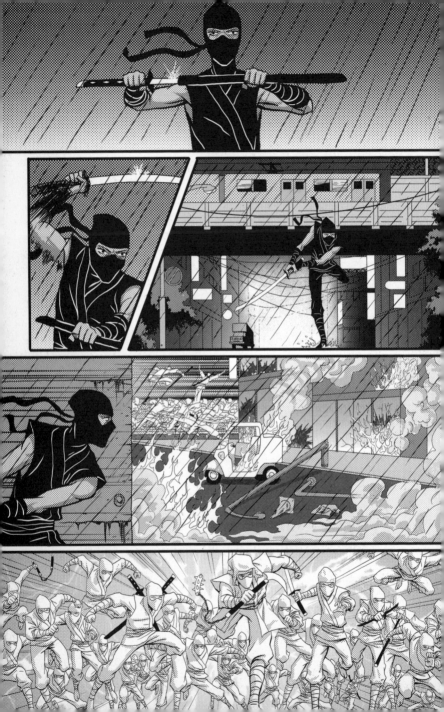

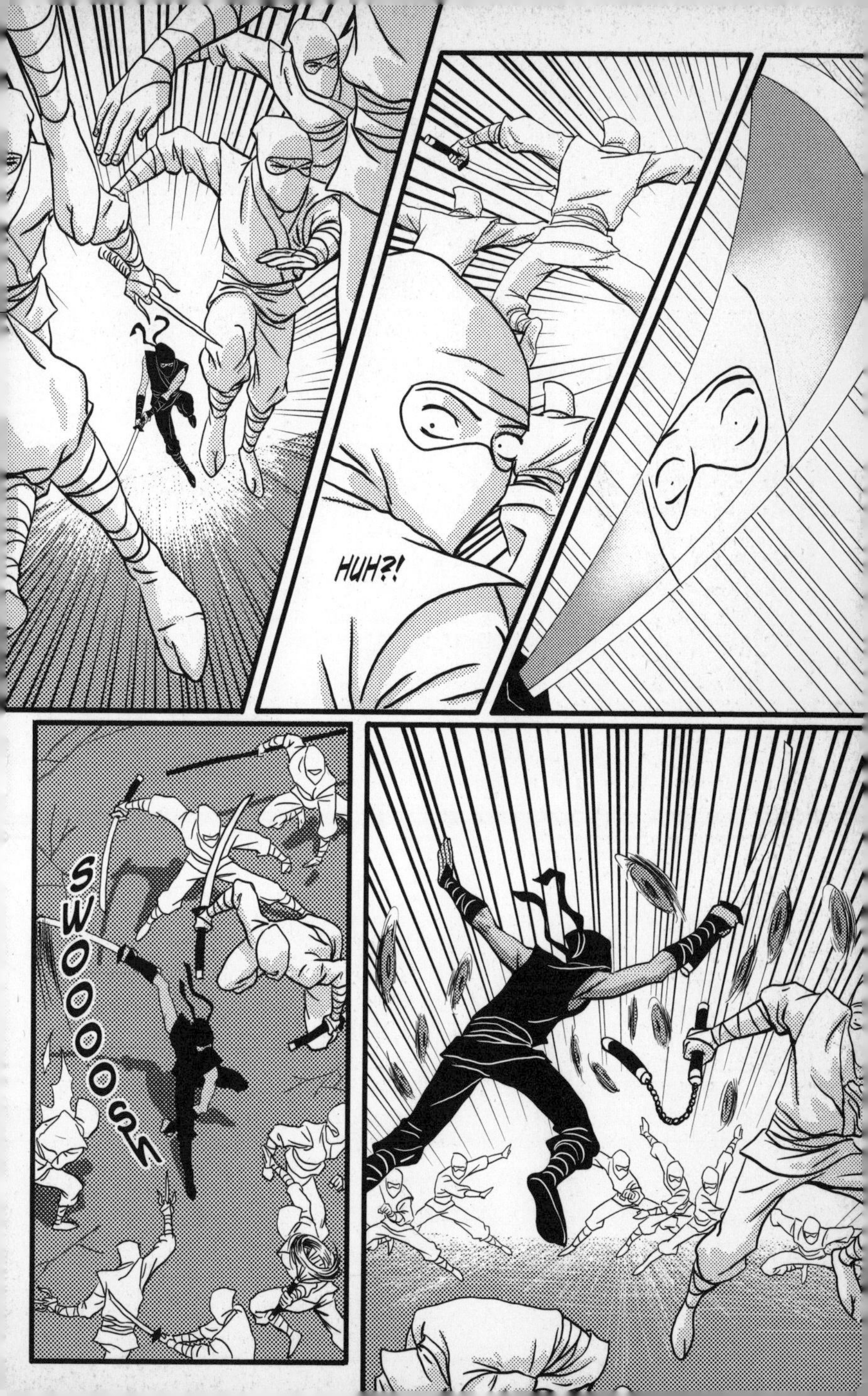
HUH?!
SWOOOOSH

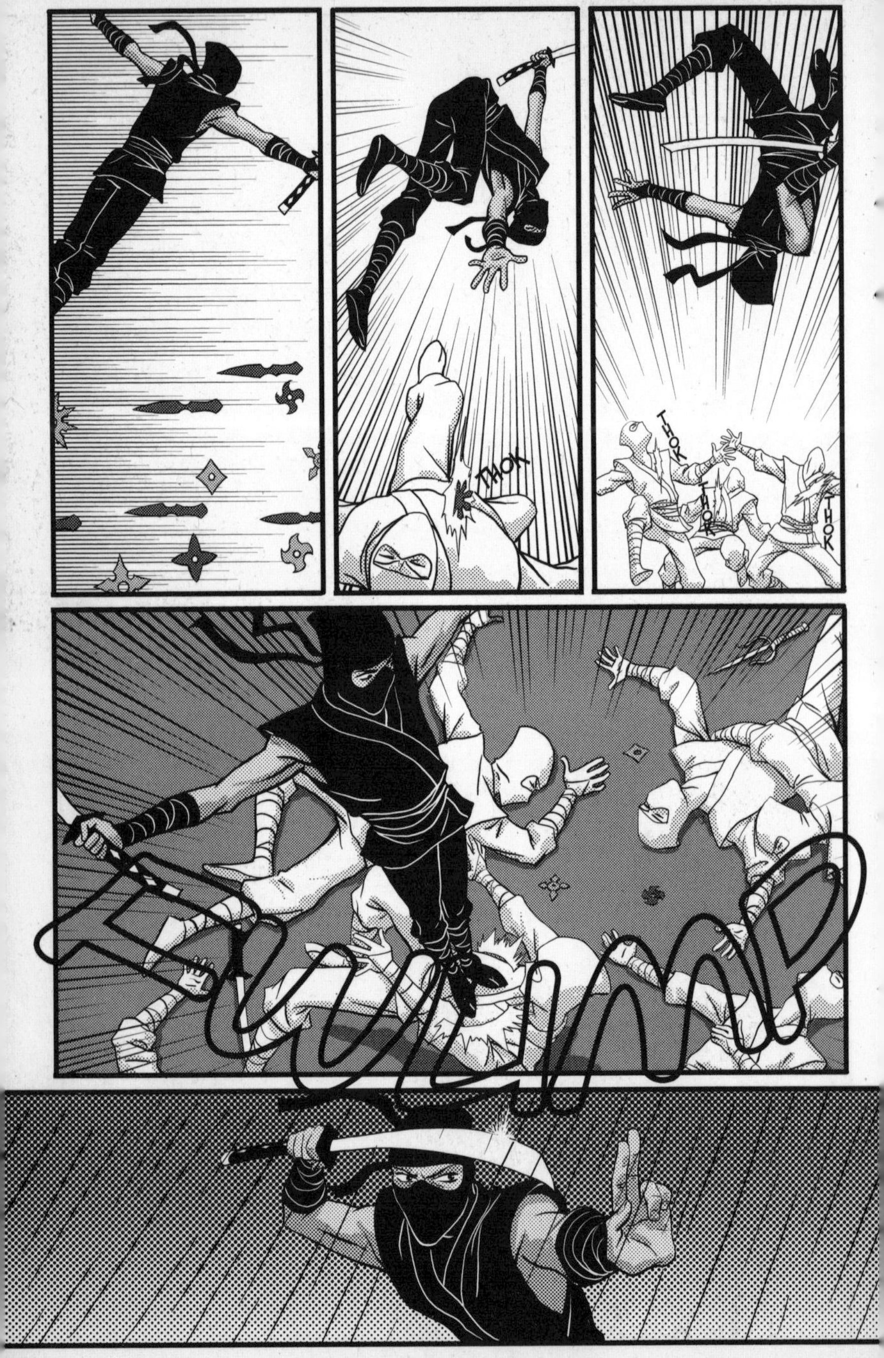
THOK
THOK
THOK
THOK
THUMP

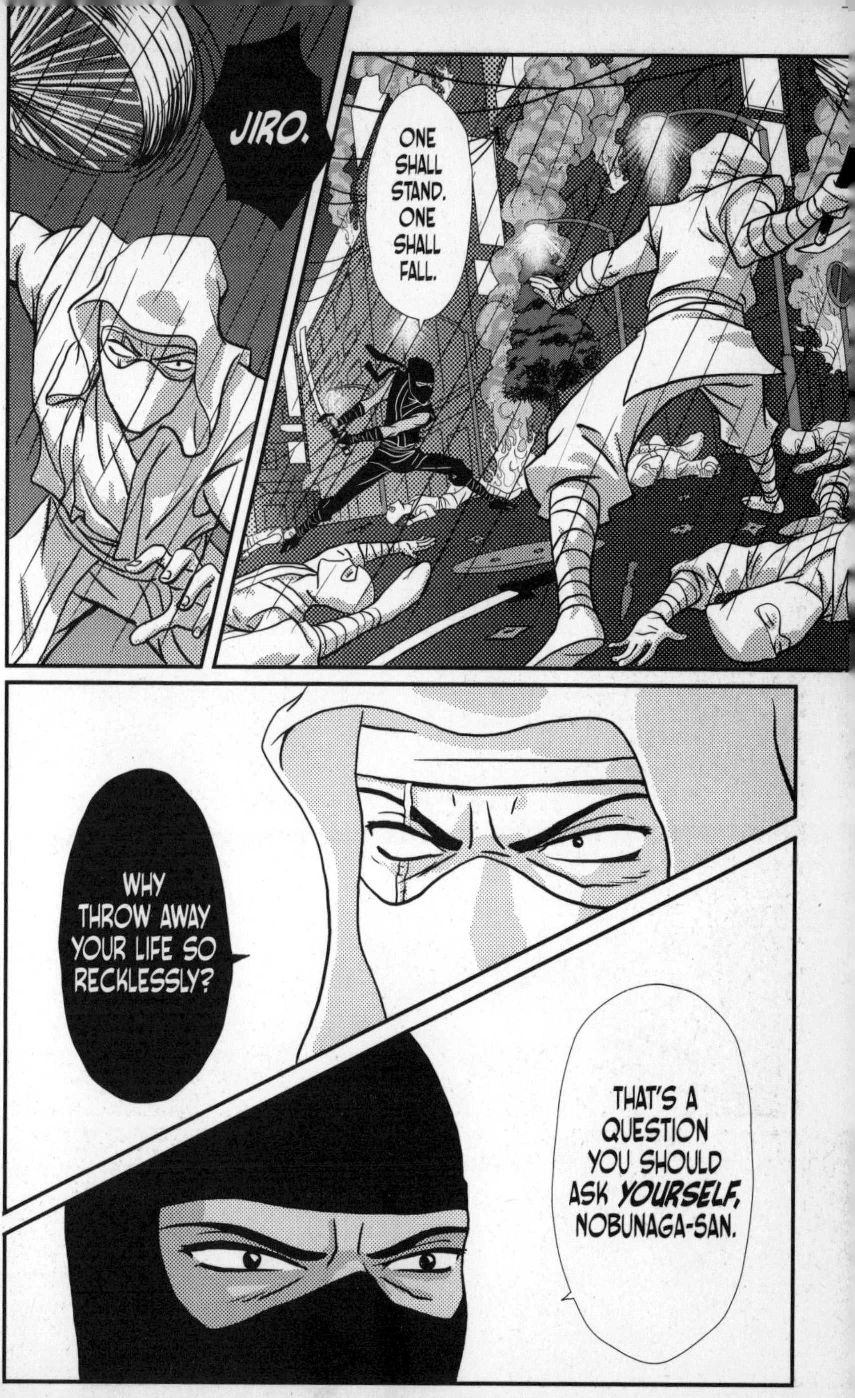
JIRO.
ONE SHALL STAND. ONE SHALL FALL.
WHY THROW AWAY YOUR LIFE SO RECKLESSLY?
THAT'S A QUESTION YOU SHOULD ASK YOURSELF, NOBUNAGA-SAN.

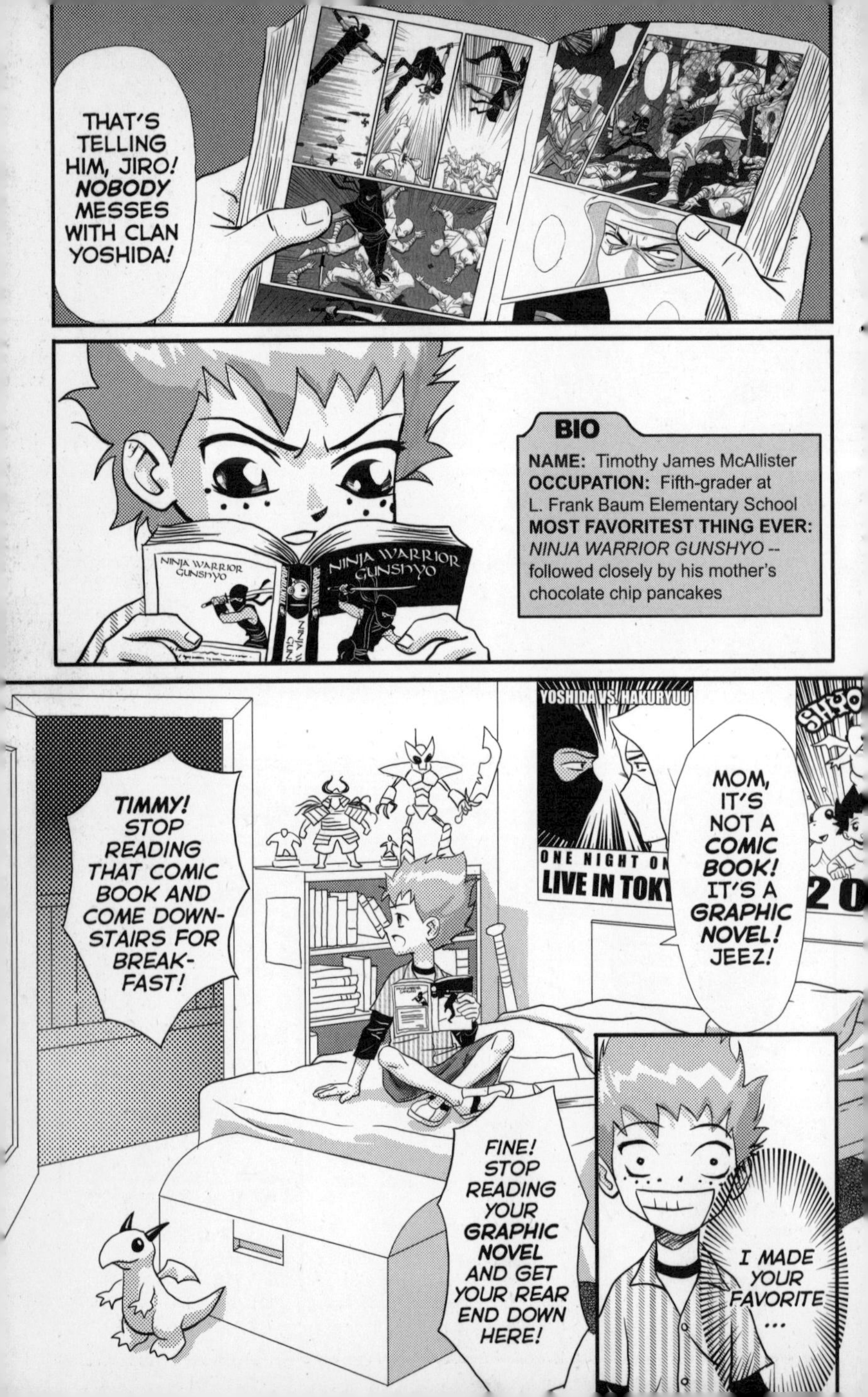
THAT'S TELLING HIM, JIRO! *NOBODY* MESSES WITH CLAN YOSHIDA!
NINJA WARRIOR GUNSHYO
NINJA WARRIOR GUNSHYO
BIO
NAME: Timothy James McAllister
OCCUPATION: Fifth-grader at L. Frank Baum Elementary School
MOST FAVORITEST THING EVER: *NINJA WARRIOR GUNSHYO* -- followed closely by his mother's chocolate chip pancakes
TIMMY! STOP READING THAT COMIC BOOK AND COME DOWN-STAIRS FOR BREAK-FAST!
YOSHIDA VS. HAKURYUU
ONE NIGHT O
LIVE IN TOK
MOM, IT'S NOT A *COMIC BOOK!* IT'S A *GRAPHIC NOVEL!* JEEZ!
FINE! STOP READING YOUR *GRAPHIC NOVEL* AND GET YOUR REAR END DOWN HERE!
I MADE YOUR FAVORITE ...

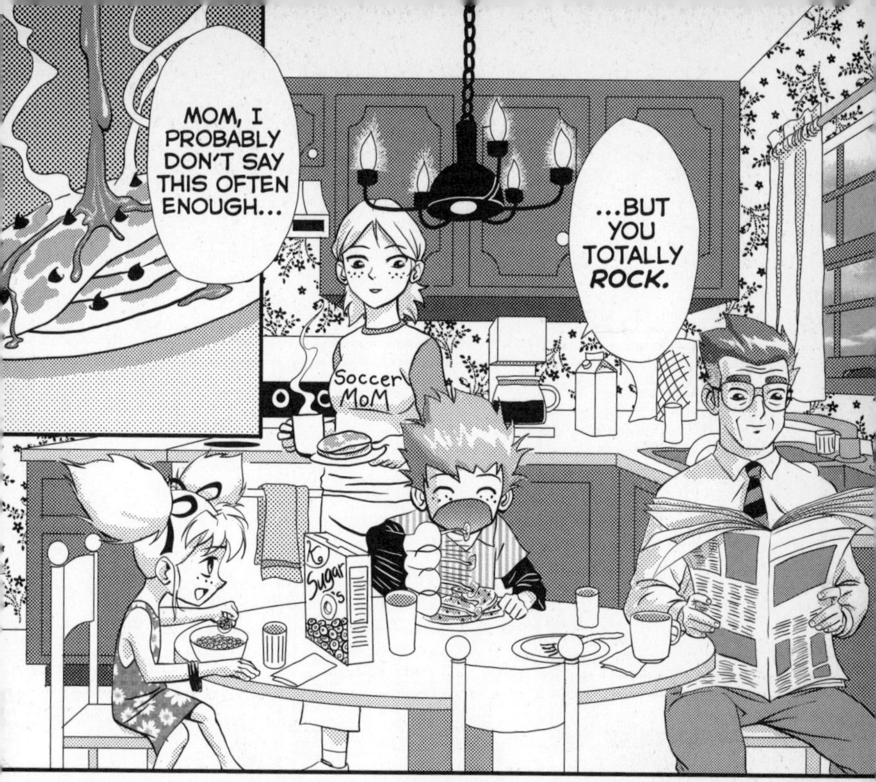
MOM, I PROBABLY DON'T SAY THIS OFTEN ENOUGH...
...BUT YOU TOTALLY *ROCK.*
Soccer MoM
Sugar O's

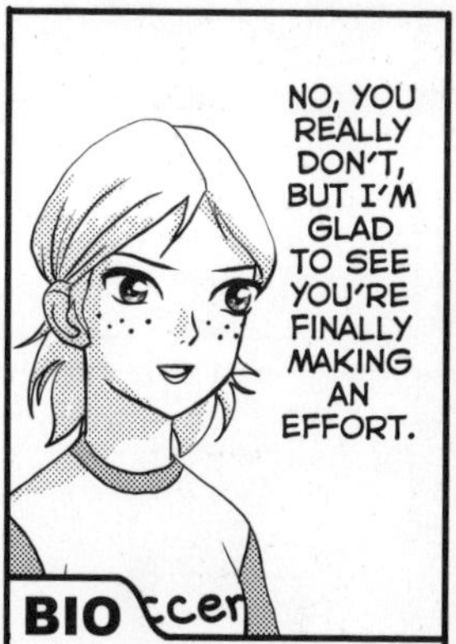
NO, YOU REALLY DON'T, BUT I'M GLAD TO SEE YOU'RE FINALLY MAKING AN EFFORT.
BIO

NAME: Carol McAllister
OCCUPATION: Homemaker
KNOWN ALIASES: Mom

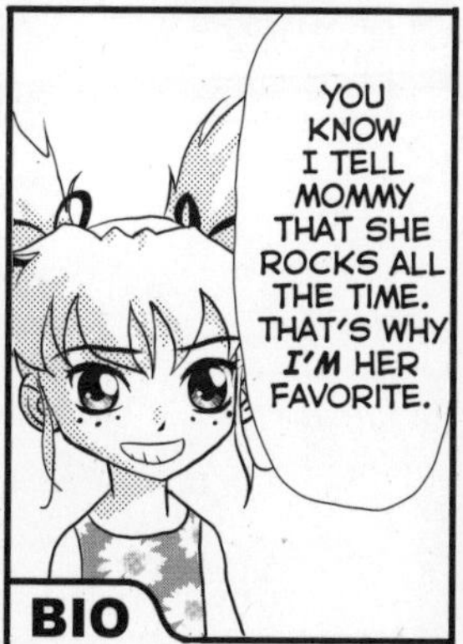
YOU KNOW I TELL MOMMY THAT SHE ROCKS ALL THE TIME. THAT'S WHY *I'M* HER FAVORITE.
BIO

NAME: Lindsay McAllister
OCCUPATION: Bratty little sister
HOBBIES: Annoying her big brother, sucking up to mom and dad, playing with her dollies

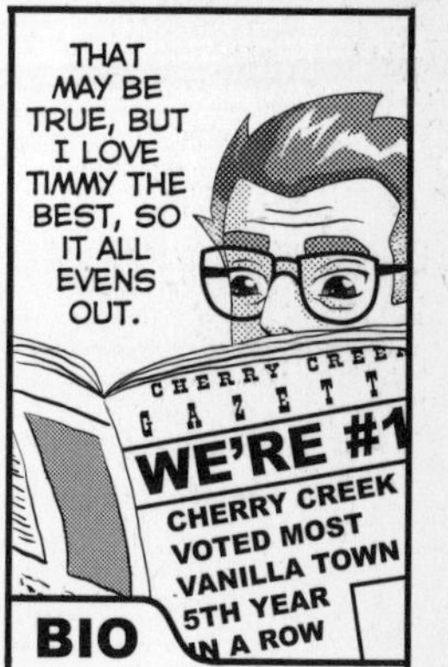
THAT MAY BE TRUE, BUT I LOVE TIMMY THE BEST, SO IT ALL EVENS OUT.
CHERRY CREEK VOTED MOST VANILLA TOWN 5TH YEAR IN A ROW
BIO

NAME: Thomas McAllister, aka Dad
OCCUPATION: Accountant
OTHER OCCUPATION: Bassist for local funk band, Funk Upside Your Head

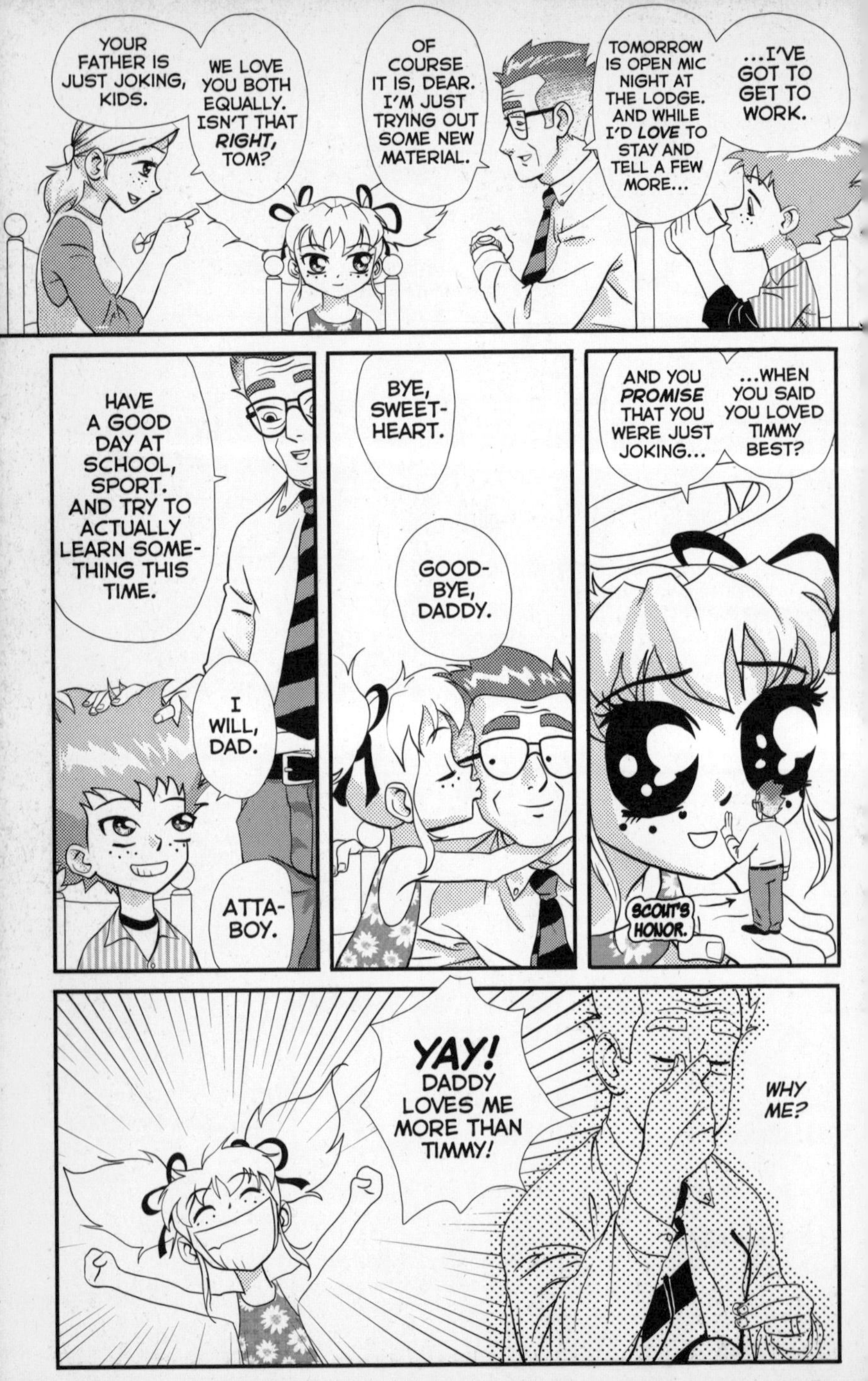
YOUR FATHER IS JUST JOKING, KIDS.
WE LOVE YOU BOTH EQUALLY. ISN'T THAT *RIGHT,* TOM?
OF COURSE IT IS, DEAR. I'M JUST TRYING OUT SOME NEW MATERIAL.
TOMORROW IS OPEN MIC NIGHT AT THE LODGE. AND WHILE I'D *LOVE* TO STAY AND TELL A FEW MORE...
...I'VE GOT TO GET TO WORK.
HAVE A GOOD DAY AT SCHOOL, SPORT. AND TRY TO ACTUALLY LEARN SOMETHING THIS TIME.
I WILL, DAD.
ATTA-BOY.
BYE, SWEET-HEART.
GOOD-BYE, DADDY.
AND YOU *PROMISE* THAT YOU WERE JUST JOKING...
...WHEN YOU SAID YOU LOVED TIMMY BEST?
SCOUT'S HONOR.
YAY! DADDY LOVES ME MORE THAN TIMMY!
WHY ME?

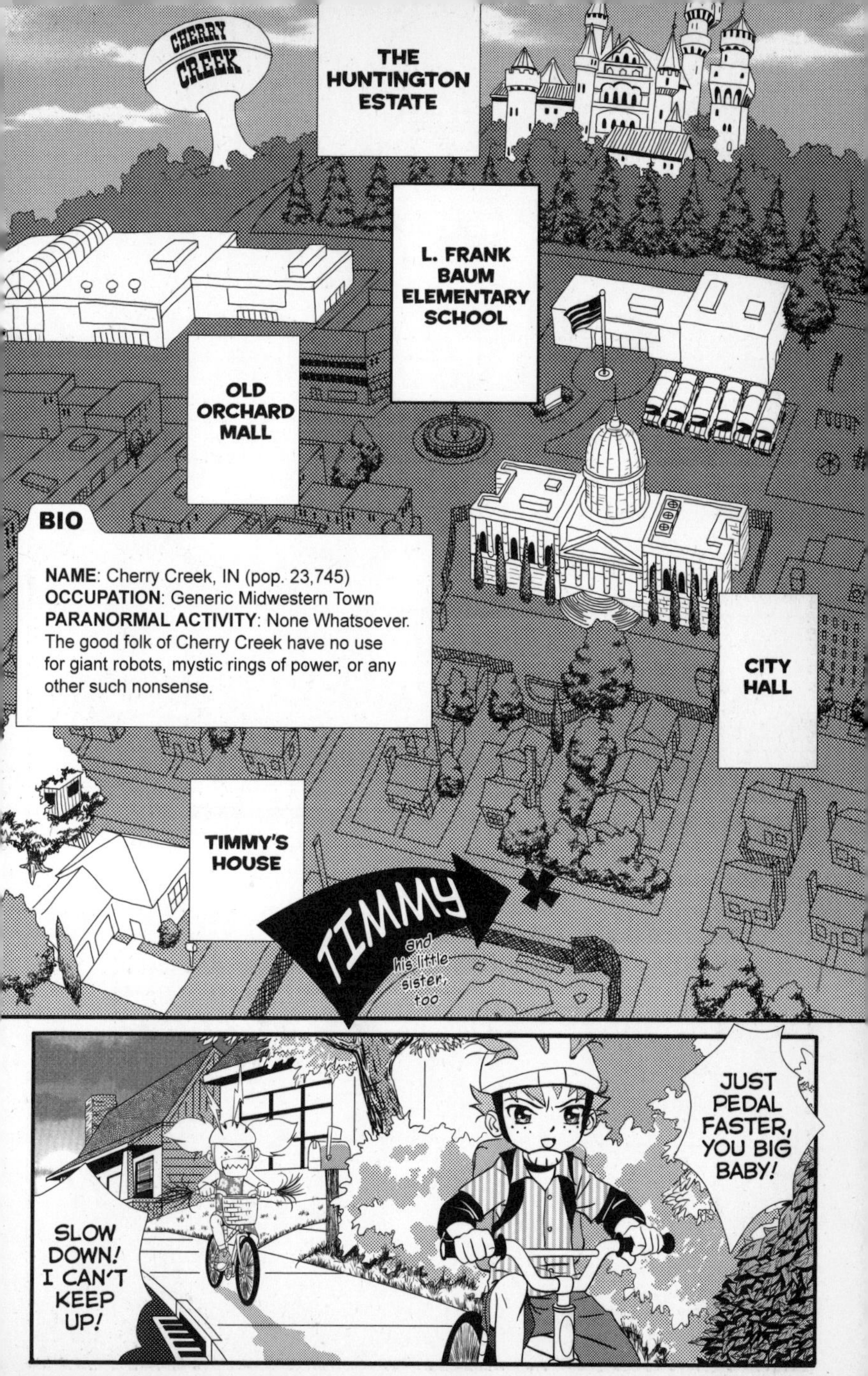
CHERRY CREEK
THE HUNTINGTON ESTATE
L. FRANK BAUM ELEMENTARY SCHOOL
OLD ORCHARD MALL
BIO
NAME: Cherry Creek, IN (pop. 23,745)
OCCUPATION: Generic Midwestern Town
PARANORMAL ACTIVITY: None Whatsoever. The good folk of Cherry Creek have no use for giant robots, mystic rings of power, or any other such nonsense.
CITY HALL
TIMMY'S HOUSE
TIMMY
and his little sister, too
SLOW DOWN! I CAN'T KEEP UP!
JUST PEDAL FASTER, YOU BIG BABY!

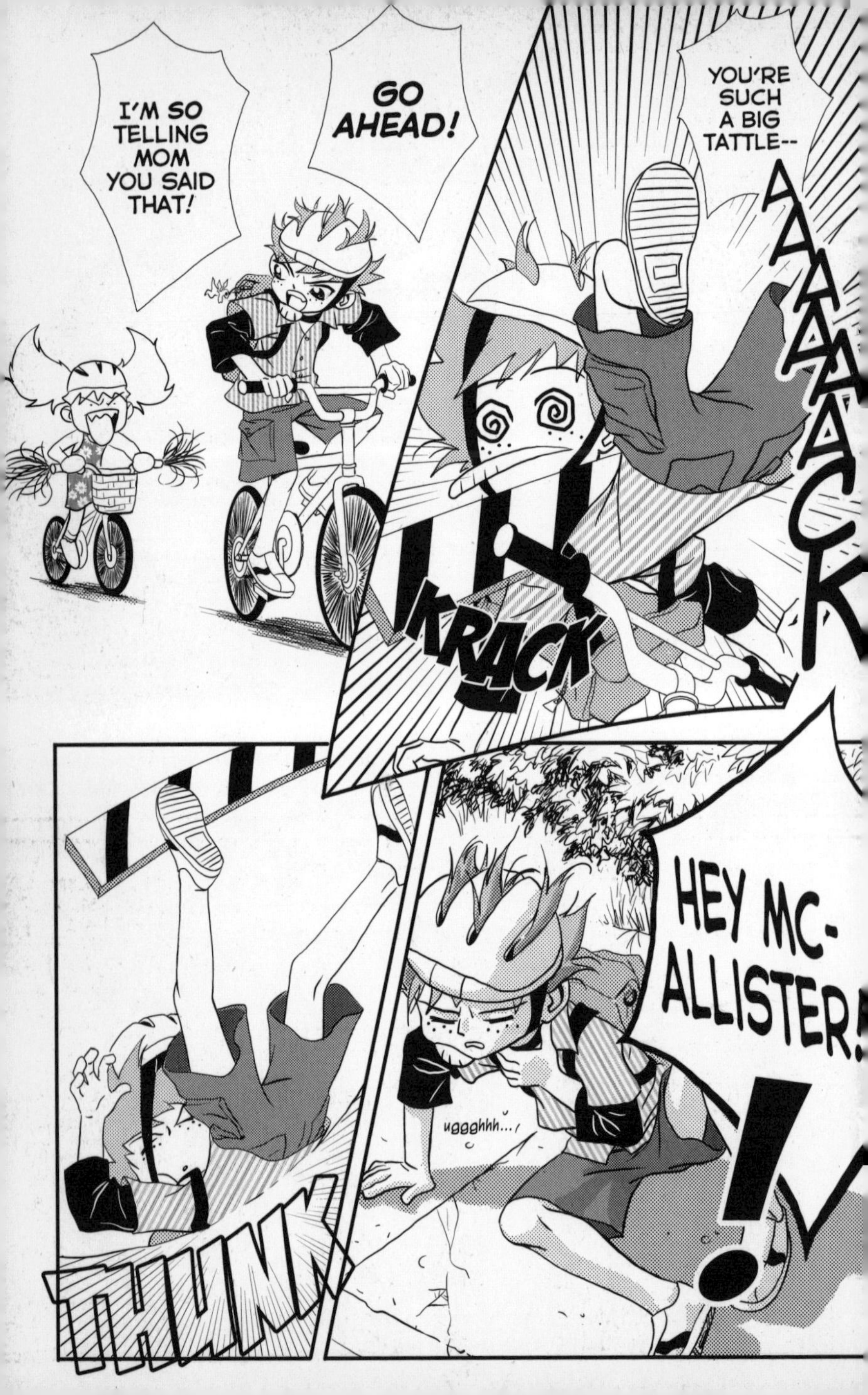
I'M SO TELLING MOM YOU SAID THAT!
GO AHEAD!
YOU'RE SUCH A BIG TATTLE--
AAAAAACK
KRACK
THUNK
HEY MC-ALLISTER!
uggghhh...!

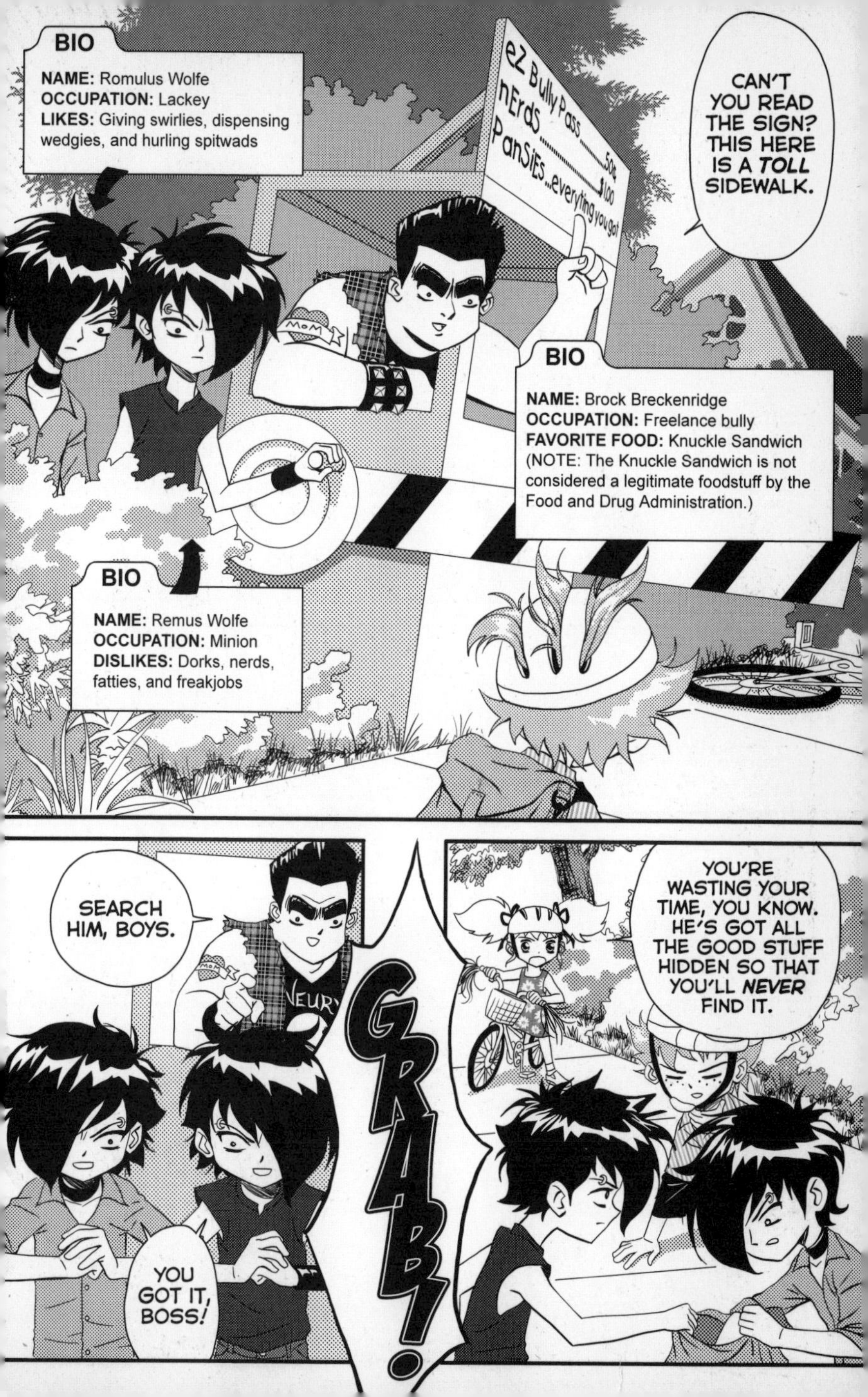

BIO
NAME: Romulus Wolfe
OCCUPATION: Lackey
LIKES: Giving swirlies, dispensing wedgies, and hurling spitwads
eZ Bully Pass
nErds........50¢
PanSiEs........$1.00
...everyting you got
CAN'T YOU READ THE SIGN? THIS HERE IS A *TOLL* SIDEWALK.
MoM
BIO
NAME: Brock Breckenridge
OCCUPATION: Freelance bully
FAVORITE FOOD: Knuckle Sandwich
(NOTE: The Knuckle Sandwich is not considered a legitimate foodstuff by the Food and Drug Administration.)
BIO
NAME: Remus Wolfe
OCCUPATION: Minion
DISLIKES: Dorks, nerds, fatties, and freakjobs
SEARCH HIM, BOYS.
YOU GOT IT, BOSS!
GRAB!
YOU'RE WASTING YOUR TIME, YOU KNOW. HE'S GOT ALL THE GOOD STUFF HIDDEN SO THAT YOU'LL *NEVER* FIND IT.

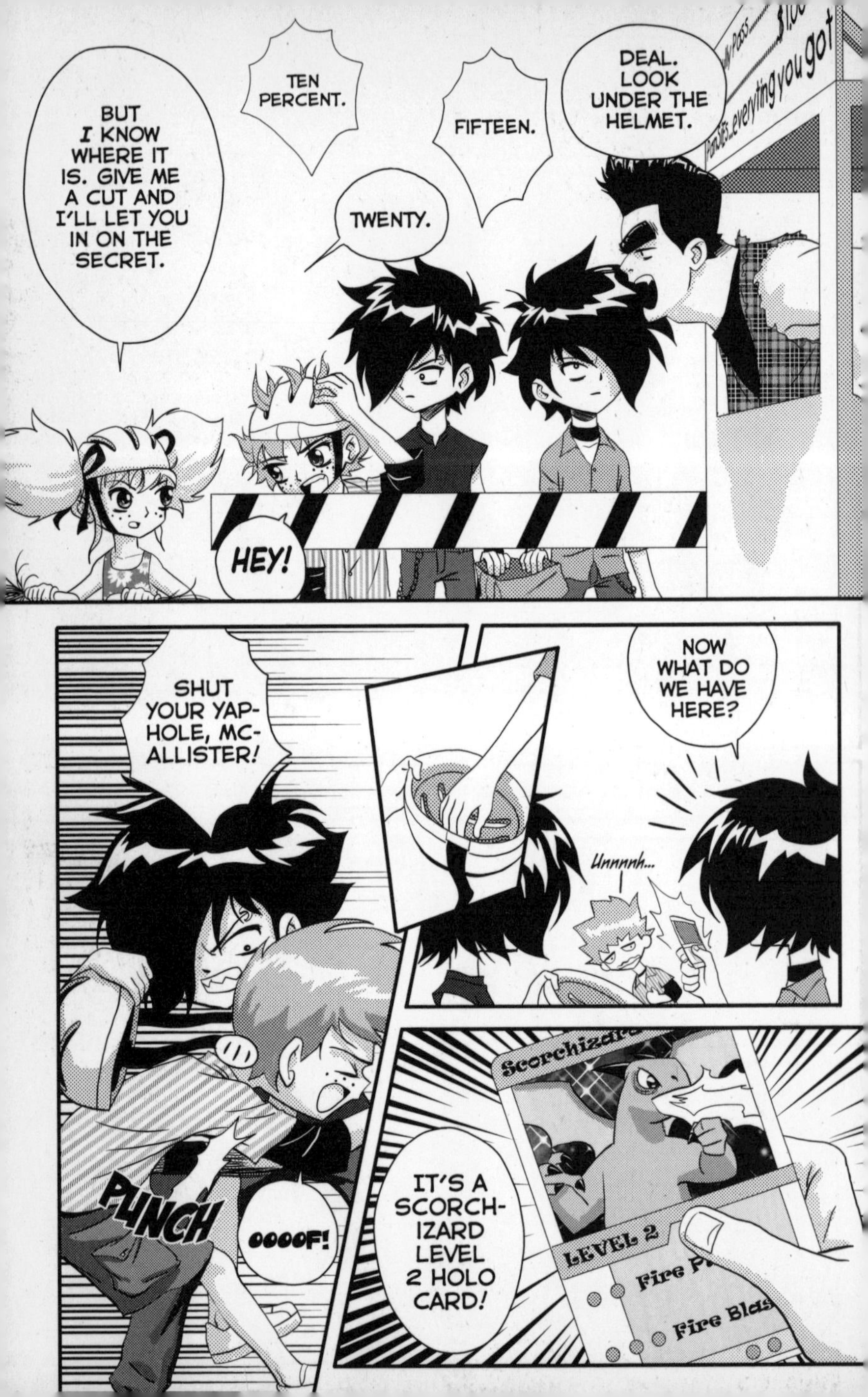

BUT I KNOW WHERE IT IS. GIVE ME A CUT AND I'LL LET YOU IN ON THE SECRET.
TEN PERCENT.
TWENTY.
FIFTEEN.
DEAL. LOOK UNDER THE HELMET.
HEY!
SHUT YOUR YAP-HOLE, MC-ALLISTER!
PUNCH
OOOOF!
NOW WHAT DO WE HAVE HERE?
Unnnnh...
IT'S A SCORCH-IZARD LEVEL 2 HOLO CARD!
LEVEL 2

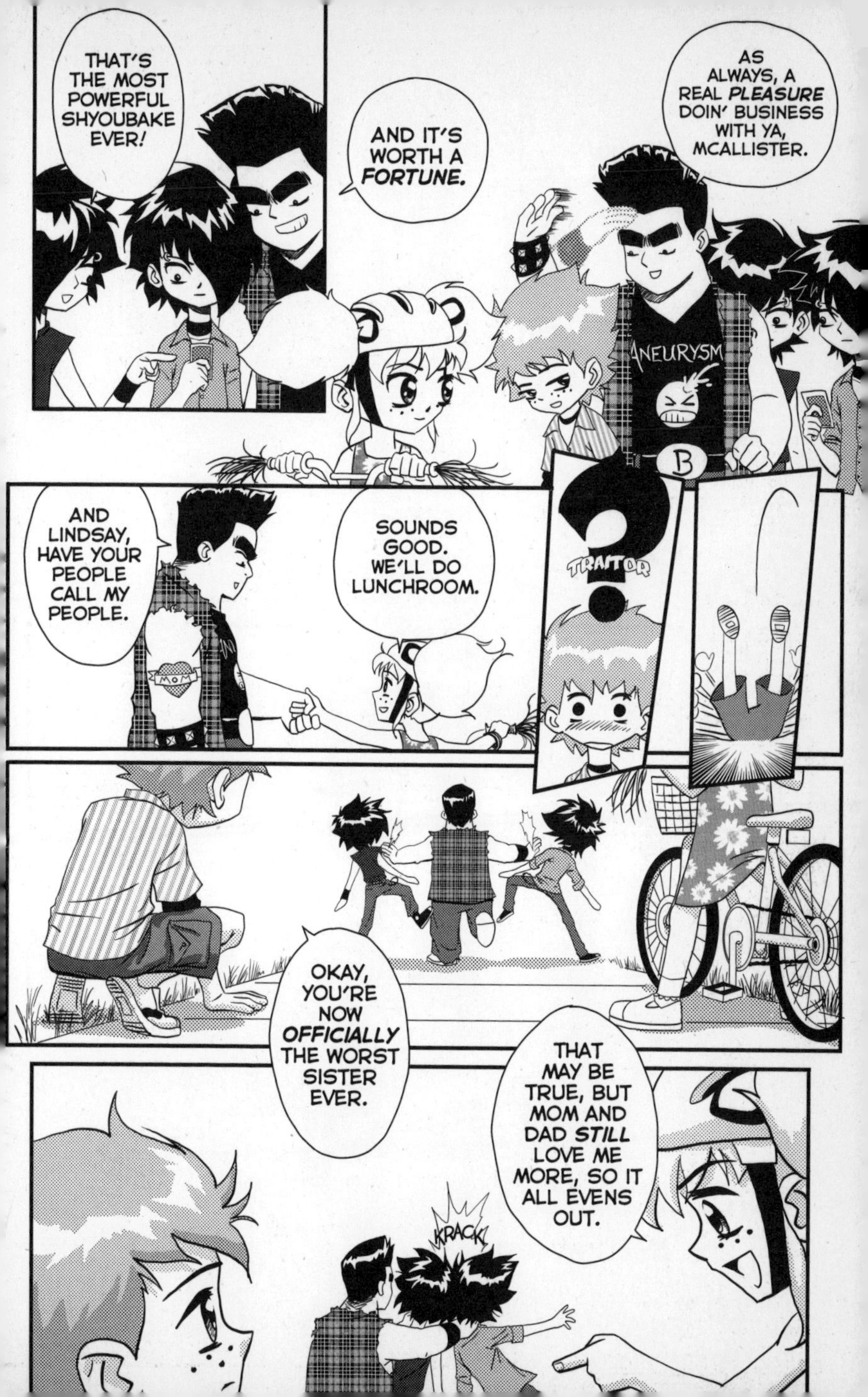
THAT'S THE MOST POWERFUL SHYOUBAKE EVER!
AND IT'S WORTH A FORTUNE.
AS ALWAYS, A REAL PLEASURE DOIN' BUSINESS WITH YA, MCALLISTER.
ANEURYSM
B
AND LINDSAY, HAVE YOUR PEOPLE CALL MY PEOPLE.
MOM
SOUNDS GOOD. WE'LL DO LUNCHROOM.
TRAITOR
OKAY, YOU'RE NOW OFFICIALLY THE WORST SISTER EVER.
THAT MAY BE TRUE, BUT MOM AND DAD STILL LOVE ME MORE, SO IT ALL EVENS OUT.
KRACK

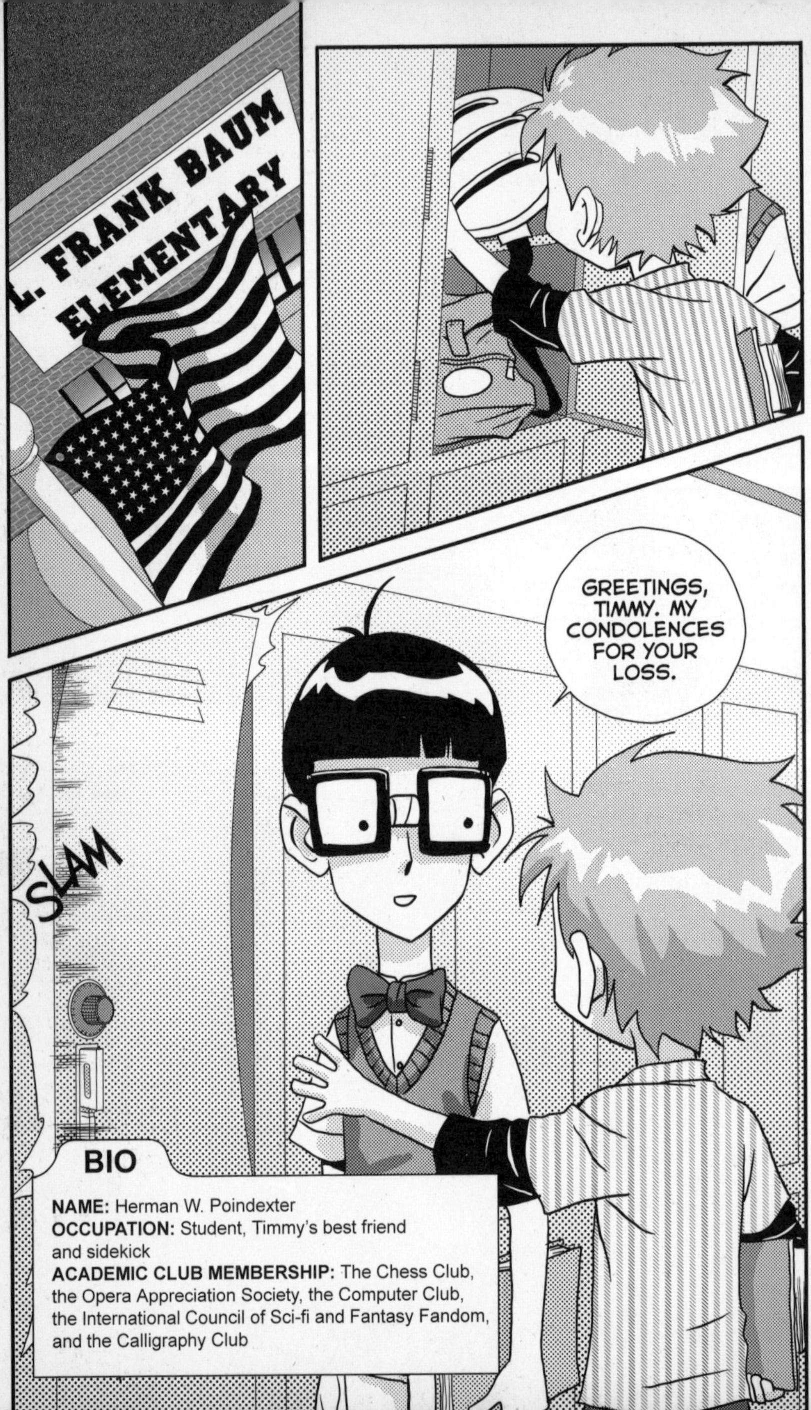
L. FRANK BAUM
ELEMENTARY
GREETINGS, TIMMY. MY CONDOLENCES FOR YOUR LOSS.
SLAM
BIO
NAME: Herman W. Poindexter
OCCUPATION: Student, Timmy's best friend and sidekick
ACADEMIC CLUB MEMBERSHIP: The Chess Club, the Opera Appreciation Society, the Computer Club, the International Council of Sci-fi and Fantasy Fandom, and the Calligraphy Club

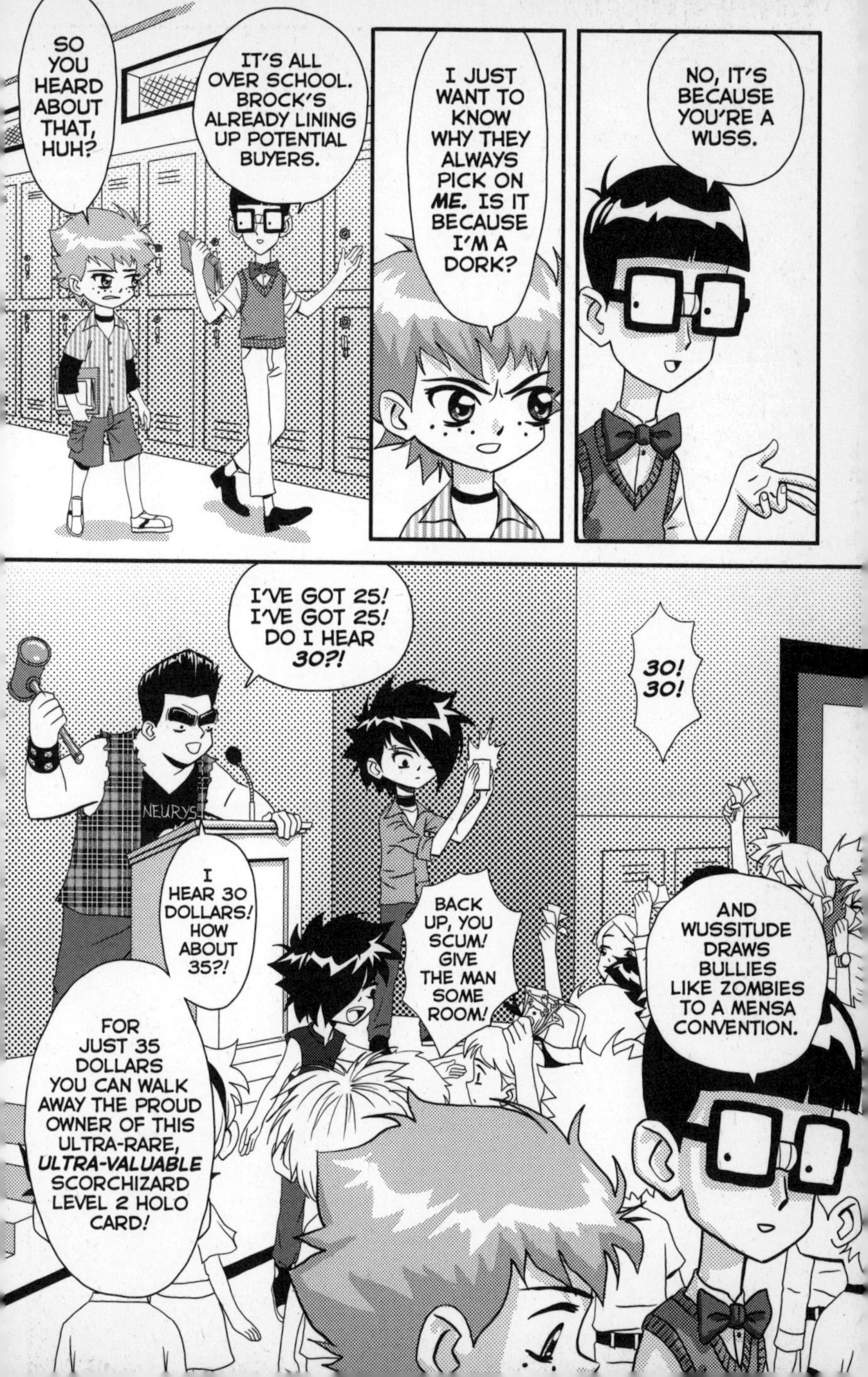
SO YOU HEARD ABOUT THAT, HUH?
IT'S ALL OVER SCHOOL. BROCK'S ALREADY LINING UP POTENTIAL BUYERS.
I JUST WANT TO KNOW WHY THEY ALWAYS PICK ON *ME.* IS IT BECAUSE I'M A DORK?
NO, IT'S BECAUSE YOU'RE A WUSS.
I'VE GOT 25! I'VE GOT 25! DO I HEAR *30?!*
30! 30!
NEURYS
I HEAR 30 DOLLARS! HOW ABOUT 35?!
BACK UP, YOU SCUM! GIVE THE MAN SOME ROOM!
AND WUSSITUDE DRAWS BULLIES LIKE ZOMBIES TO A MENSA CONVENTION.
FOR JUST 35 DOLLARS YOU CAN WALK AWAY THE PROUD OWNER OF THIS ULTRA-RARE, *ULTRA-VALUABLE* SCORCHIZARD LEVEL 2 HOLO CARD!

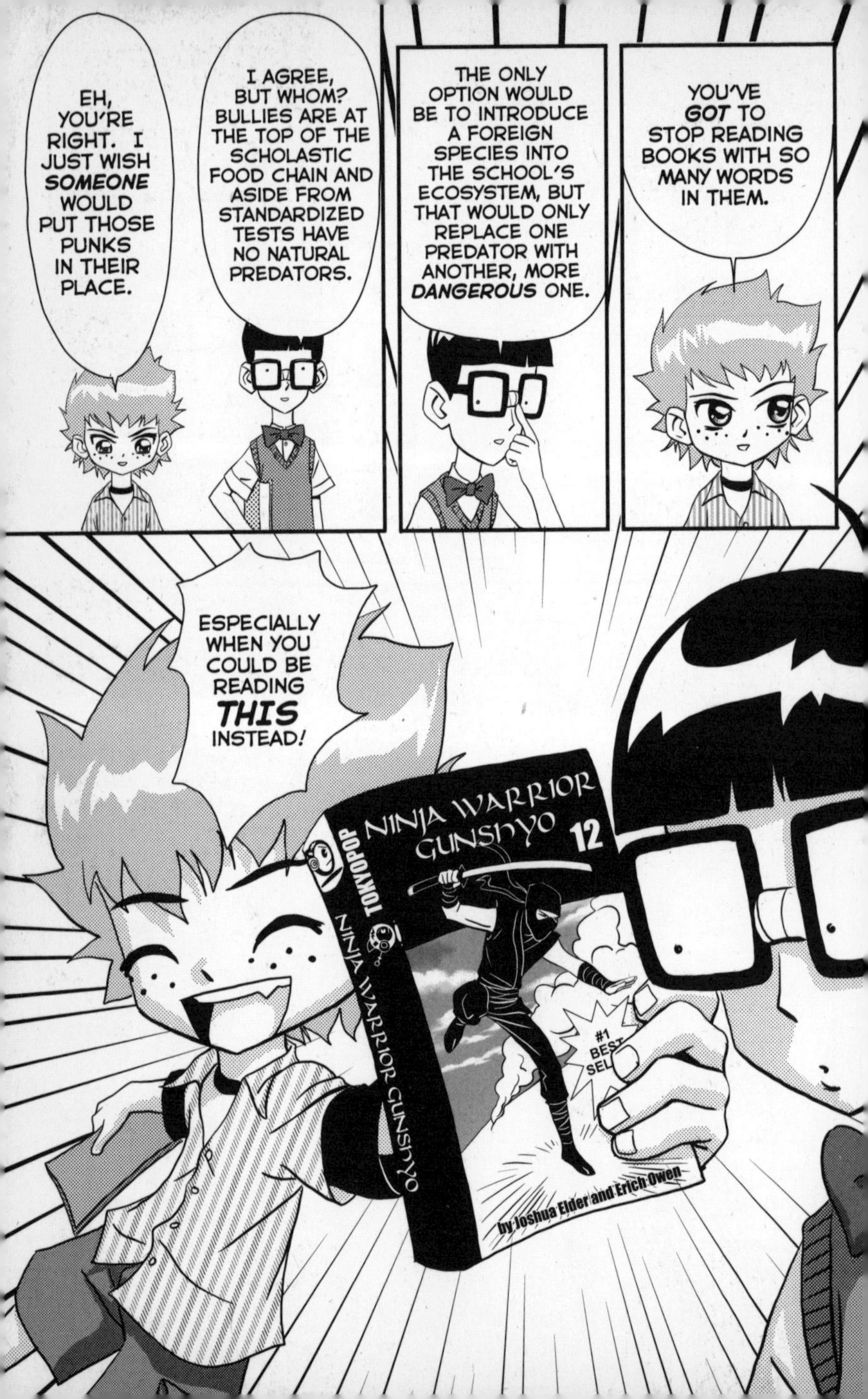
EH, YOU'RE RIGHT. I JUST WISH SOMEONE WOULD PUT THOSE PUNKS IN THEIR PLACE.
I AGREE, BUT WHOM? BULLIES ARE AT THE TOP OF THE SCHOLASTIC FOOD CHAIN AND ASIDE FROM STANDARDIZED TESTS HAVE NO NATURAL PREDATORS.
THE ONLY OPTION WOULD BE TO INTRODUCE A FOREIGN SPECIES INTO THE SCHOOL'S ECOSYSTEM, BUT THAT WOULD ONLY REPLACE ONE PREDATOR WITH ANOTHER, MORE DANGEROUS ONE.
YOU'VE GOT TO STOP READING BOOKS WITH SO MANY WORDS IN THEM.
ESPECIALLY WHEN YOU COULD BE READING THIS INSTEAD!
NINJA WARRIOR GUNSHYO 12
TOKYOPOP
NINJA WARRIOR GUNSHYO
by Joshua Elder and Erich Owen

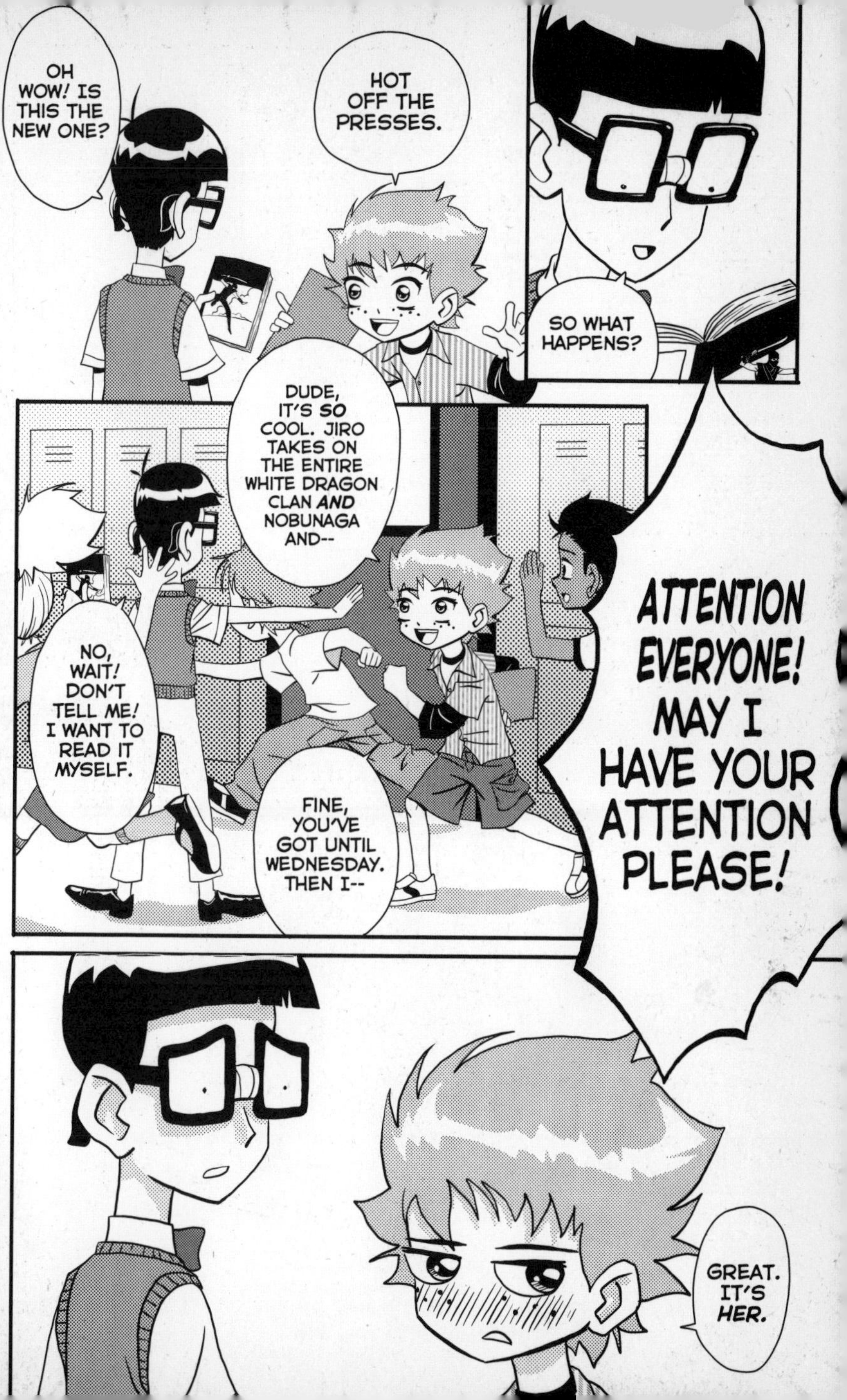
OH WOW! IS THIS THE NEW ONE?
HOT OFF THE PRESSES.
SO WHAT HAPPENS?
DUDE, IT'S *SO* COOL. JIRO TAKES ON THE ENTIRE WHITE DRAGON CLAN *AND* NOBUNAGA AND--
NO, WAIT! DON'T TELL ME! I WANT TO READ IT MYSELF.
FINE, YOU'VE GOT UNTIL WEDNESDAY. THEN I--
ATTENTION EVERYONE! MAY I HAVE YOUR ATTENTION PLEASE!
GREAT. IT'S *HER*.

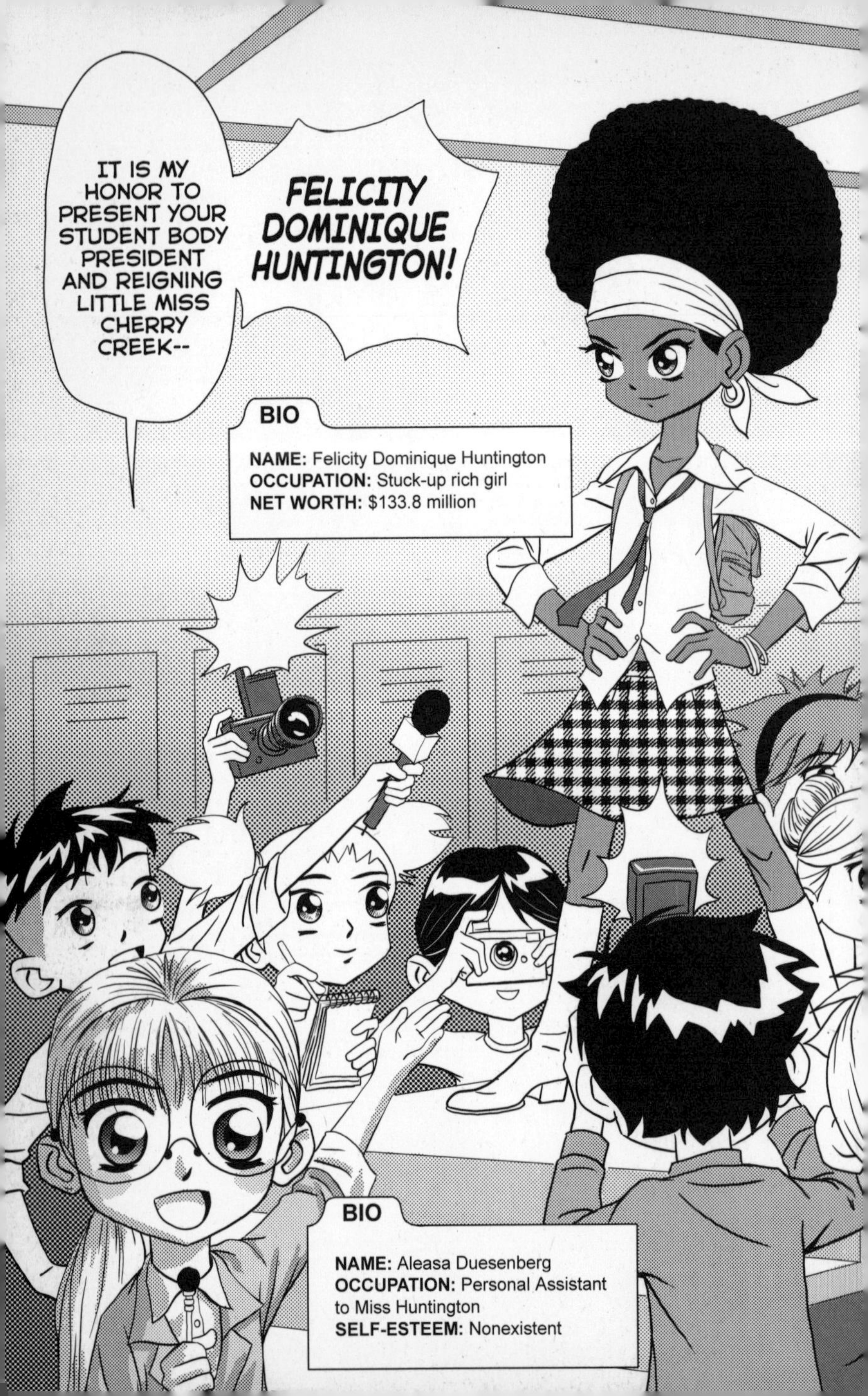
IT IS MY HONOR TO PRESENT YOUR STUDENT BODY PRESIDENT AND REIGNING LITTLE MISS CHERRY CREEK--
FELICITY DOMINIQUE HUNTINGTON!
BIO
NAME: Felicity Dominique Huntington
OCCUPATION: Stuck-up rich girl
NET WORTH: $133.8 million
BIO
NAME: Aleasa Duesenberg
OCCUPATION: Personal Assistant to Miss Huntington
SELF-ESTEEM: Nonexistent

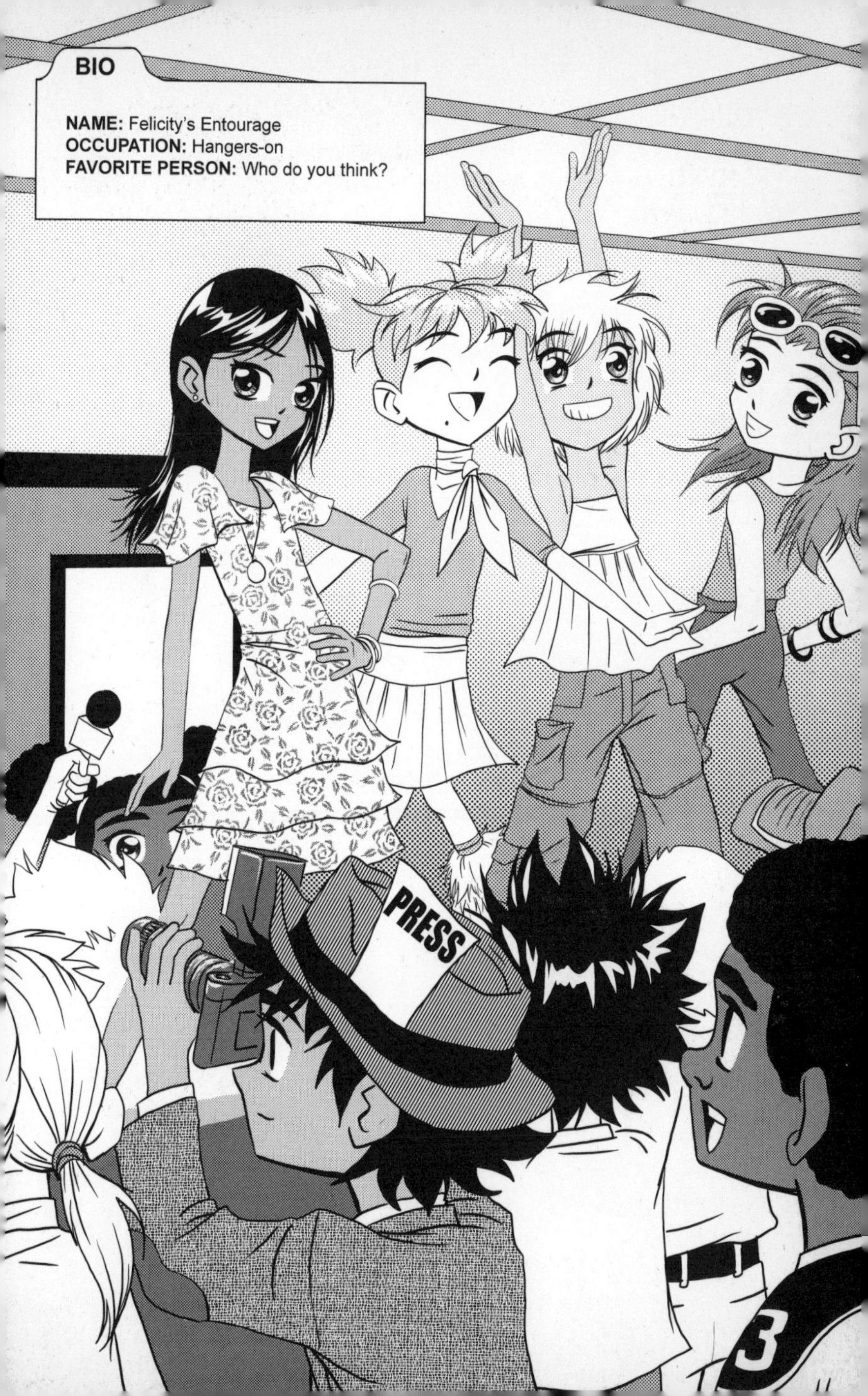
BIO
NAME: Felicity's Entourage
OCCUPATION: Hangers-on
FAVORITE PERSON: Who do you think?
PRESS
3

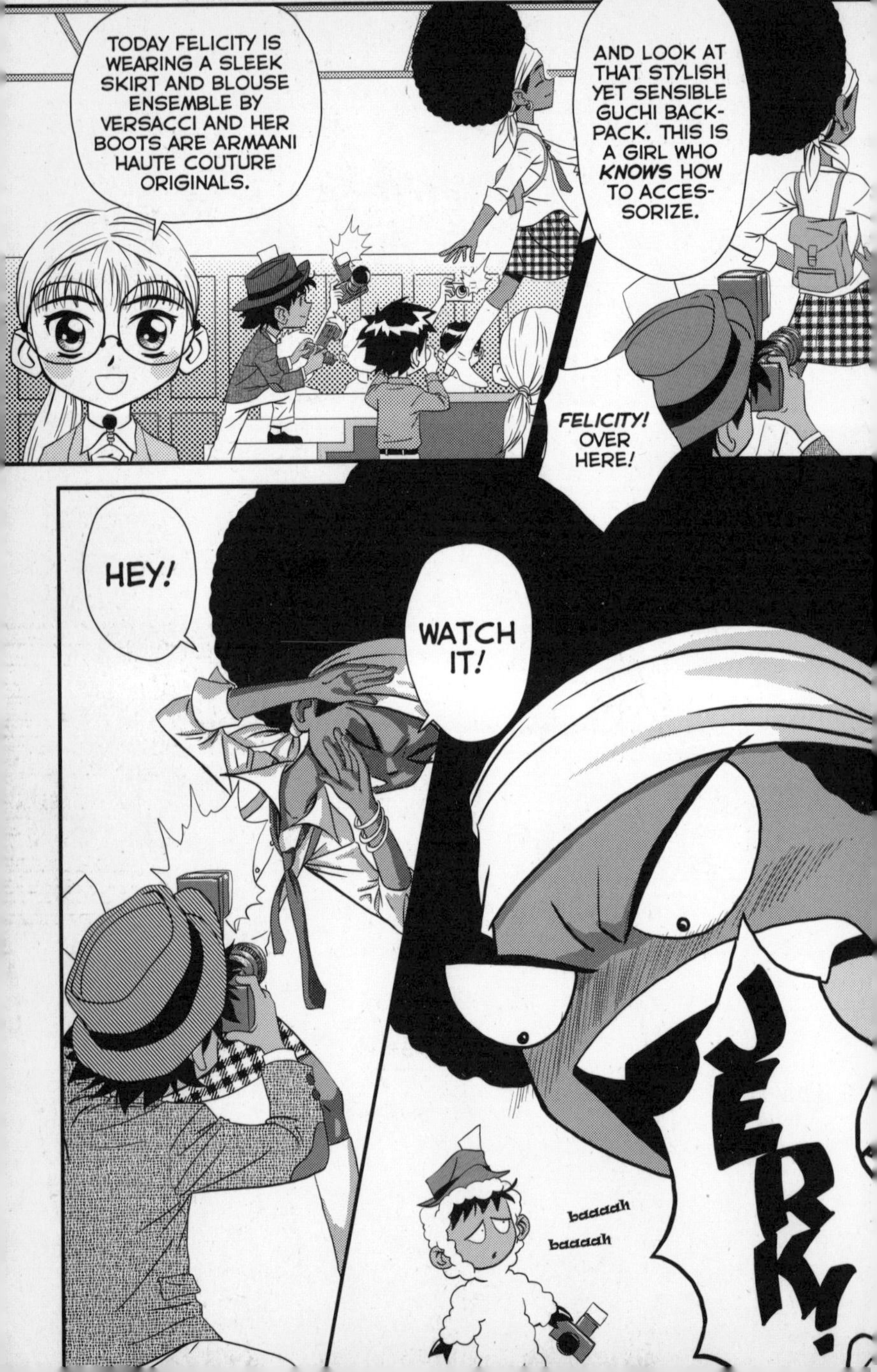
TODAY FELICITY IS WEARING A SLEEK SKIRT AND BLOUSE ENSEMBLE BY VERSACCI AND HER BOOTS ARE ARMAANI HAUTE COUTURE ORIGINALS.
AND LOOK AT THAT STYLISH YET SENSIBLE GUCHI BACK-PACK. THIS IS A GIRL WHO *KNOWS* HOW TO ACCES-SORIZE.
FELICITY! OVER HERE!
HEY!
WATCH IT!
JERK!
baaaah
baaaah

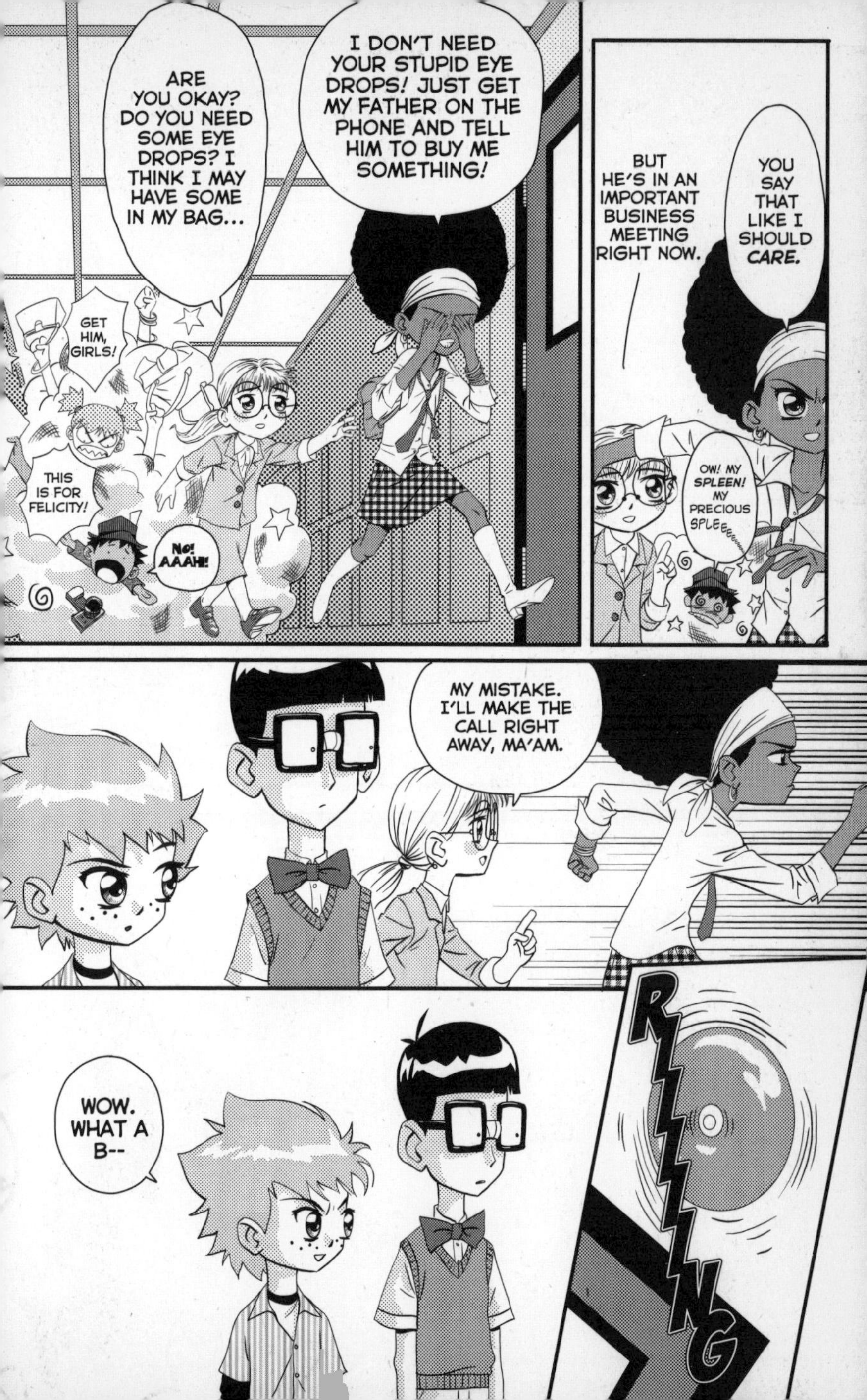
ARE YOU OKAY? DO YOU NEED SOME EYE DROPS? I THINK I MAY HAVE SOME IN MY BAG...
GET HIM, GIRLS!
THIS IS FOR FELICITY!
NO! AAAH!
I DON'T NEED YOUR STUPID EYE DROPS! JUST GET MY FATHER ON THE PHONE AND TELL HIM TO BUY ME SOMETHING!
BUT HE'S IN AN IMPORTANT BUSINESS MEETING RIGHT NOW.
YOU SAY THAT LIKE I SHOULD CARE.
OW! MY SPLEEN! MY PRECIOUS SPLEEEEEE
MY MISTAKE. I'LL MAKE THE CALL RIGHT AWAY, MA'AM.
WOW. WHAT A B--
RIIIING

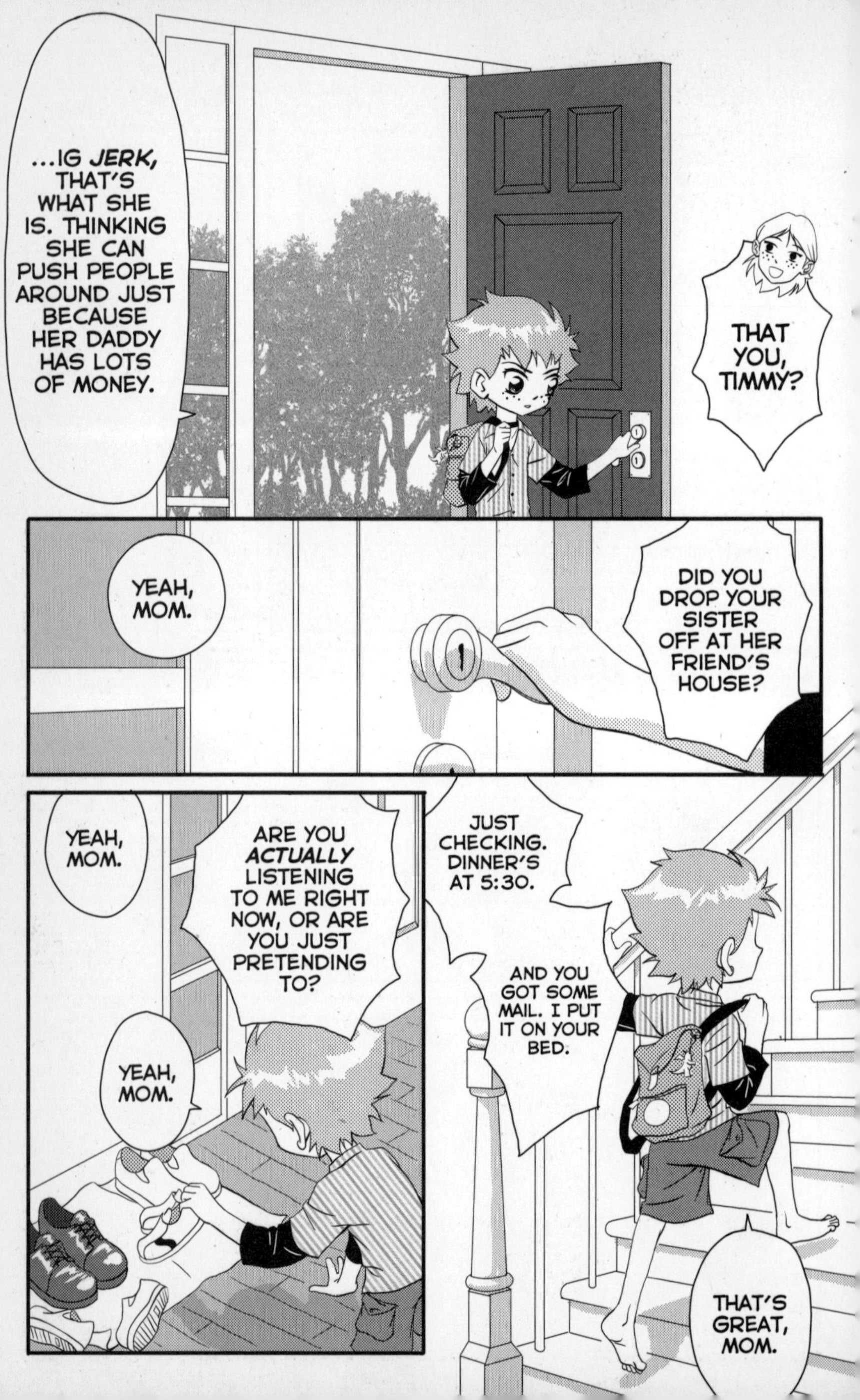
...IG *JERK*, THAT'S WHAT SHE IS. THINKING SHE CAN PUSH PEOPLE AROUND JUST BECAUSE HER DADDY HAS LOTS OF MONEY.
THAT YOU, TIMMY?
YEAH, MOM.
DID YOU DROP YOUR SISTER OFF AT HER FRIEND'S HOUSE?
YEAH, MOM.
ARE YOU *ACTUALLY* LISTENING TO ME RIGHT NOW, OR ARE YOU JUST PRETENDING TO?
YEAH, MOM.
JUST CHECKING. DINNER'S AT 5:30.
AND YOU GOT SOME MAIL. I PUT IT ON YOUR BED.
THAT'S GREAT, MOM.

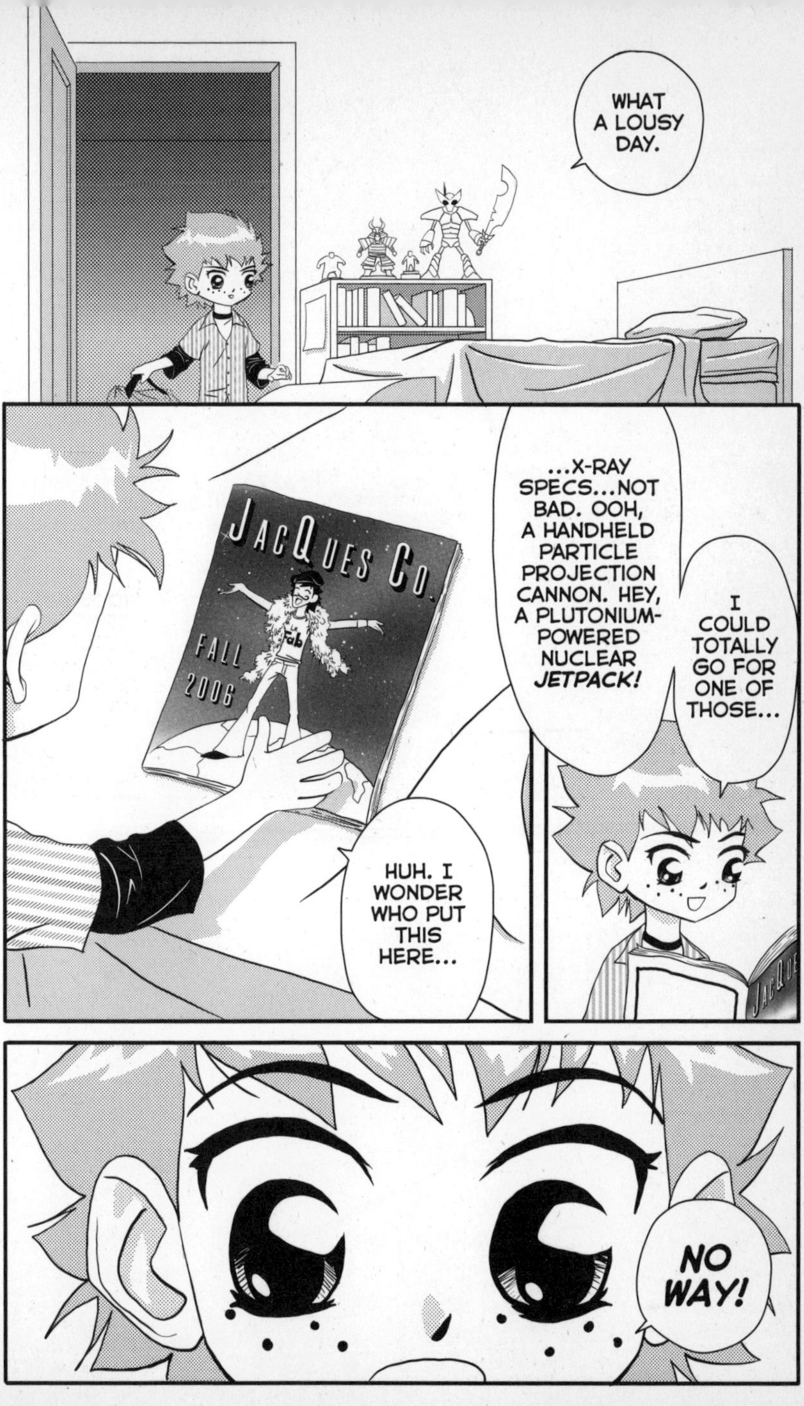
WHAT A LOUSY DAY.
JACQUES CO.
FALL 2006
HUH. I WONDER WHO PUT THIS HERE...
...X-RAY SPECS...NOT BAD. OOH, A HANDHELD PARTICLE PROJECTION CANNON. HEY, A PLUTONIUM-POWERED NUCLEAR *JETPACK!*
I COULD TOTALLY GO FOR ONE OF THOSE...
NO WAY!

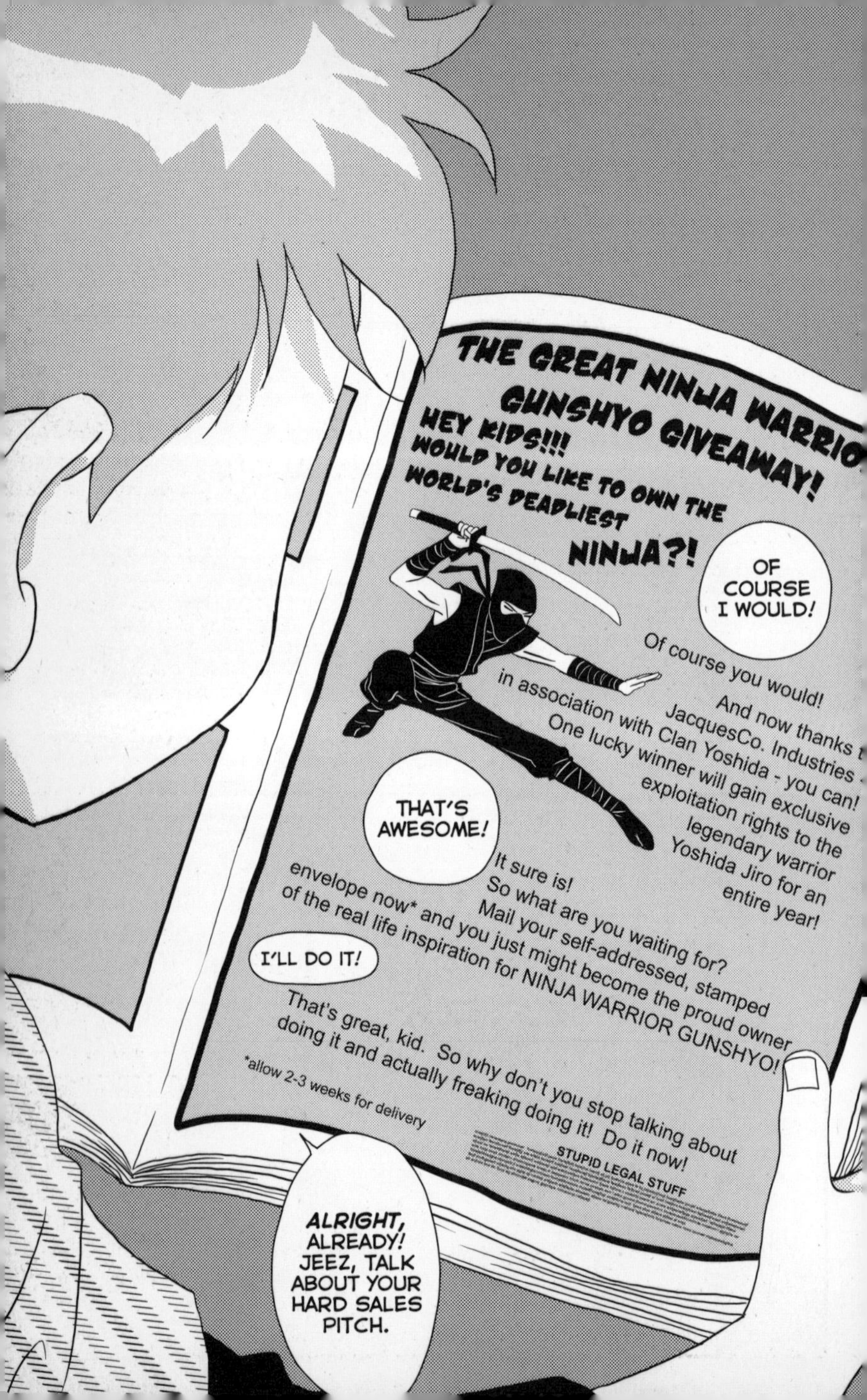
THE GREAT NINJA WARRIO
GUNSHYO GIVEAWAY!
HEY KIDS!!!
WOULD YOU LIKE TO OWN THE
WORLD'S DEADLIEST
NINJA?!
OF COURSE I WOULD!
Of course you would!
And now thanks
JacquesCo. Industries
in association with Clan Yoshida - you can!
One lucky winner will gain exclusive
exploitation rights to the
legendary warrior
Yoshida Jiro for an
entire year!
THAT'S AWESOME!
It sure is!
So what are you waiting for?
Mail your self-addressed, stamped
envelope now* and you just might become the proud owner
of the real life inspiration for NINJA WARRIOR GUNSHYO!
I'LL DO IT!
That's great, kid. So why don't you stop talking about
doing it and actually freaking doing it! Do it now!
*allow 2-3 weeks for delivery
STUPID LEGAL STUFF
ALRIGHT, ALREADY! JEEZ, TALK ABOUT YOUR HARD SALES PITCH.

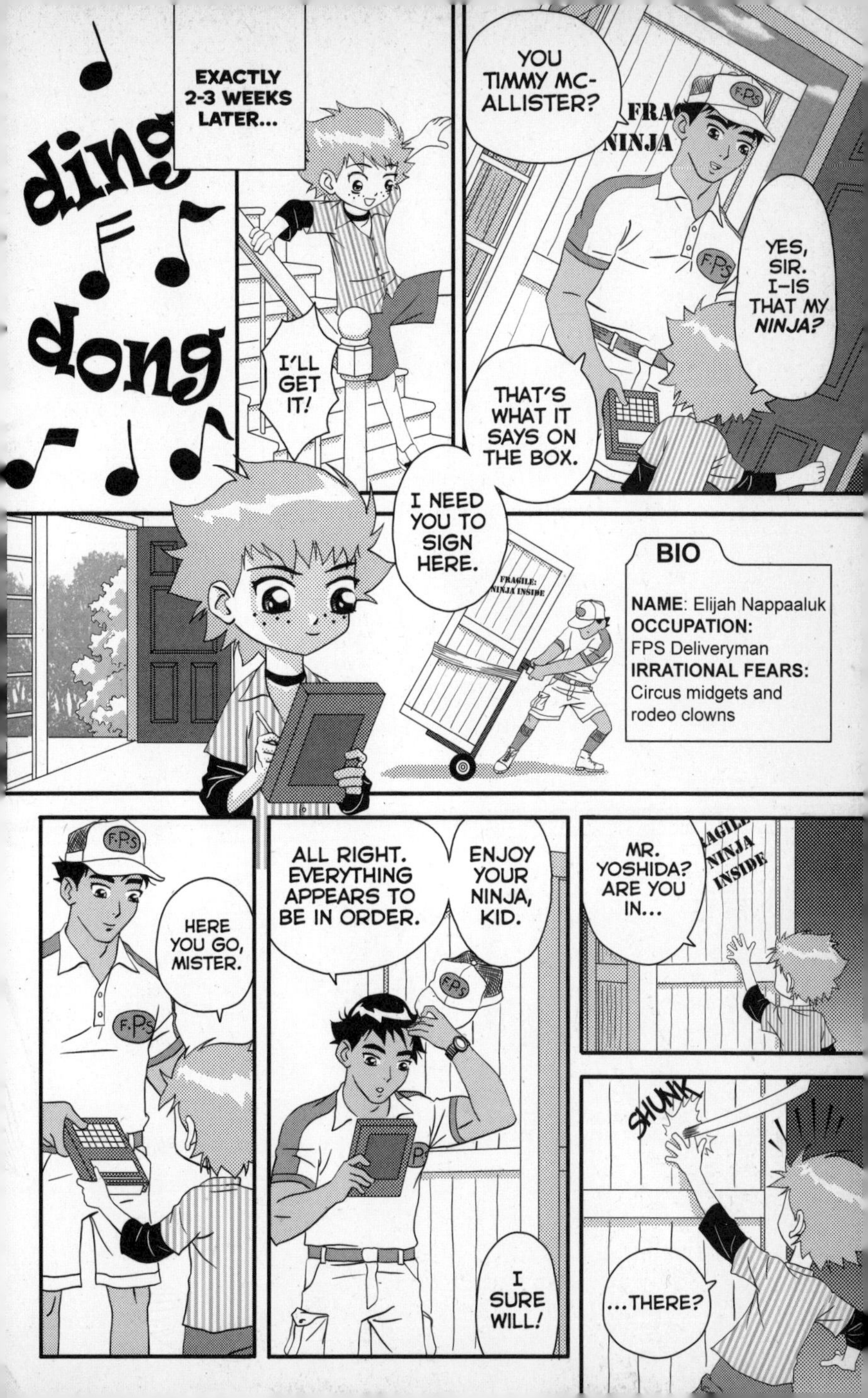
ding
dong
EXACTLY 2-3 WEEKS LATER...
I'LL GET IT!
YOU TIMMY MC-ALLISTER?
FRA
NINJA
YES, SIR. I—IS THAT MY *NINJA?*
THAT'S WHAT IT SAYS ON THE BOX.
I NEED YOU TO SIGN HERE.
FRAGILE: NINJA INSIDE
BIO
NAME: Elijah Nappaaluk
OCCUPATION: FPS Deliveryman
IRRATIONAL FEARS: Circus midgets and rodeo clowns
HERE YOU GO, MISTER.
ALL RIGHT. EVERYTHING APPEARS TO BE IN ORDER.
ENJOY YOUR NINJA, KID.
I SURE WILL!
MR. YOSHIDA? ARE YOU IN...
AGILE NINJA INSIDE
SHUNK
...THERE?

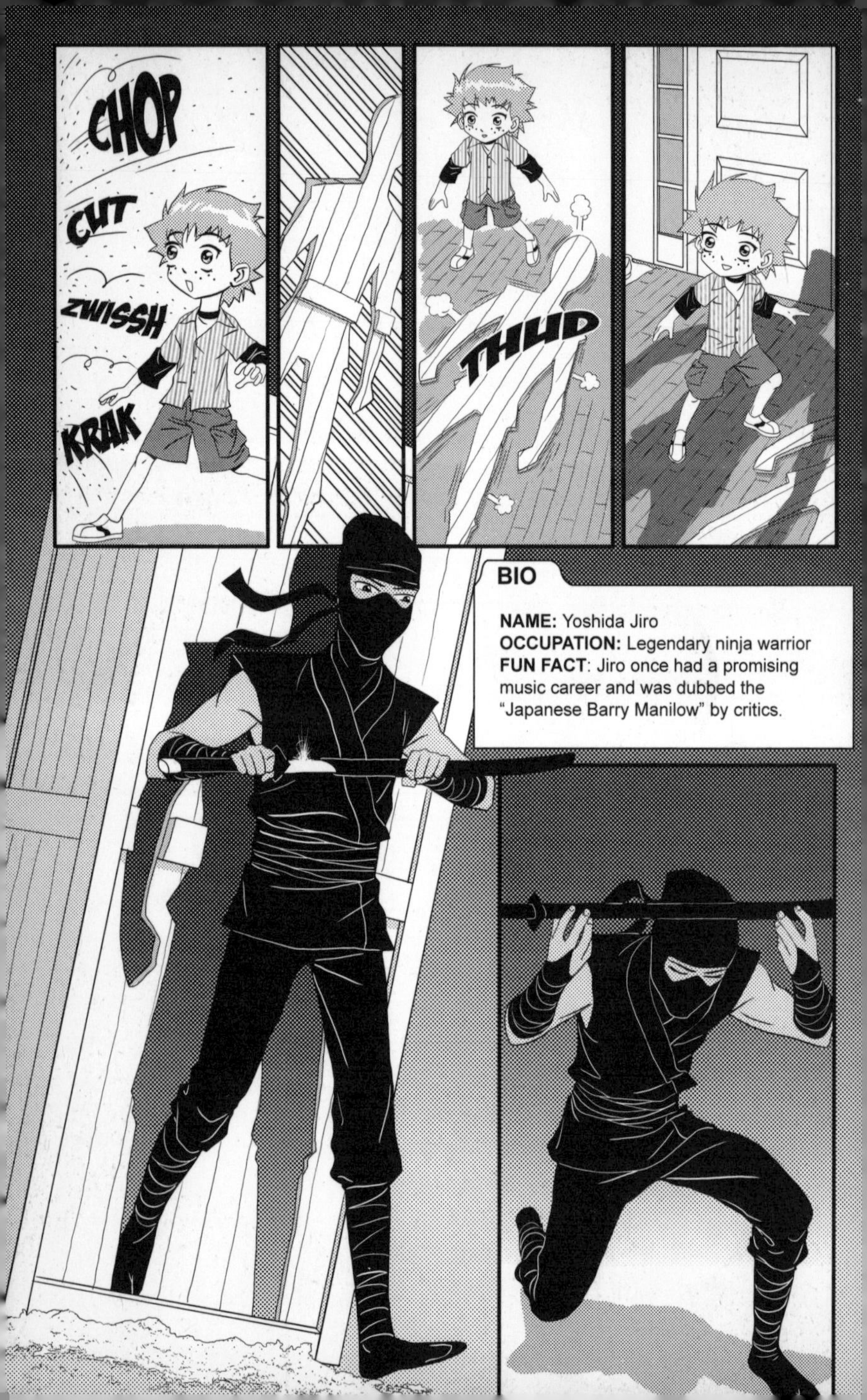
CHOP
CUT
ZWISSH
KRAK
THUD
BIO
NAME: Yoshida Jiro
OCCUPATION: Legendary ninja warrior
FUN FACT: Jiro once had a promising music career and was dubbed the "Japanese Barry Manilow" by critics.

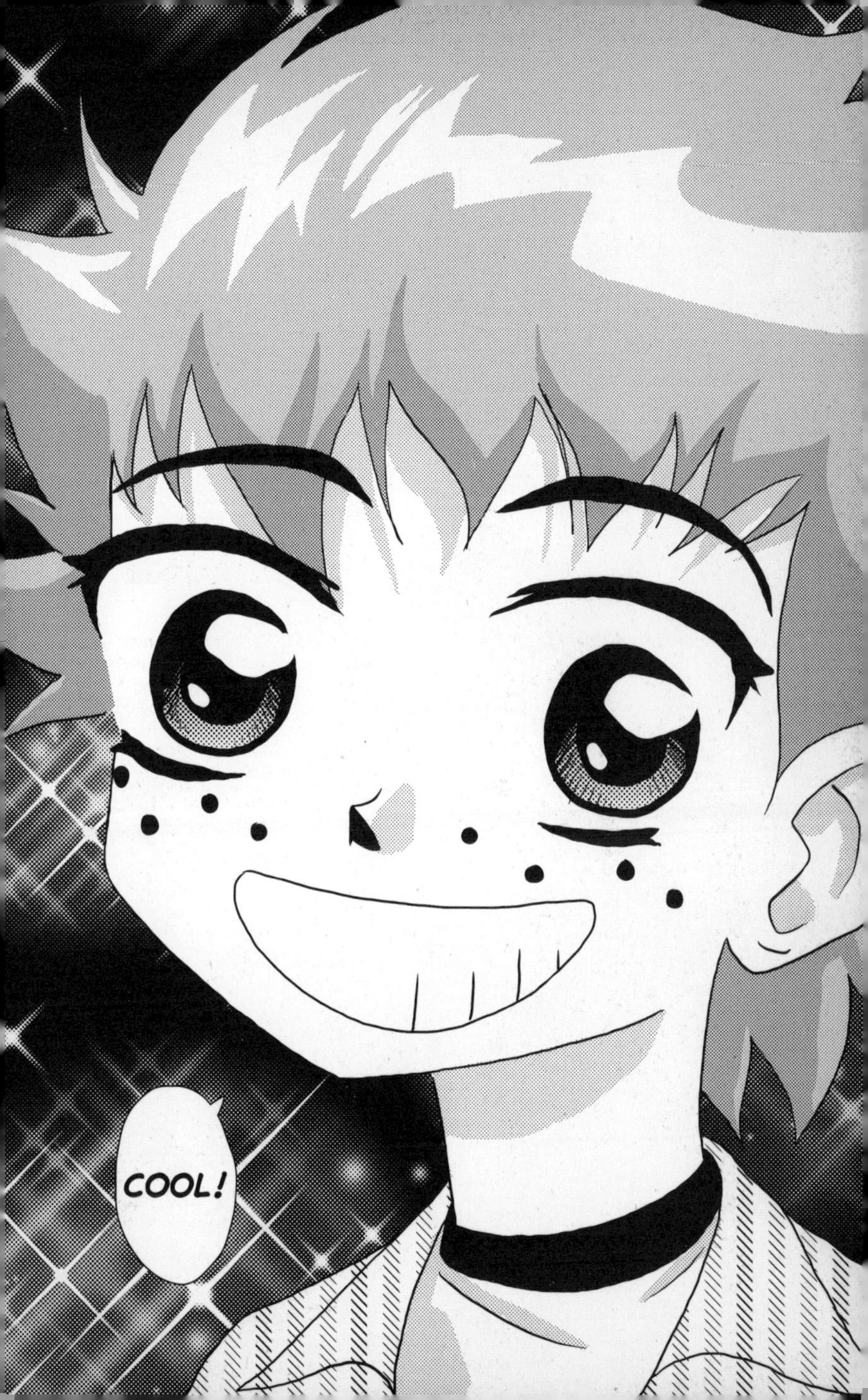
COOL!

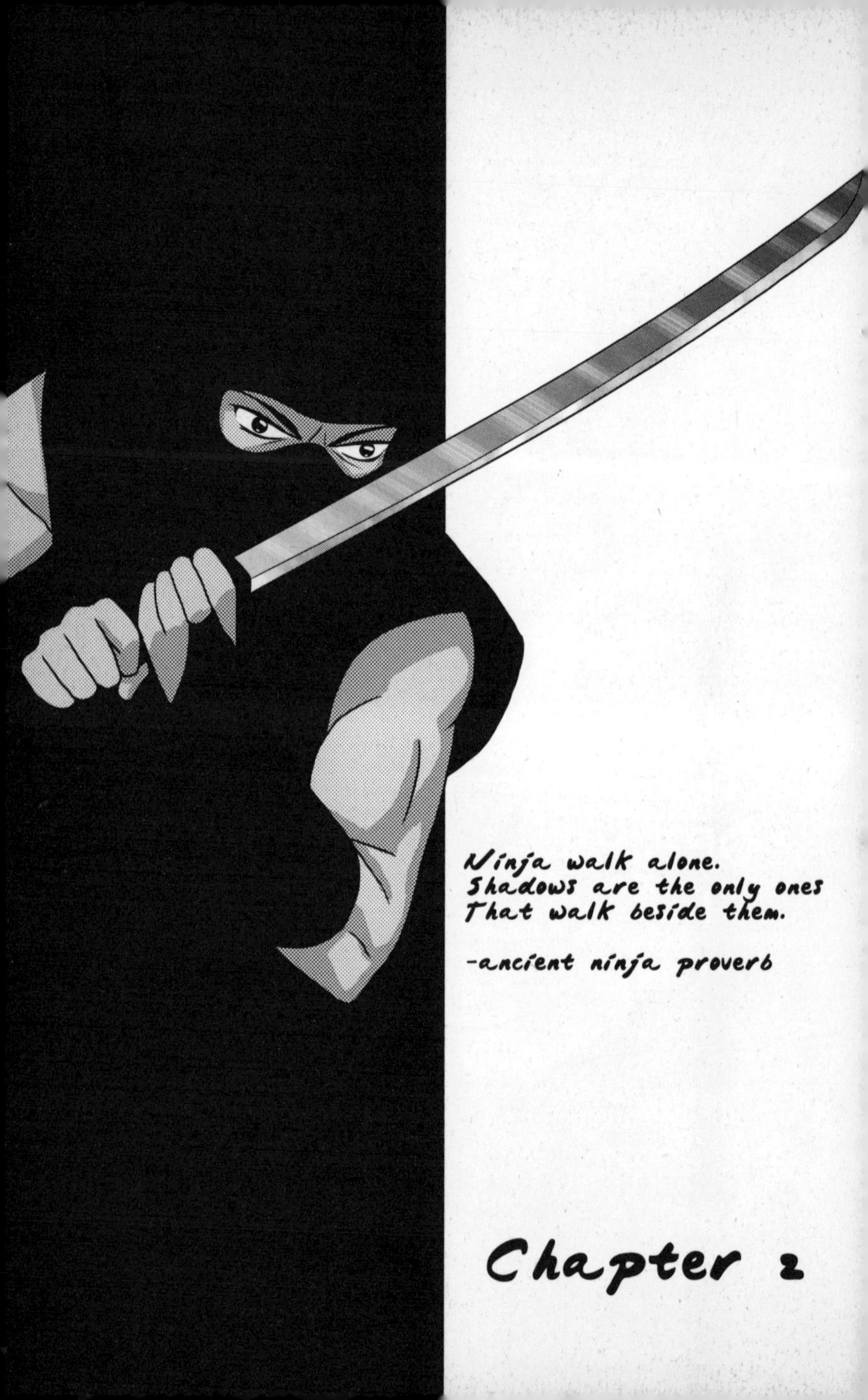

Ninja walk alone.
Shadows are the only ones
That walk beside them.

-ancient ninja proverb

Chapter 2

THE FOLLOWING
IS A PAID ADVERTISEMENT
FOR JACQUES CO.
INDUSTRIES.
IT DOES NOT REFLECT
THE VIEWS OR OPINIONS
OF THIS GRAPHIC NOVEL,
ITS PARENT COMPANY
OR ITS ADVERTISERS.

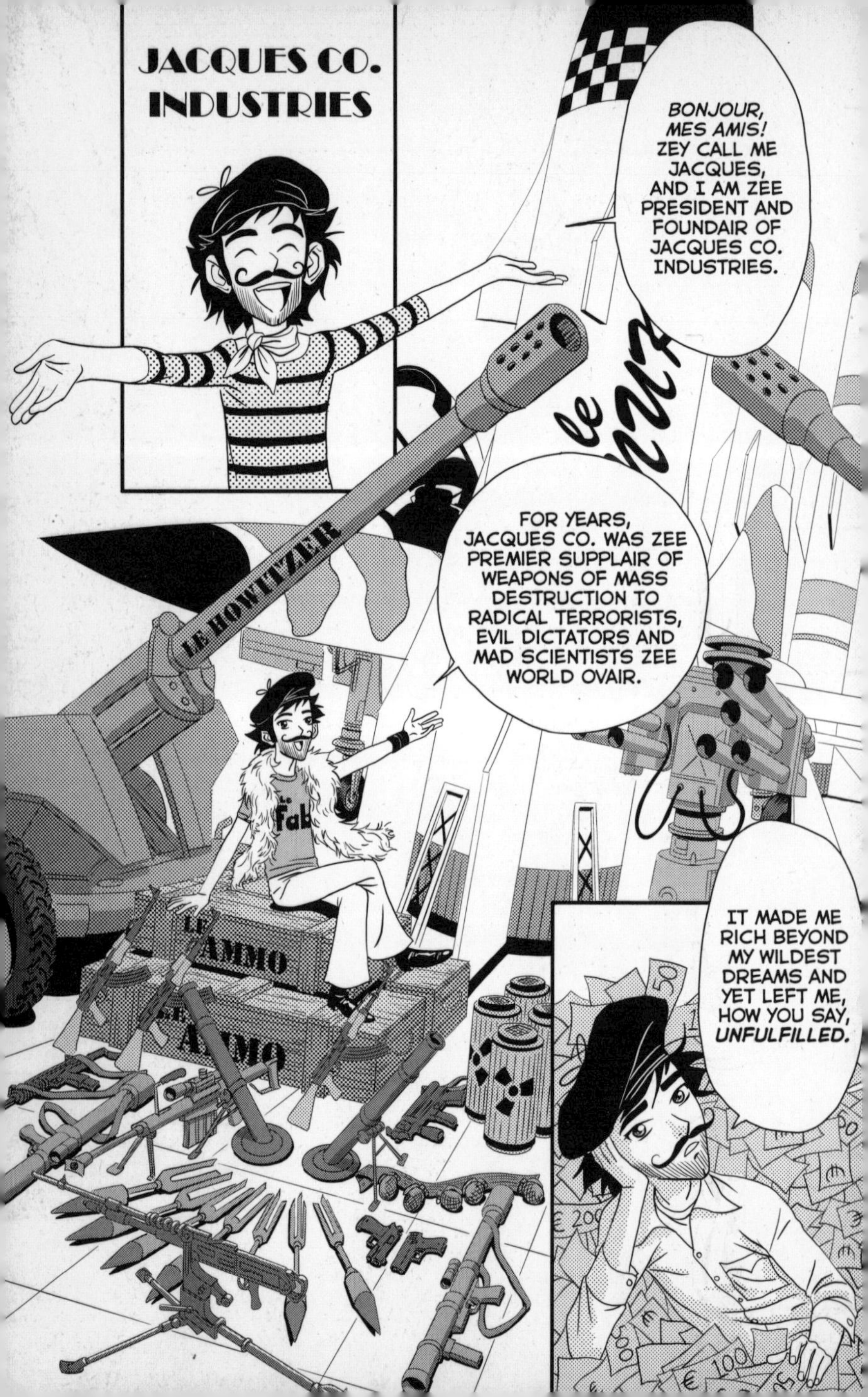
JACQUES CO. INDUSTRIES
BONJOUR, MES AMIS! ZEY CALL ME JACQUES, AND I AM ZEE PRESIDENT AND FOUNDAIR OF JACQUES CO. INDUSTRIES.
FOR YEARS, JACQUES CO. WAS ZEE PREMIER SUPPLAIR OF WEAPONS OF MASS DESTRUCTION TO RADICAL TERRORISTS, EVIL DICTATORS AND MAD SCIENTISTS ZEE WORLD OVAIR.
LE HOWITZER
LE AMMO
LE AMMO
IT MADE ME RICH BEYOND MY WILDEST DREAMS AND YET LEFT ME, HOW YOU SAY, *UNFULFILLED.*

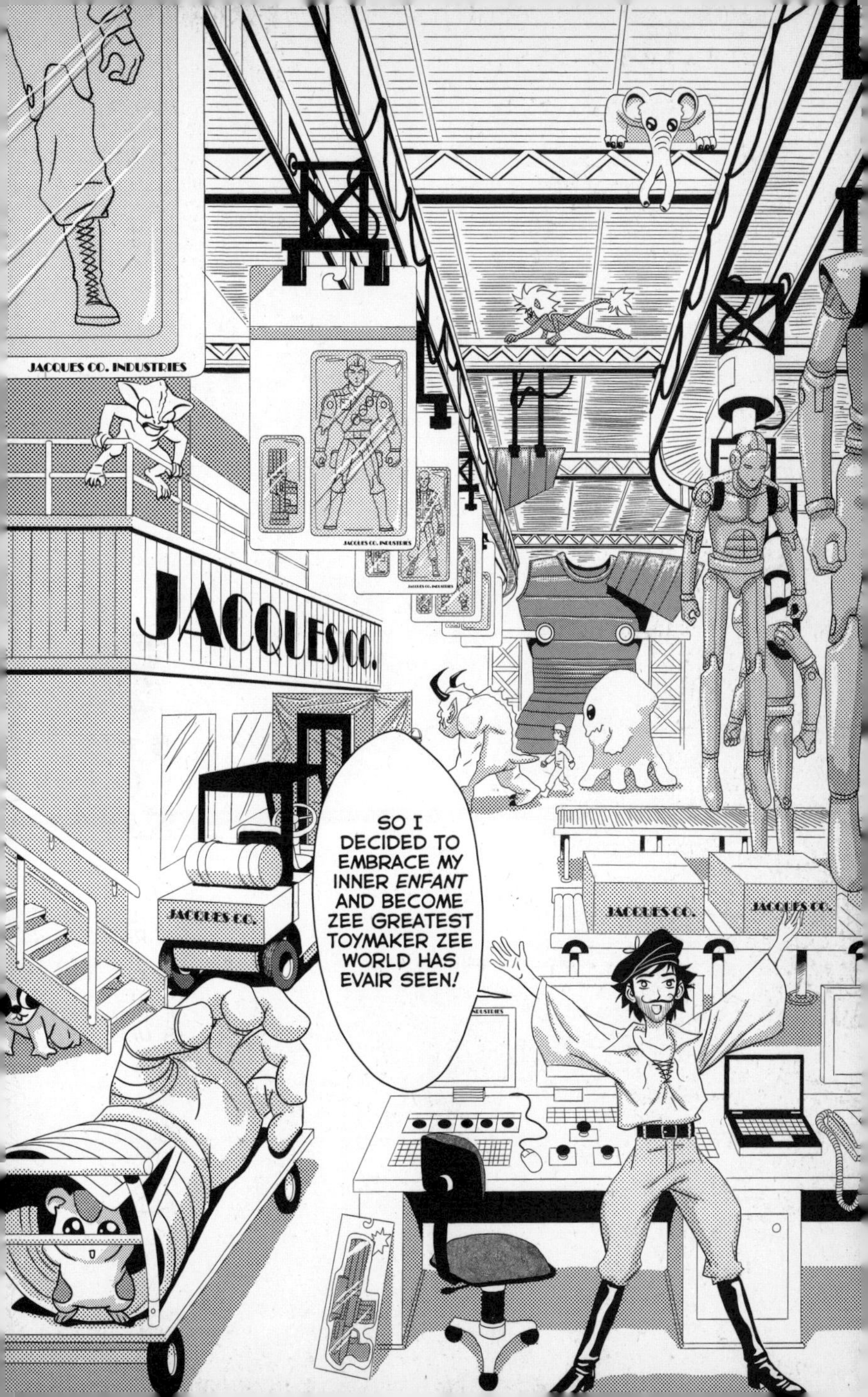
JACQUES CO. INDUSTRIES
JACQUES CO. INDUSTRIES
JACQUES CO.
JACQUES CO.
SO I DECIDED TO EMBRACE MY INNER *ENFANT* AND BECOME ZEE GREATEST TOYMAKER ZEE WORLD HAS EVAIR SEEN!
JACQUES CO.
JACQUES CO.

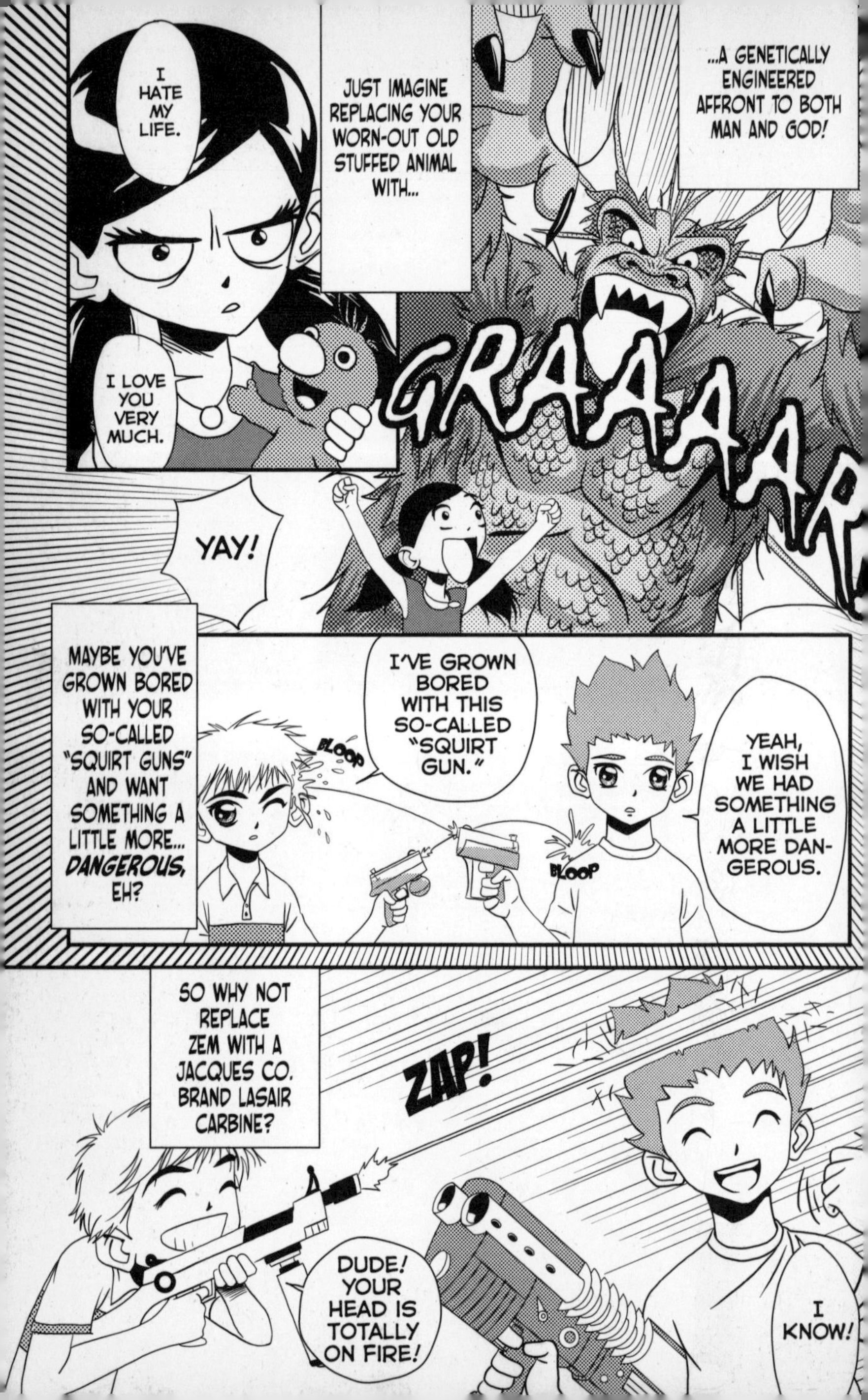
I HATE MY LIFE.
I LOVE YOU VERY MUCH.
JUST IMAGINE REPLACING YOUR WORN-OUT OLD STUFFED ANIMAL WITH...
...A GENETICALLY ENGINEERED AFFRONT TO BOTH MAN AND GOD!
GRAAAAAR
YAY!
MAYBE YOU'VE GROWN BORED WITH YOUR SO-CALLED "SQUIRT GUNS" AND WANT SOMETHING A LITTLE MORE... DANGEROUS, EH?
BLOOP
I'VE GROWN BORED WITH THIS SO-CALLED "SQUIRT GUN."
BLOOP
YEAH, I WISH WE HAD SOMETHING A LITTLE MORE DAN-GEROUS.
SO WHY NOT REPLACE ZEM WITH A JACQUES CO. BRAND LASAIR CARBINE?
ZAP!
DUDE! YOUR HEAD IS TOTALLY ON FIRE!
I KNOW!

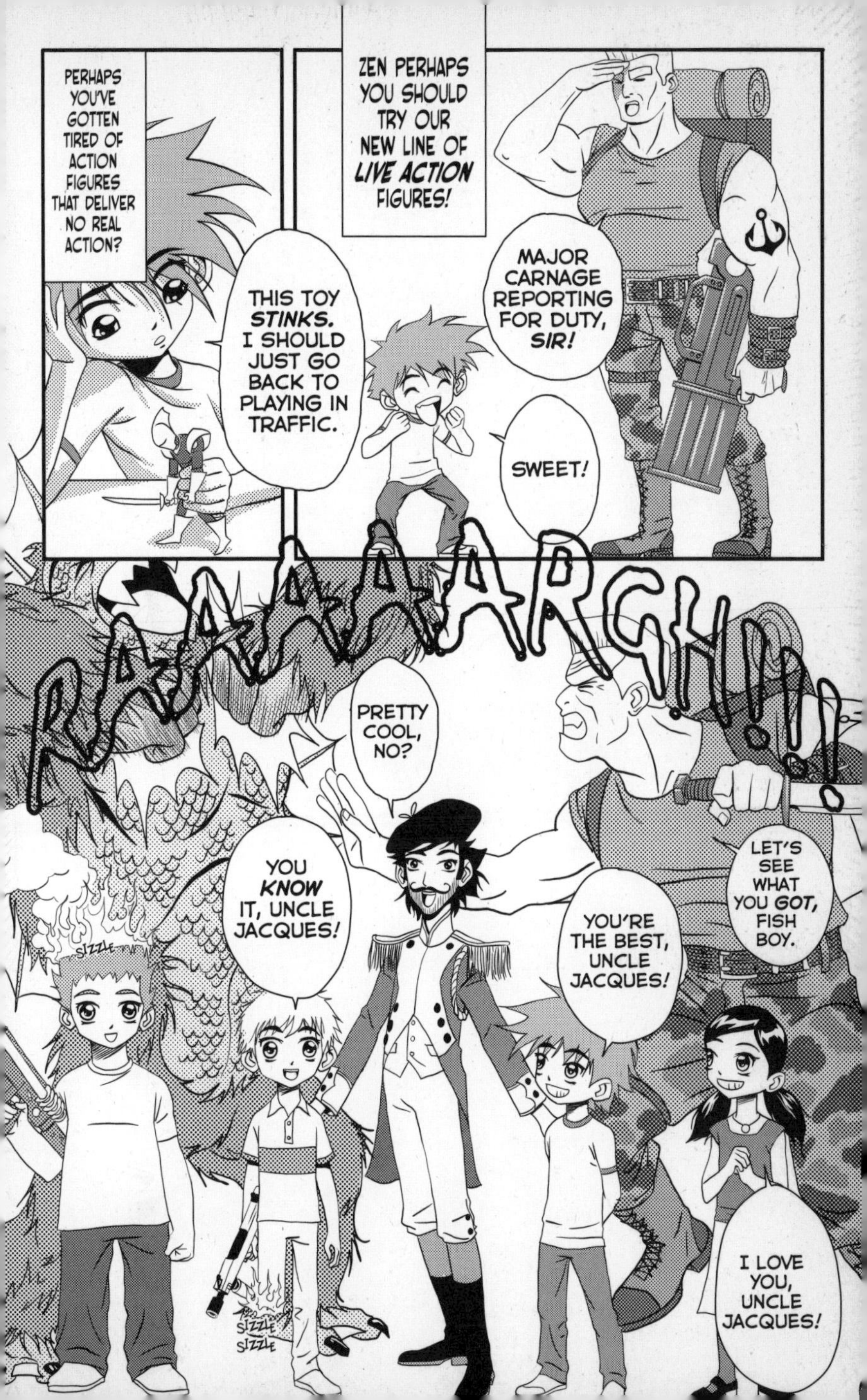
PERHAPS YOU'VE GOTTEN TIRED OF ACTION FIGURES THAT DELIVER NO REAL ACTION?
THIS TOY STINKS. I SHOULD JUST GO BACK TO PLAYING IN TRAFFIC.
ZEN PERHAPS YOU SHOULD TRY OUR NEW LINE OF LIVE ACTION FIGURES!
MAJOR CARNAGE REPORTING FOR DUTY, SIR!
SWEET!
RAAAAARGH!!!
PRETTY COOL, NO?
YOU KNOW IT, UNCLE JACQUES!
SIZZLE
YOU'RE THE BEST, UNCLE JACQUES!
LET'S SEE WHAT YOU GOT, FISH BOY.
SIZZLE SIZZLE
I LOVE YOU, UNCLE JACQUES!

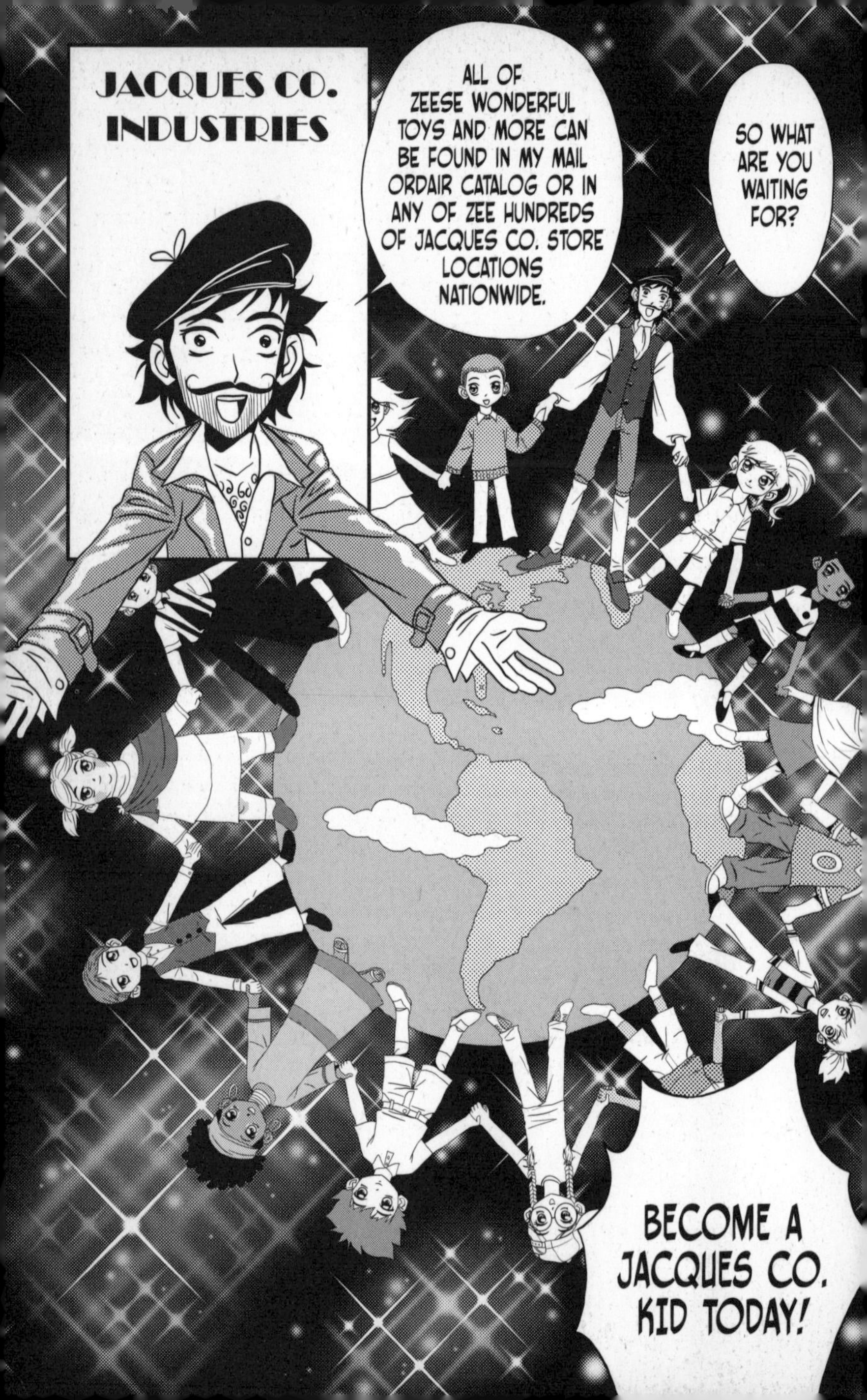
JACQUES CO. INDUSTRIES
ALL OF ZEESE WONDERFUL TOYS AND MORE CAN BE FOUND IN MY MAIL ORDAIR CATALOG OR IN ANY OF ZEE HUNDREDS OF JACQUES CO. STORE LOCATIONS NATIONWIDE.
SO WHAT ARE YOU WAITING FOR?
BECOME A JACQUES CO. KID TODAY!

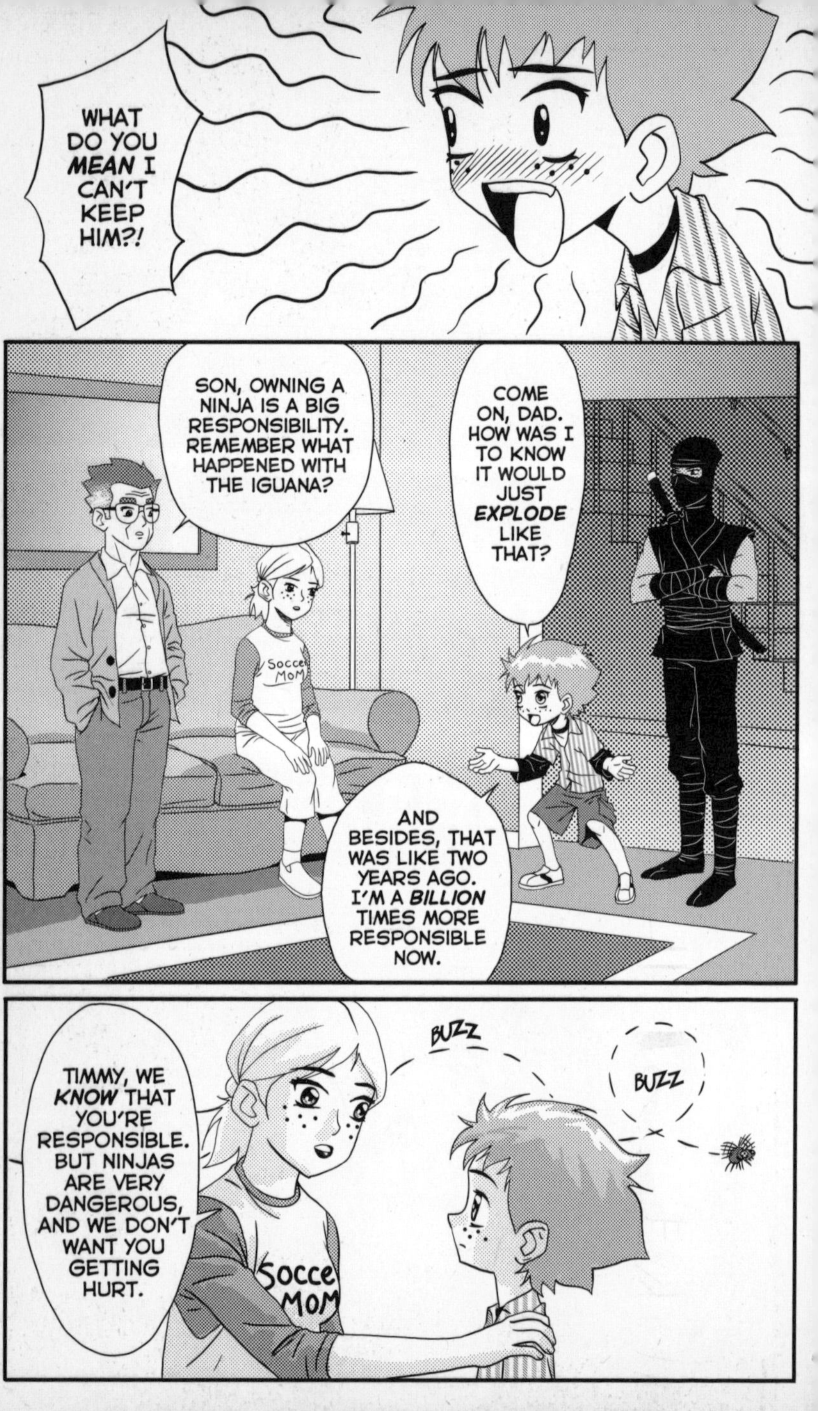
WHAT DO YOU *MEAN* I CAN'T KEEP HIM?!
SON, OWNING A NINJA IS A BIG RESPONSIBILITY. REMEMBER WHAT HAPPENED WITH THE IGUANA?
SOCCER MOM
COME ON, DAD. HOW WAS I TO KNOW IT WOULD JUST *EXPLODE* LIKE THAT?
AND BESIDES, THAT WAS LIKE TWO YEARS AGO. I'M A *BILLION* TIMES MORE RESPONSIBLE NOW.
TIMMY, WE *KNOW* THAT YOU'RE RESPONSIBLE. BUT NINJAS ARE VERY DANGEROUS, AND WE DON'T WANT YOU GETTING HURT.
BUZZ
BUZZ
SOCCE MOM

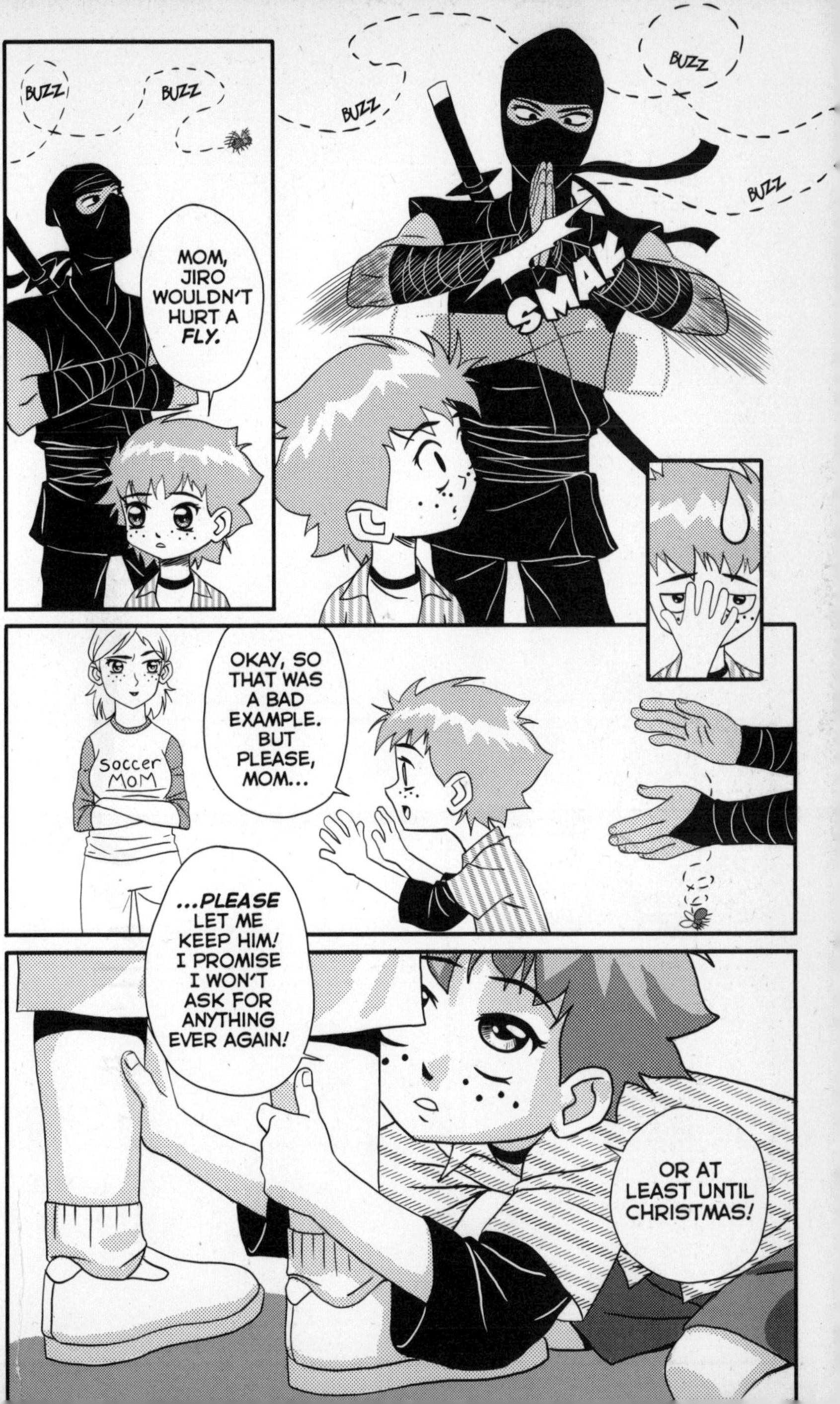
BUZZ
BUZZ
BUZZ
BUZZ
BUZZ
MOM, JIRO WOULDN'T HURT A *FLY.*
SMAK
OKAY, SO THAT WAS A BAD EXAMPLE. BUT PLEASE, MOM...
Soccer MOM
...PLEASE LET ME KEEP HIM! I PROMISE I WON'T ASK FOR ANYTHING EVER AGAIN!
OR AT LEAST UNTIL CHRISTMAS!

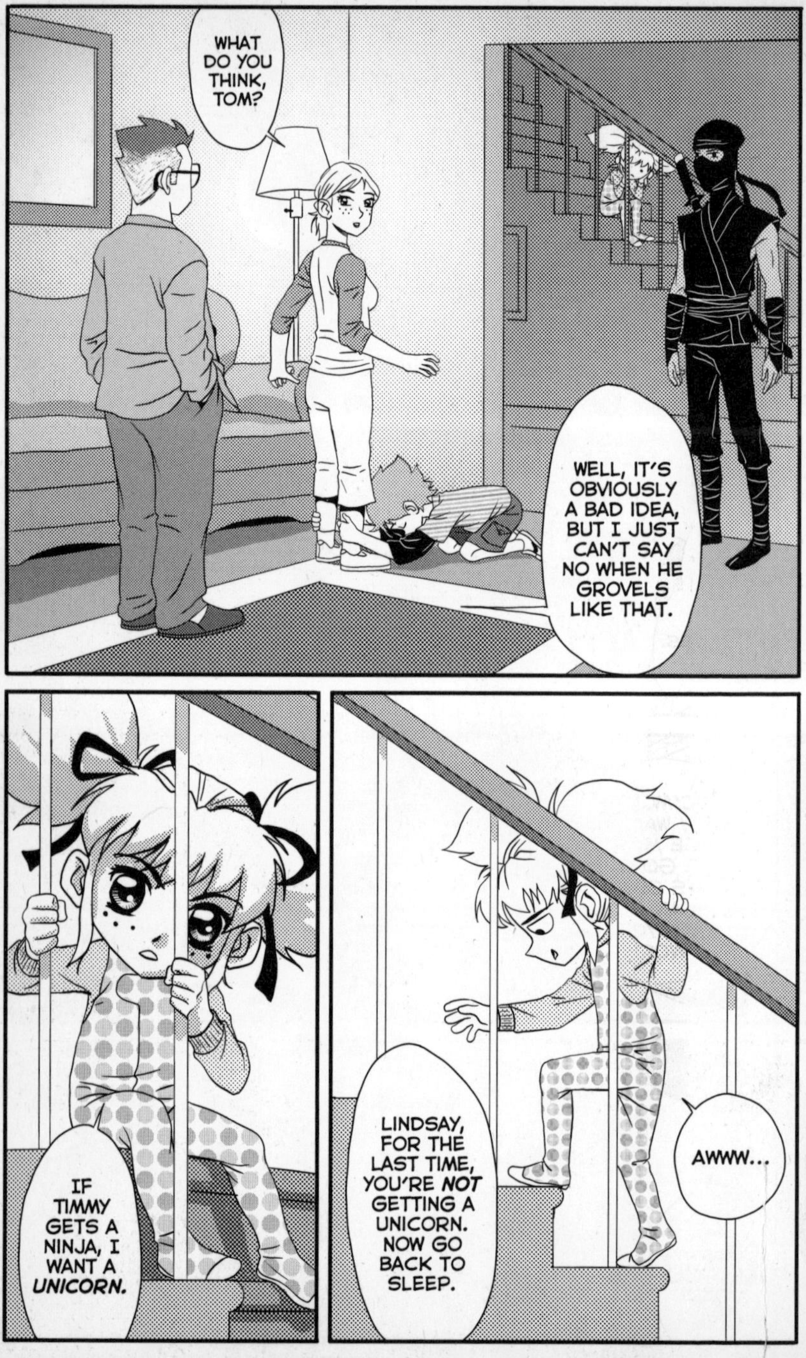
WHAT DO YOU THINK, TOM?
WELL, IT'S OBVIOUSLY A BAD IDEA, BUT I JUST CAN'T SAY NO WHEN HE GROVELS LIKE THAT.
IF TIMMY GETS A NINJA, I WANT A *UNICORN.*
LINDSAY, FOR THE LAST TIME, YOU'RE ***NOT*** GETTING A UNICORN. NOW GO BACK TO SLEEP.
AWWW...

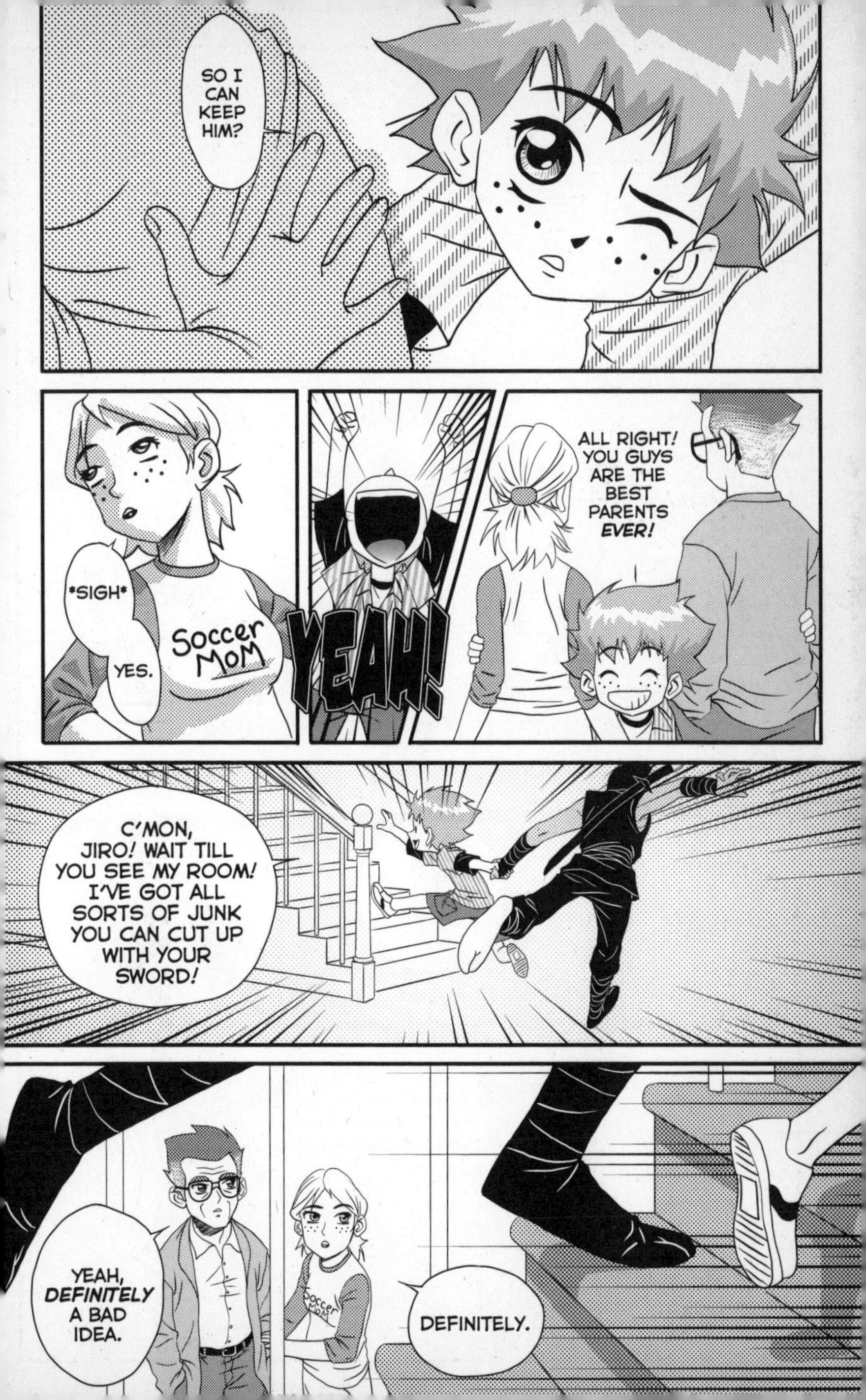
SO I CAN KEEP HIM?
SIGH
YES.
Soccer MoM
YEAH!
ALL RIGHT! YOU GUYS ARE THE BEST PARENTS *EVER!*
C'MON, JIRO! WAIT TILL YOU SEE MY ROOM! I'VE GOT ALL SORTS OF JUNK YOU CAN CUT UP WITH YOUR SWORD!
YEAH, *DEFINITELY* A BAD IDEA.
Soccer MoM
DEFINITELY.

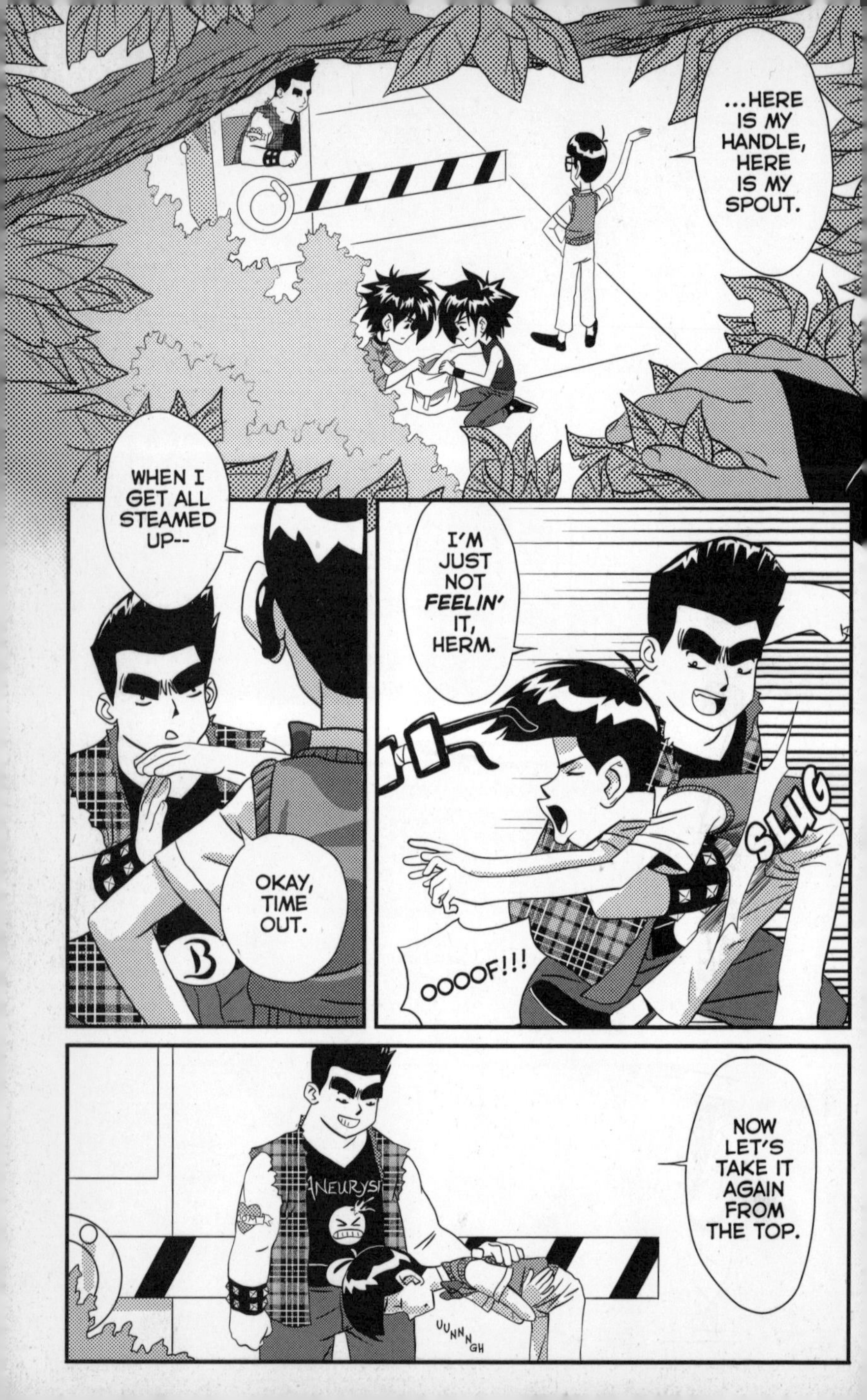
...HERE IS MY HANDLE, HERE IS MY SPOUT.
WHEN I GET ALL STEAMED UP--
OKAY, TIME OUT.
I'M JUST NOT FEELIN' IT, HERM.
SLUG
OOOOF!!!
NOW LET'S TAKE IT AGAIN FROM THE TOP.
UUNNNGH

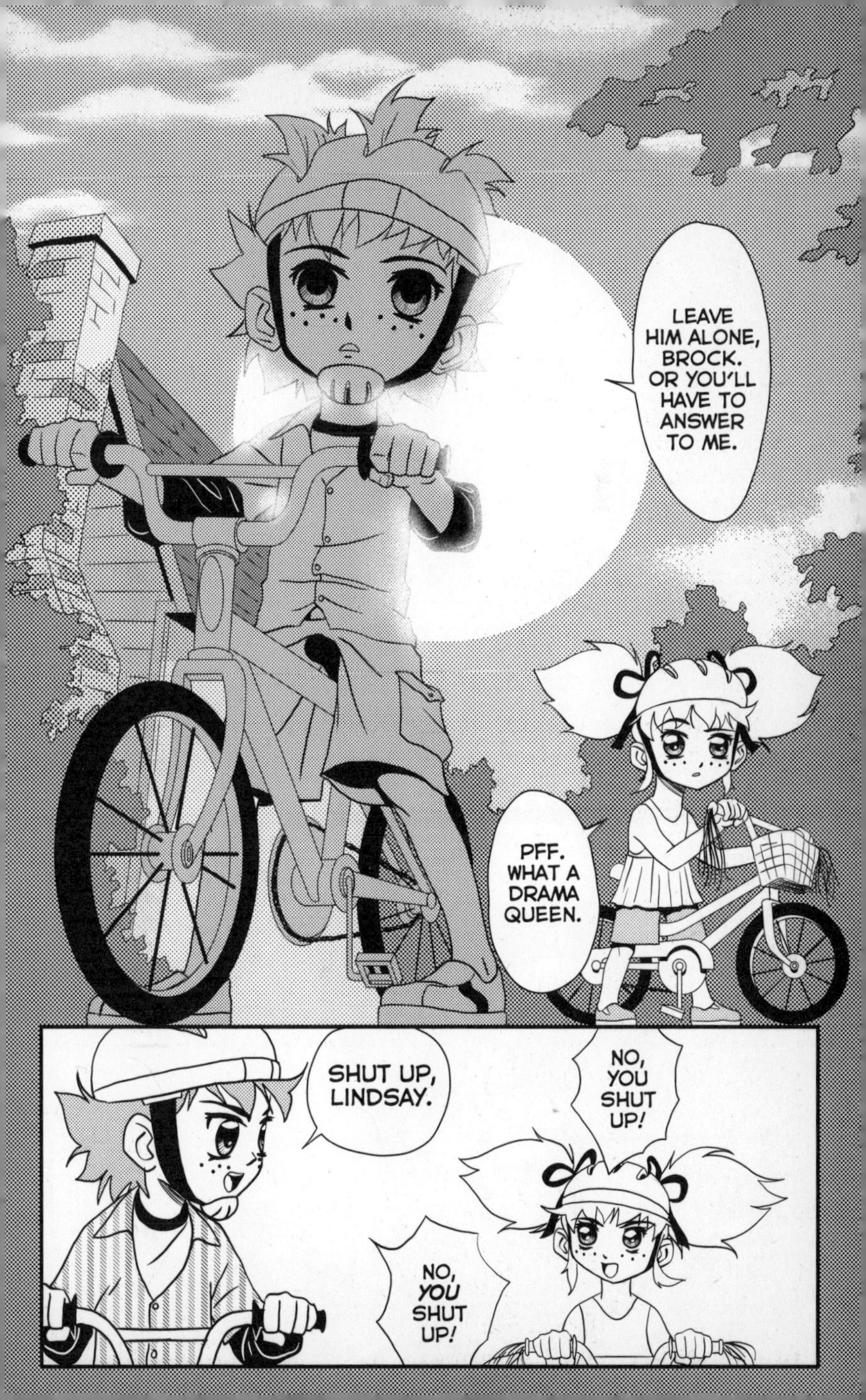
LEAVE HIM ALONE, BROCK. OR YOU'LL HAVE TO ANSWER TO ME.
PFF. WHAT A DRAMA QUEEN.
SHUT UP, LINDSAY.
NO, YOU SHUT UP!
NO, *YOU* SHUT UP!

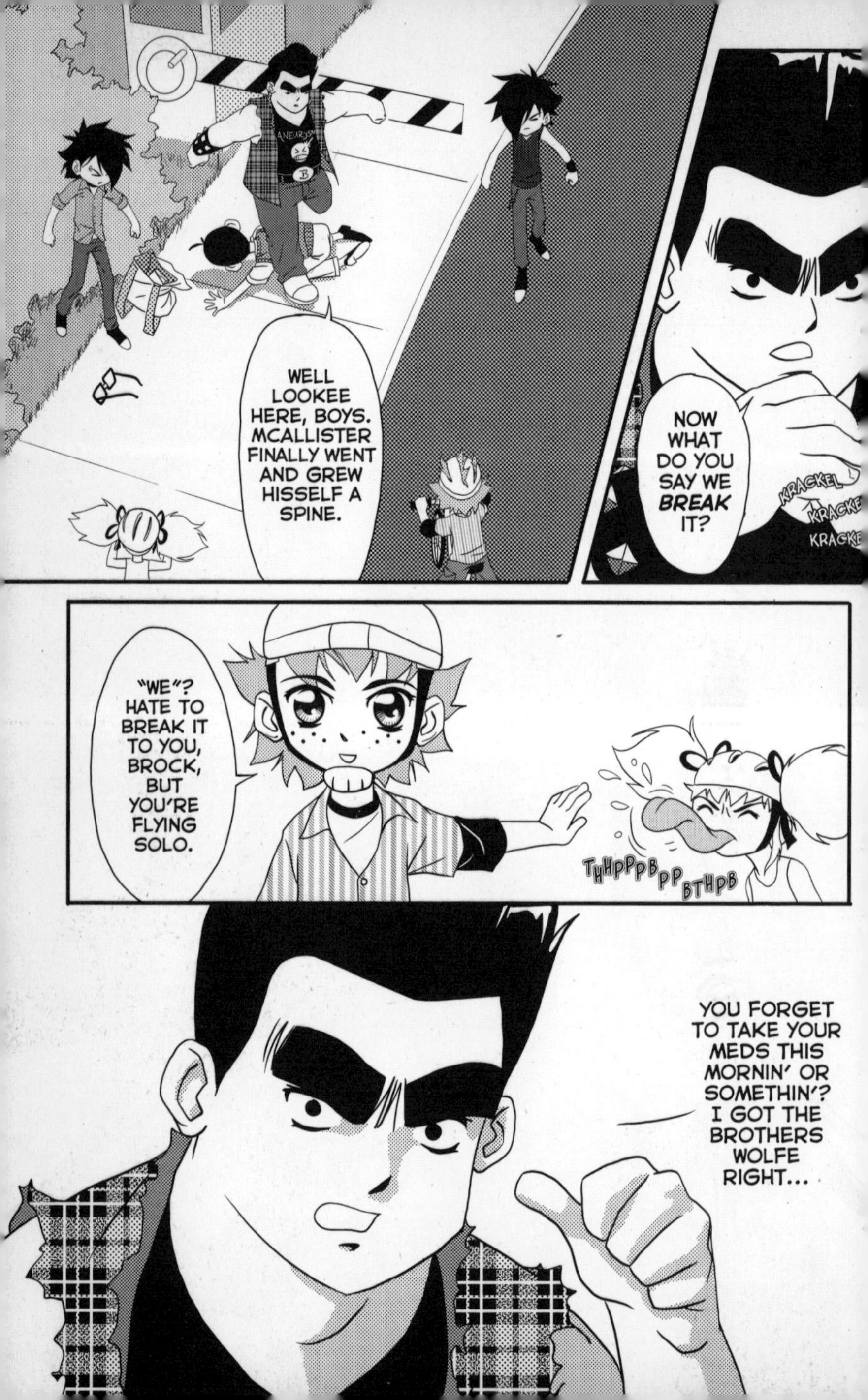
WELL LOOKEE HERE, BOYS. MCALLISTER FINALLY WENT AND GREW HISSELF A SPINE.
NOW WHAT DO YOU SAY WE *BREAK* IT?
KRACKEL KRACKE KRACKE
"WE"? HATE TO BREAK IT TO YOU, BROCK, BUT YOU'RE FLYING SOLO.
THHPPPB PP BTHPB
YOU FORGET TO TAKE YOUR MEDS THIS MORNIN' OR SOMETHIN'? I GOT THE BROTHERS WOLFE RIGHT...

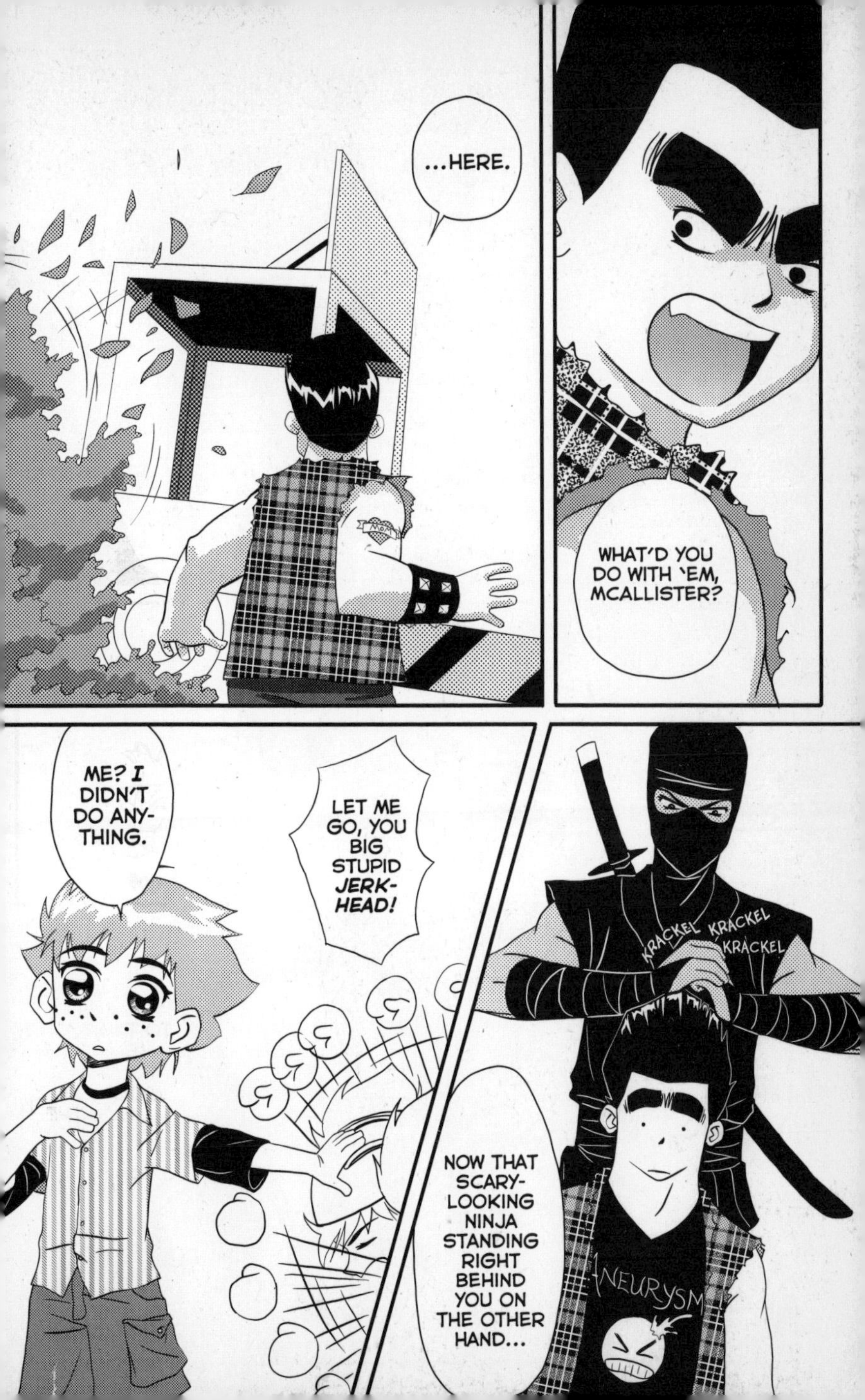
...HERE.
WHAT'D YOU DO WITH 'EM, MCALLISTER?
ME? I DIDN'T DO ANY-THING.
LET ME GO, YOU BIG STUPID *JERK-HEAD!*
KRACKEL KRACKEL KRACKEL
NOW THAT SCARY-LOOKING NINJA STANDING RIGHT BEHIND YOU ON THE OTHER HAND...
ANEURYSM

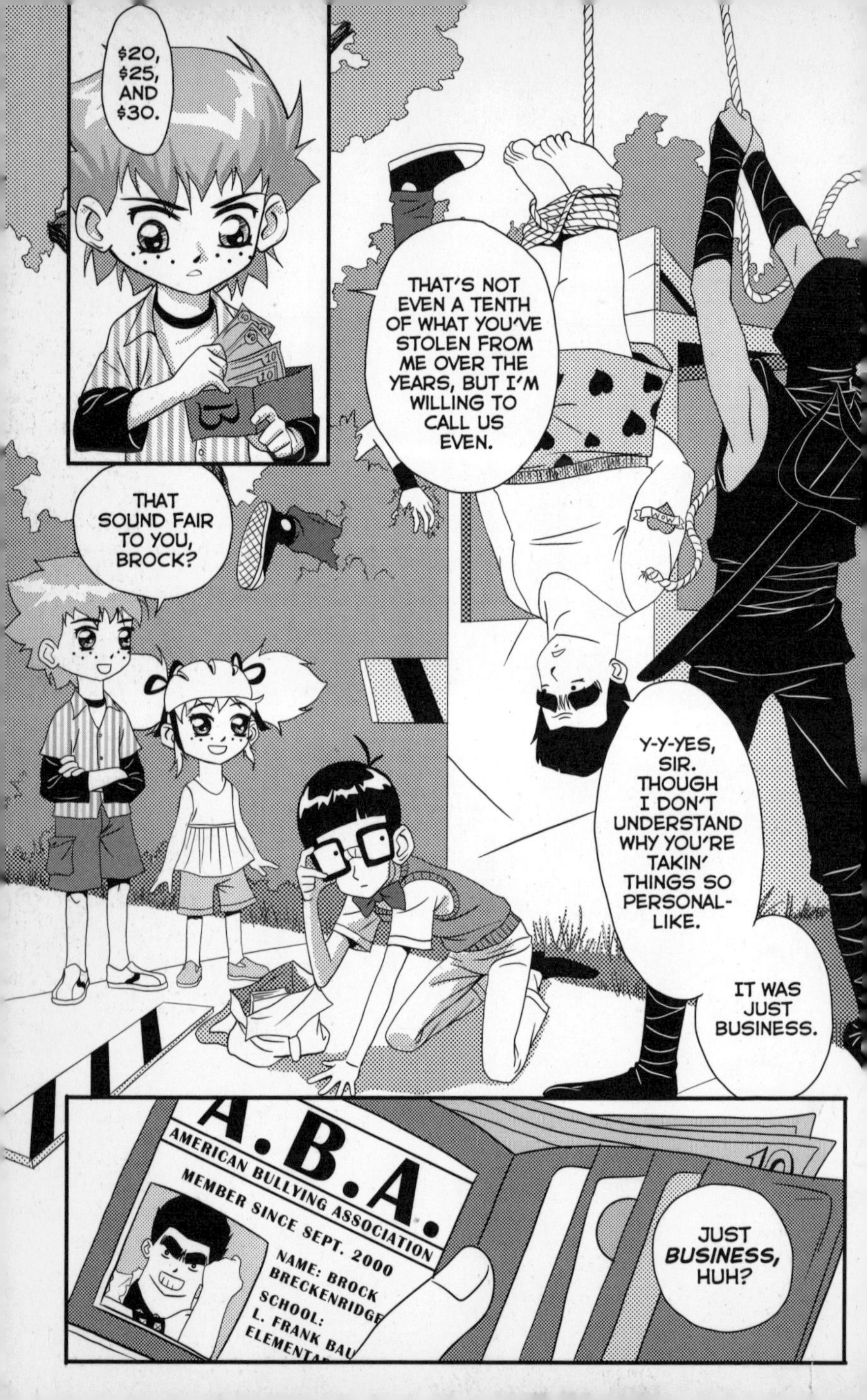
$20, $25, AND $30.
THAT'S NOT EVEN A TENTH OF WHAT YOU'VE STOLEN FROM ME OVER THE YEARS, BUT I'M WILLING TO CALL US EVEN.
THAT SOUND FAIR TO YOU, BROCK?
Y-Y-YES, SIR. THOUGH I DON'T UNDERSTAND WHY YOU'RE TAKIN' THINGS SO PERSONAL-LIKE.
IT WAS JUST BUSINESS.
A.B.A.
AMERICAN BULLYING ASSOCIATION
MEMBER SINCE SEPT. 2000
NAME: BROCK BRECKENRIDGE
SCHOOL: L. FRANK BAU
ELEMENTA
JUST *BUSINESS*, HUH?

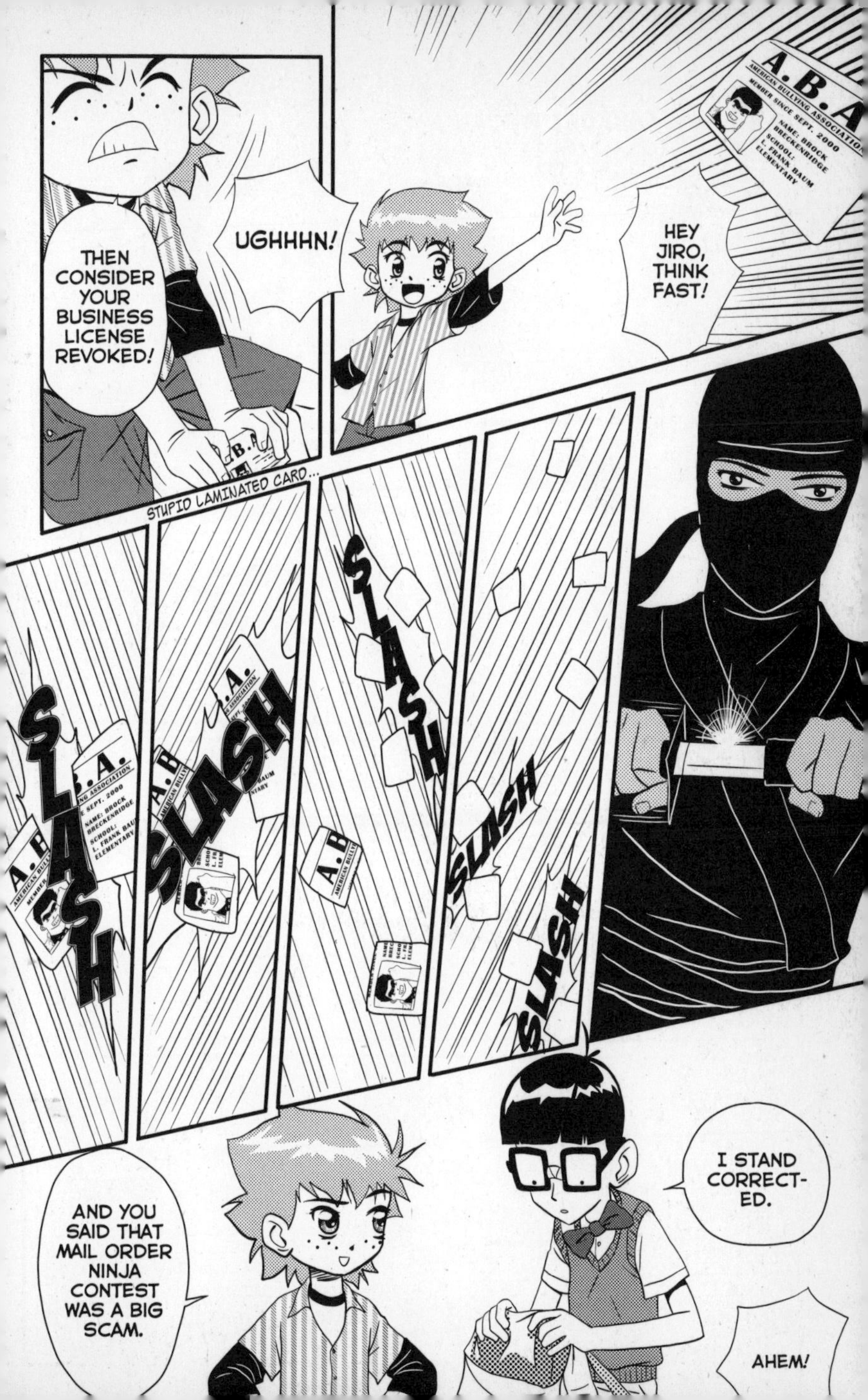
THEN CONSIDER YOUR BUSINESS LICENSE REVOKED!
UGHHHN!
A.B.A.
AMERICAN BULLYING ASSOCIATION
MEMBER SINCE SEPT. 2000
NAME: BROCK BRECKENRIDGE
SCHOOL: L. FRANK BAUM ELEMENTARY
HEY JIRO, THINK FAST!
STUPID LAMINATED CARD...
SLASH
SLASH
SLASH
SLASH
SLASH
AND YOU SAID THAT MAIL ORDER NINJA CONTEST WAS A BIG SCAM.
I STAND CORRECT-ED.
AHEM!

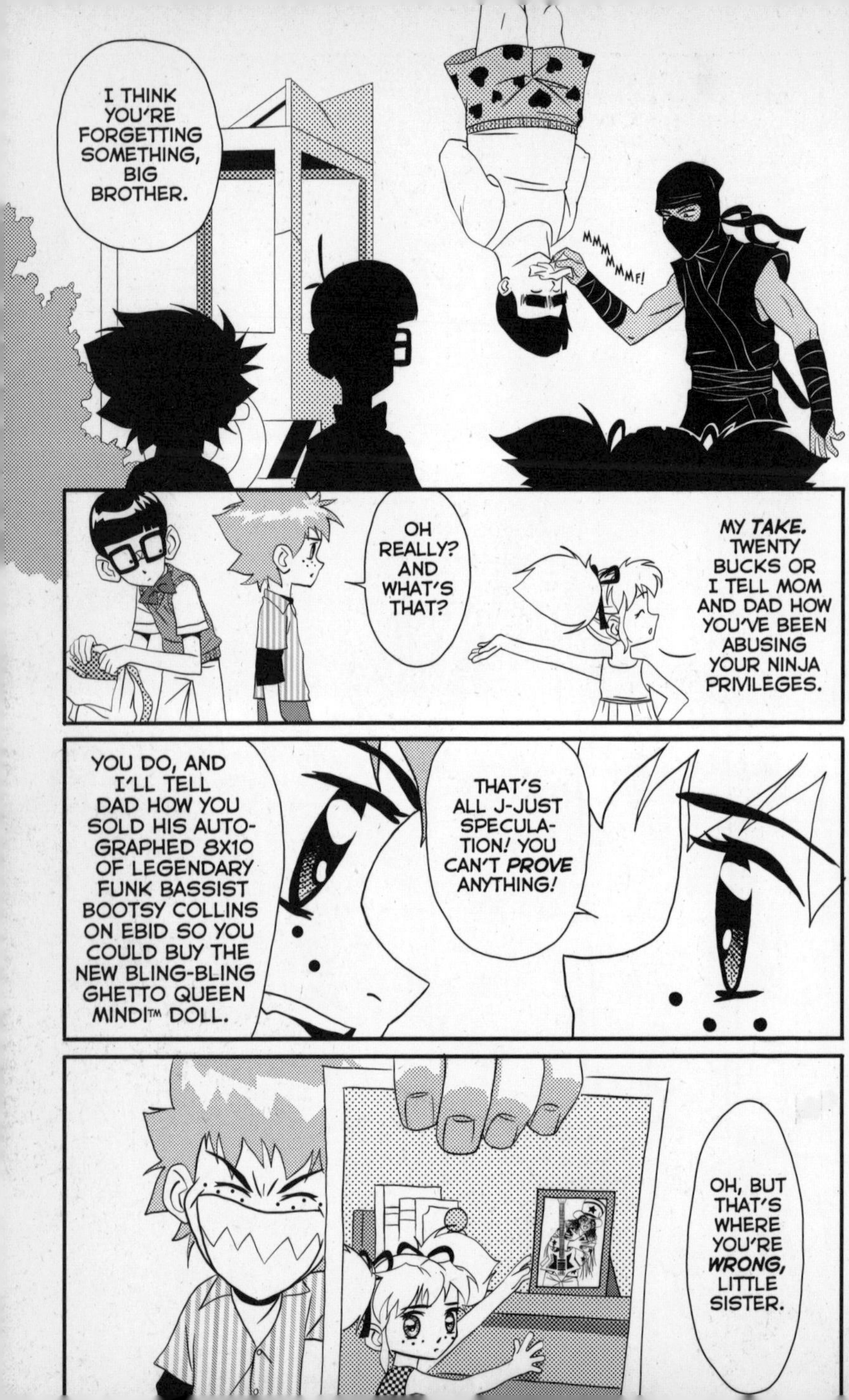
I THINK YOU'RE FORGETTING SOMETHING, BIG BROTHER.
MMMMMMF!
OH REALLY? AND WHAT'S THAT?
MY *TAKE.* TWENTY BUCKS OR I TELL *MOM* AND DAD HOW YOU'VE BEEN ABUSING YOUR NINJA PRIVILEGES.
YOU DO, AND I'LL TELL DAD HOW YOU SOLD HIS AUTO-GRAPHED 8X10 OF LEGENDARY FUNK BASSIST BOOTSY COLLINS ON EBID SO YOU COULD BUY THE NEW BLING-BLING GHETTO QUEEN MINDI™ DOLL.
THAT'S ALL J-JUST SPECULA-TION! YOU CAN'T *PROVE* ANYTHING!
OH, BUT THAT'S WHERE YOU'RE *WRONG,* LITTLE SISTER.

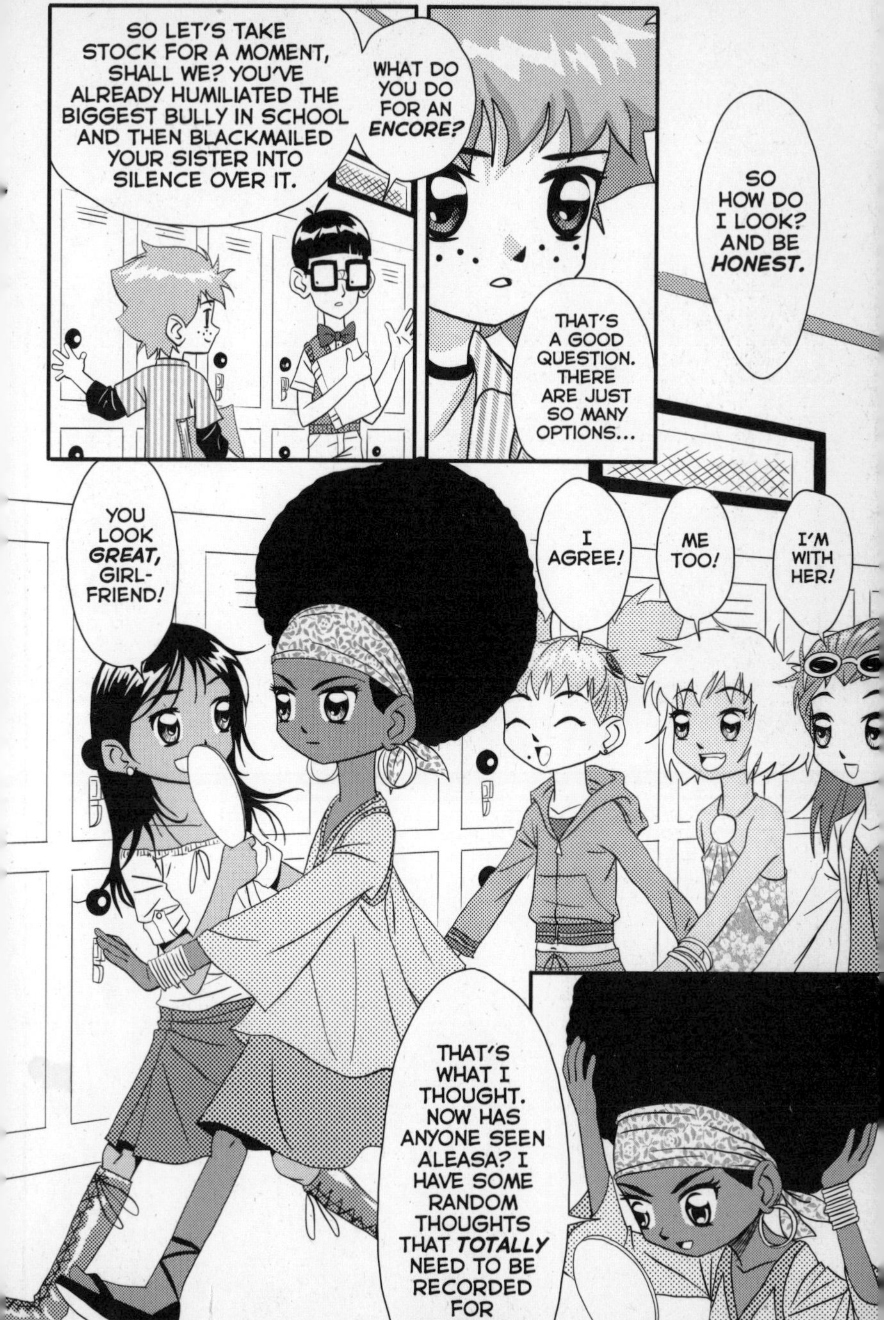
SO LET'S TAKE STOCK FOR A MOMENT, SHALL WE? YOU'VE ALREADY HUMILIATED THE BIGGEST BULLY IN SCHOOL AND THEN BLACKMAILED YOUR SISTER INTO SILENCE OVER IT.
WHAT DO YOU DO FOR AN *ENCORE?*
THAT'S A GOOD QUESTION. THERE ARE JUST SO MANY OPTIONS...
SO HOW DO I LOOK? AND BE ***HONEST.***
YOU LOOK ***GREAT,*** GIRL-FRIEND!
I AGREE!
ME TOO!
I'M WITH HER!
THAT'S WHAT I THOUGHT. NOW HAS ANYONE SEEN ALEASA? I HAVE SOME RANDOM THOUGHTS THAT ***TOTALLY*** NEED TO BE RECORDED FOR POSTERITY.

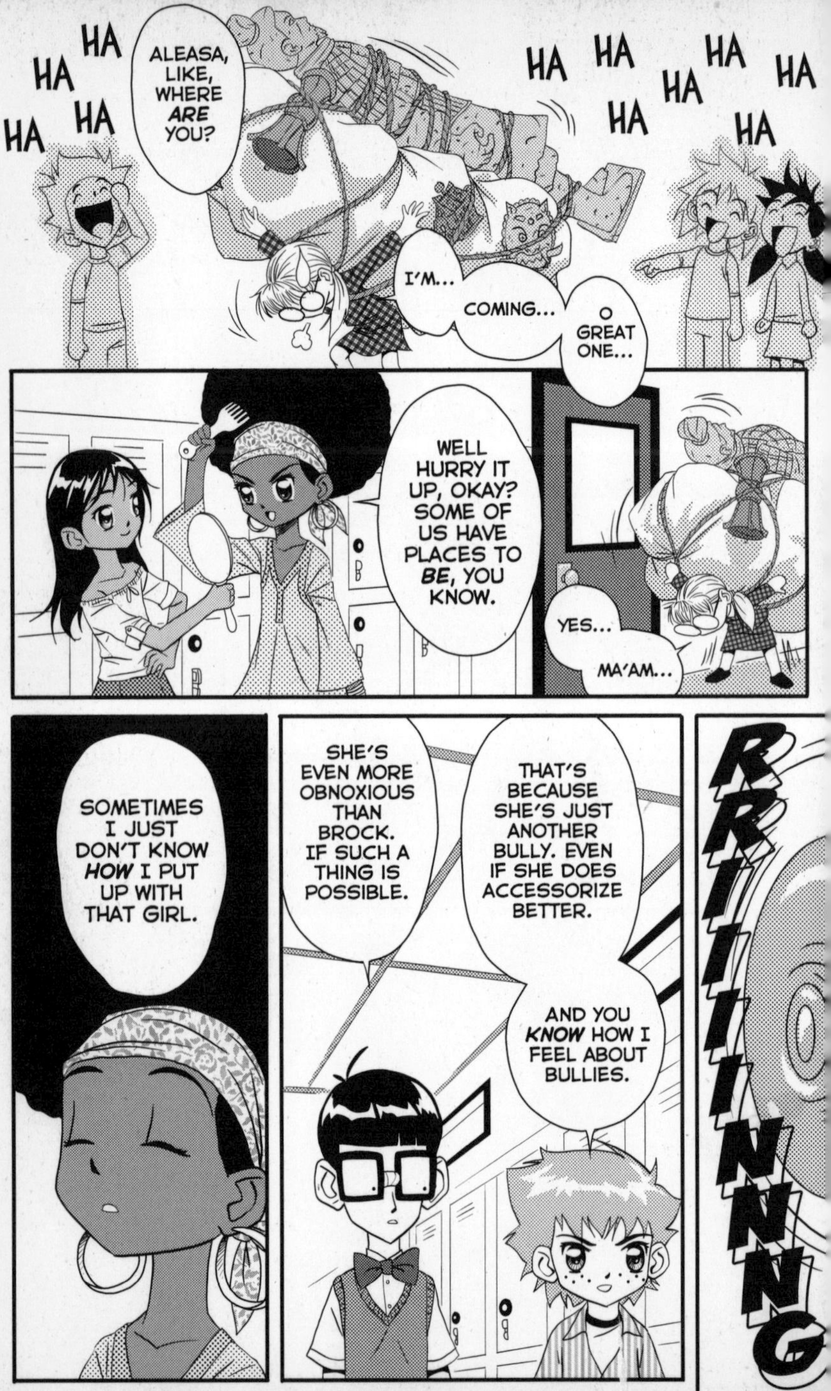
HA HA HA HA HA
ALEASA, LIKE, WHERE *ARE* YOU?
HA HA HA HA HA HA HA
I'M...
COMING...
O GREAT ONE...
WELL HURRY IT UP, OKAY? SOME OF US HAVE PLACES TO *BE*, YOU KNOW.
YES...
MA'AM...
SOMETIMES I JUST DON'T KNOW *HOW* I PUT UP WITH THAT GIRL.
SHE'S EVEN MORE OBNOXIOUS THAN BROCK. IF SUCH A THING IS POSSIBLE.
THAT'S BECAUSE SHE'S JUST ANOTHER BULLY. EVEN IF SHE DOES ACCESSORIZE BETTER.
AND YOU *KNOW* HOW I FEEL ABOUT BULLIES.
RRIIIINNNG

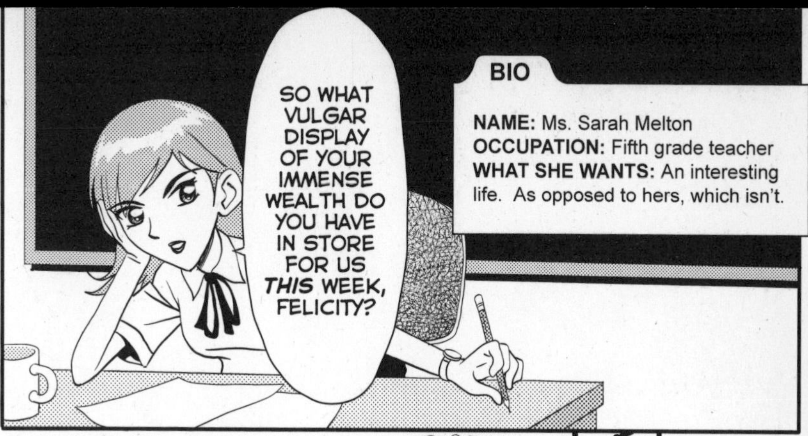
BIO
NAME: Ms. Sarah Melton
OCCUPATION: Fifth grade teacher
WHAT SHE WANTS: An interesting life. As opposed to hers, which isn't.
SO WHAT VULGAR DISPLAY OF YOUR IMMENSE WEALTH DO YOU HAVE IN STORE FOR US *THIS* WEEK, FELICITY?

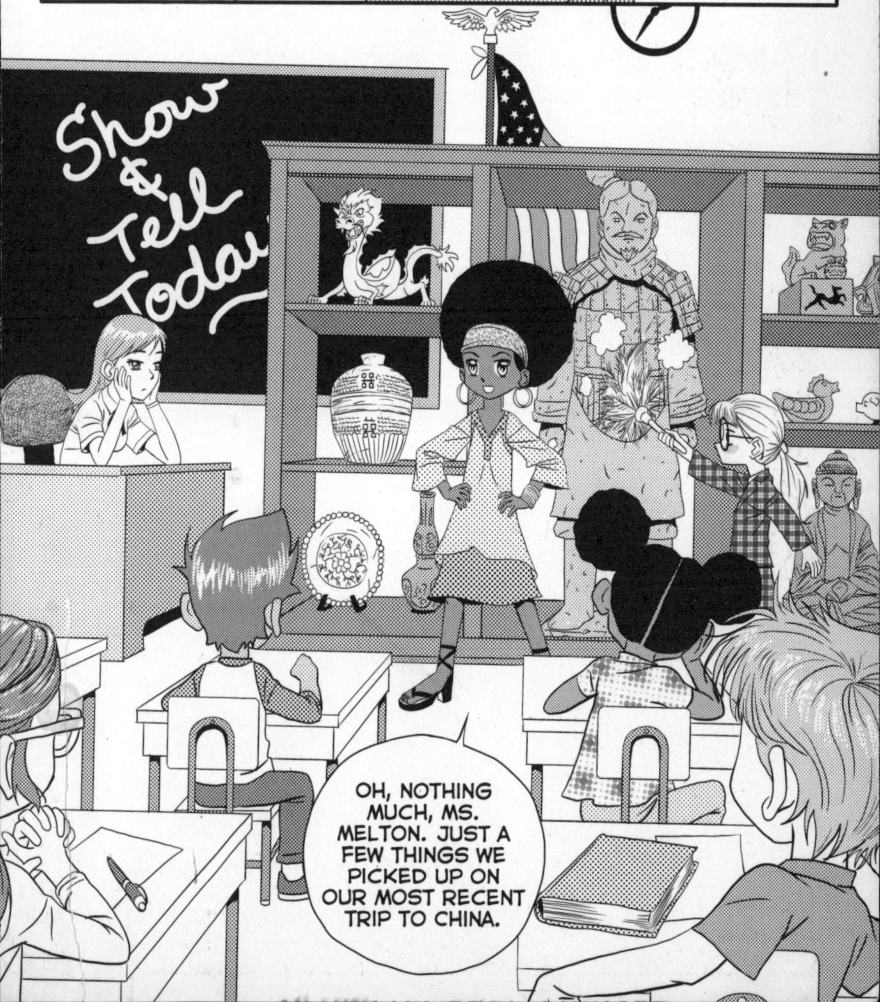
Show & Tell Today
OH, NOTHING MUCH, MS. MELTON. JUST A FEW THINGS WE PICKED UP ON OUR MOST RECENT TRIP TO CHINA.

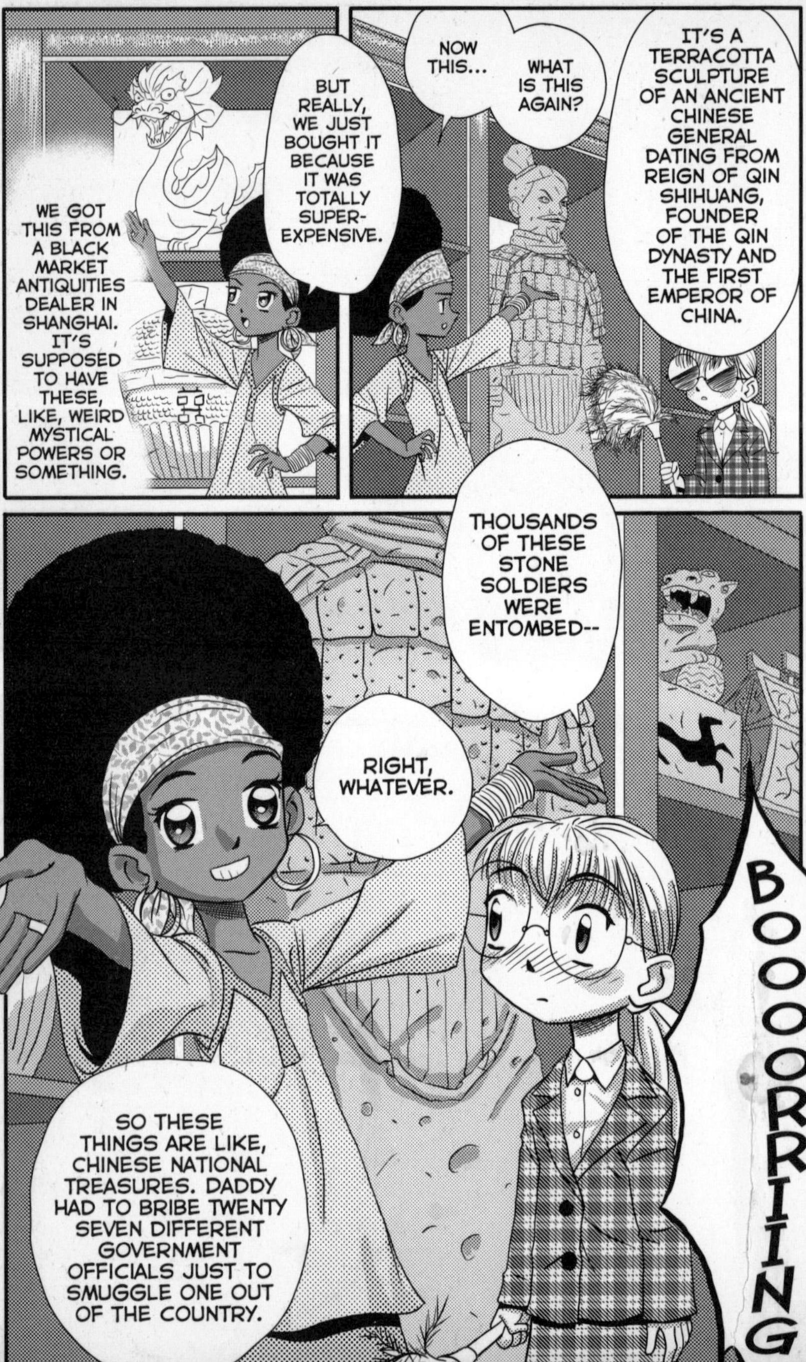
WE GOT THIS FROM A BLACK MARKET ANTIQUITIES DEALER IN SHANGHAI. IT'S SUPPOSED TO HAVE THESE, LIKE, WEIRD MYSTICAL POWERS OR SOMETHING.
BUT REALLY, WE JUST BOUGHT IT BECAUSE IT WAS TOTALLY SUPER-EXPENSIVE.
NOW THIS...
WHAT IS THIS AGAIN?
IT'S A TERRACOTTA SCULPTURE OF AN ANCIENT CHINESE GENERAL DATING FROM REIGN OF QIN SHIHUANG, FOUNDER OF THE QIN DYNASTY AND THE FIRST EMPEROR OF CHINA.
THOUSANDS OF THESE STONE SOLDIERS WERE ENTOMBED--
RIGHT, WHATEVER.
SO THESE THINGS ARE LIKE, CHINESE NATIONAL TREASURES. DADDY HAD TO BRIBE TWENTY SEVEN DIFFERENT GOVERNMENT OFFICIALS JUST TO SMUGGLE ONE OUT OF THE COUNTRY.
BOOOOORRIING

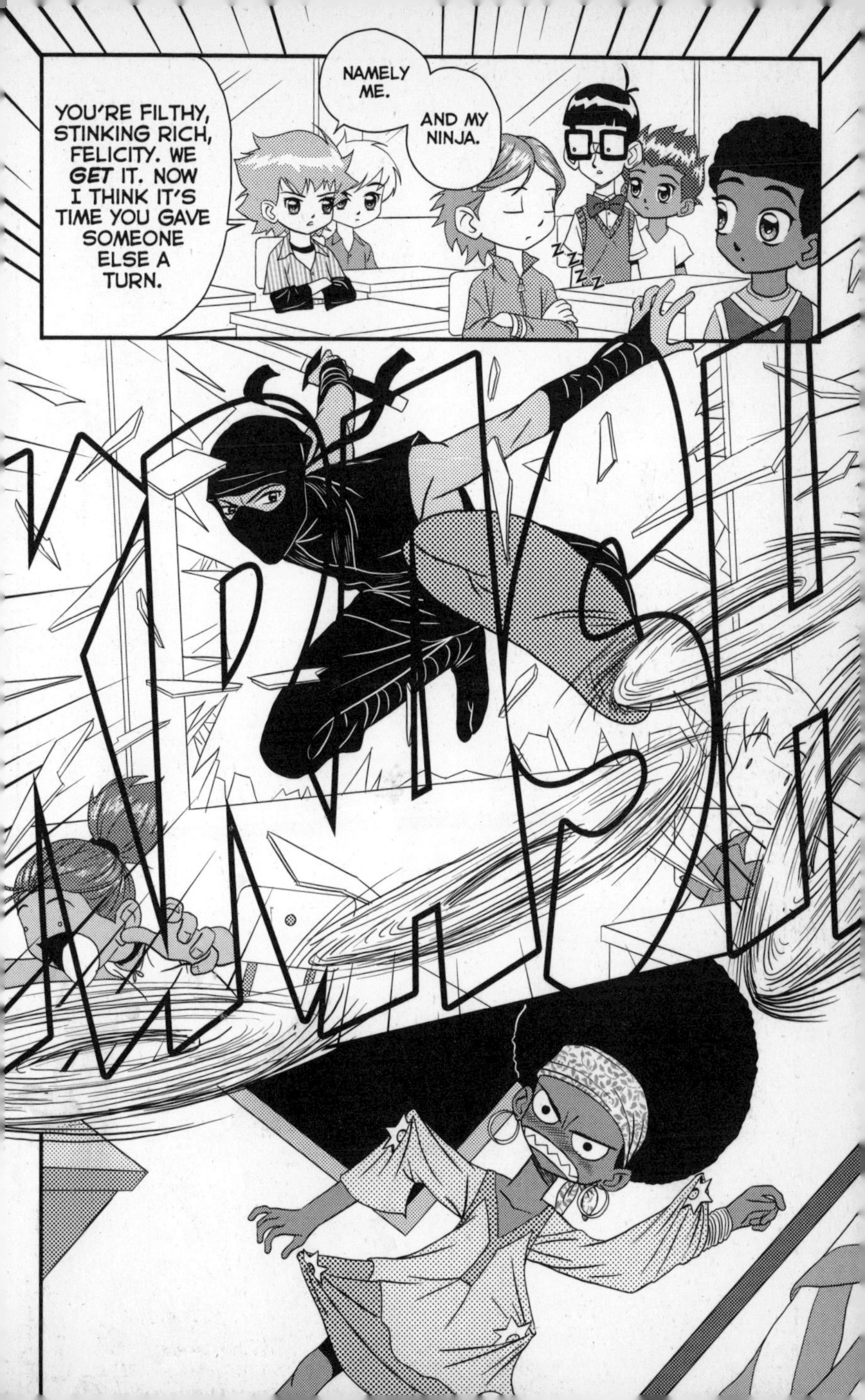
YOU'RE FILTHY, STINKING RICH, FELICITY. WE *GET* IT. NOW I THINK IT'S TIME YOU GAVE SOMEONE ELSE A TURN.
NAMELY ME.
AND MY NINJA.

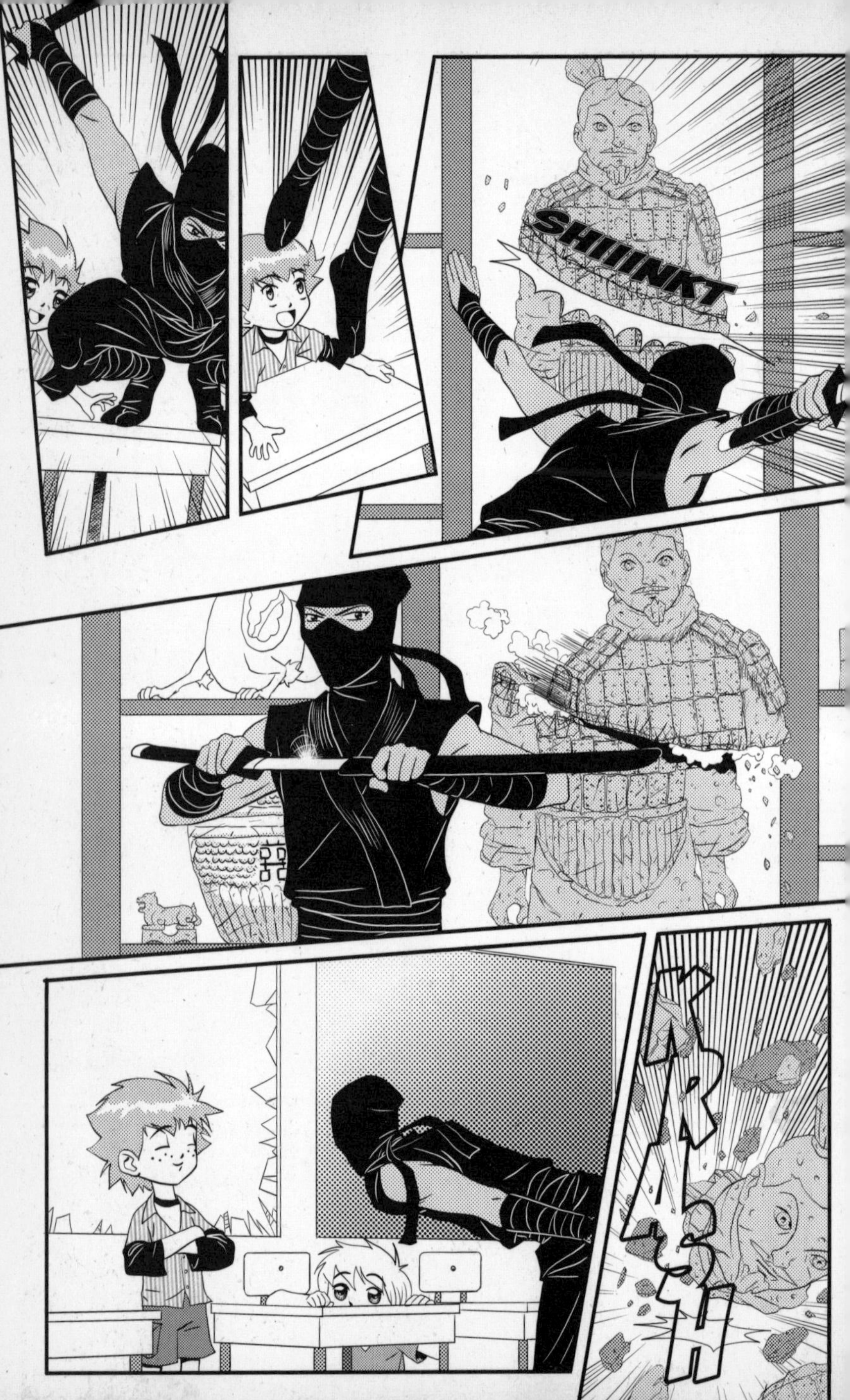
SHIIINKT
KRASH

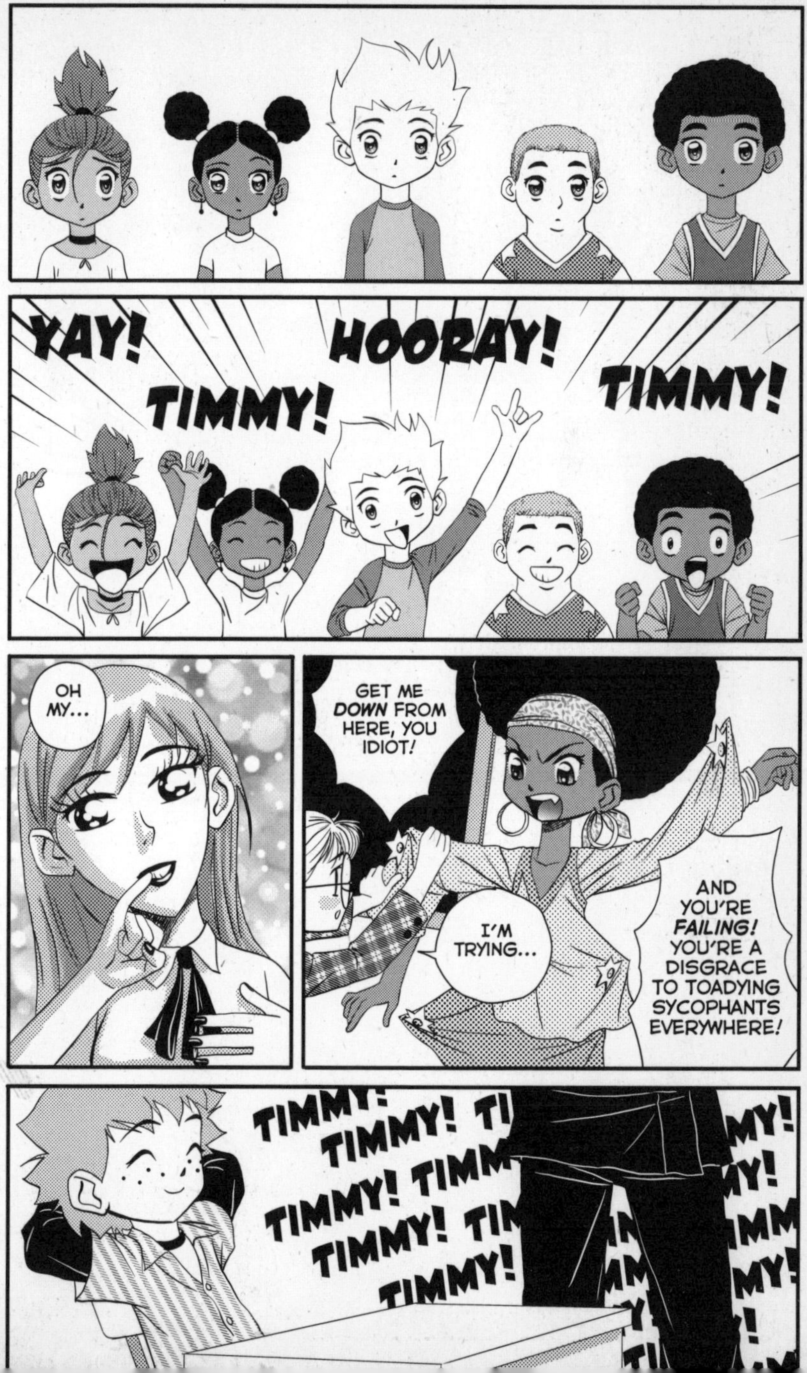
YAY!
HOORAY!
TIMMY!
TIMMY!
OH MY...
GET ME *DOWN* FROM HERE, YOU IDIOT!
I'M TRYING...
AND YOU'RE *FAILING!* YOU'RE A DISGRACE TO TOADYING SYCOPHANTS EVERYWHERE!
TIMMY!
TIMMY!
TIMMY!
TIMMY!
TIMMY!
TIMMY!

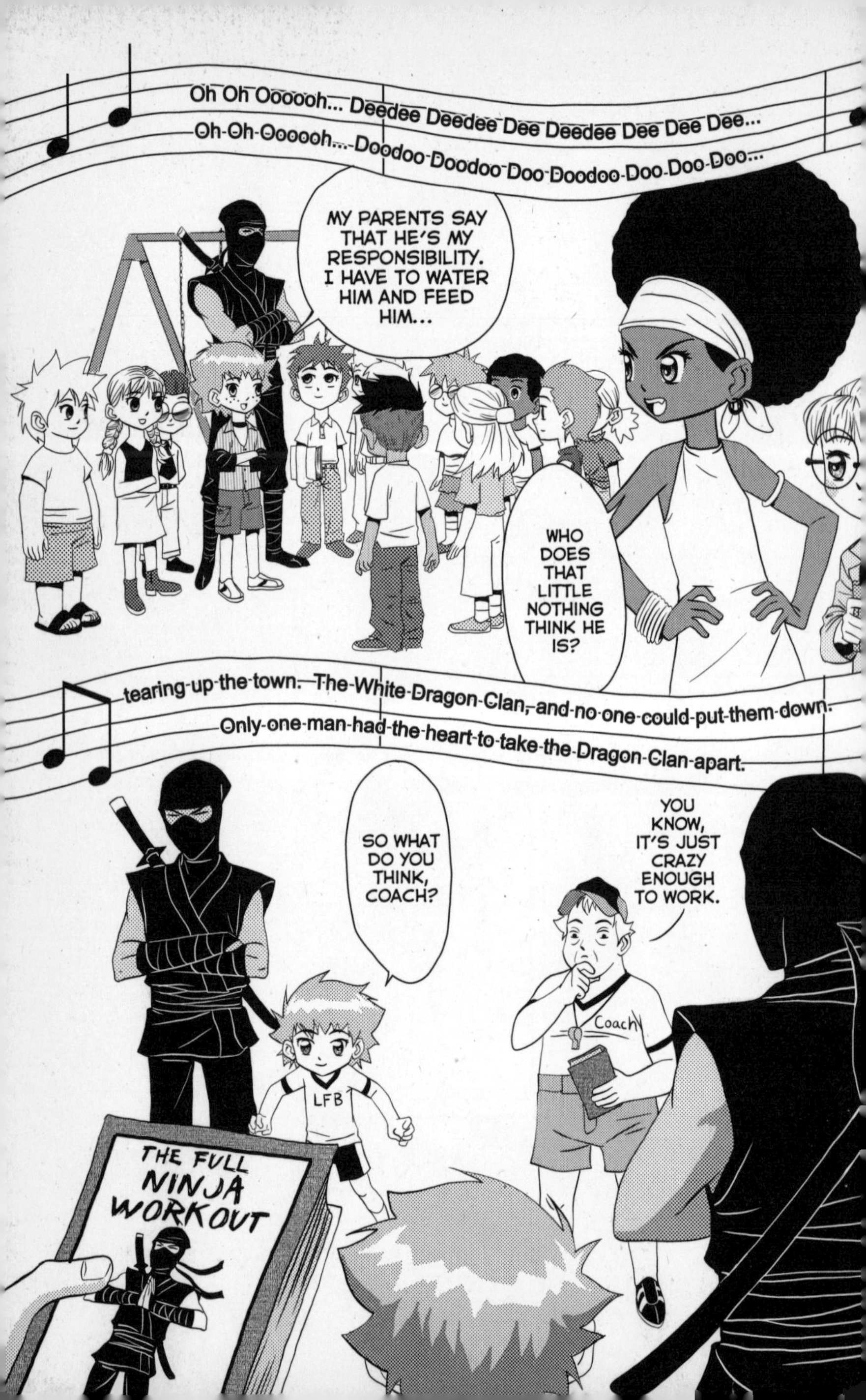

Oh Oh Oooooh... Deedee Deedee Dee Deedee Dee Dee Dee...
Oh-Oh-Oooooh...-Doodoo-Doodoo-Doo-Doodoo-Doo-Doo-Doo...
MY PARENTS SAY THAT HE'S MY RESPONSIBILITY. I HAVE TO WATER HIM AND FEED HIM...
WHO DOES THAT LITTLE NOTHING THINK HE IS?
tearing-up-the-town. The-White-Dragon-Clan, and-no-one-could-put-them-down.
Only-one-man-had-the-heart-to-take-the-Dragon-Clan-apart.
SO WHAT DO YOU THINK, COACH?
YOU KNOW, IT'S JUST CRAZY ENOUGH TO WORK.
Coach
LFB
THE FULL NINJA WORKOUT

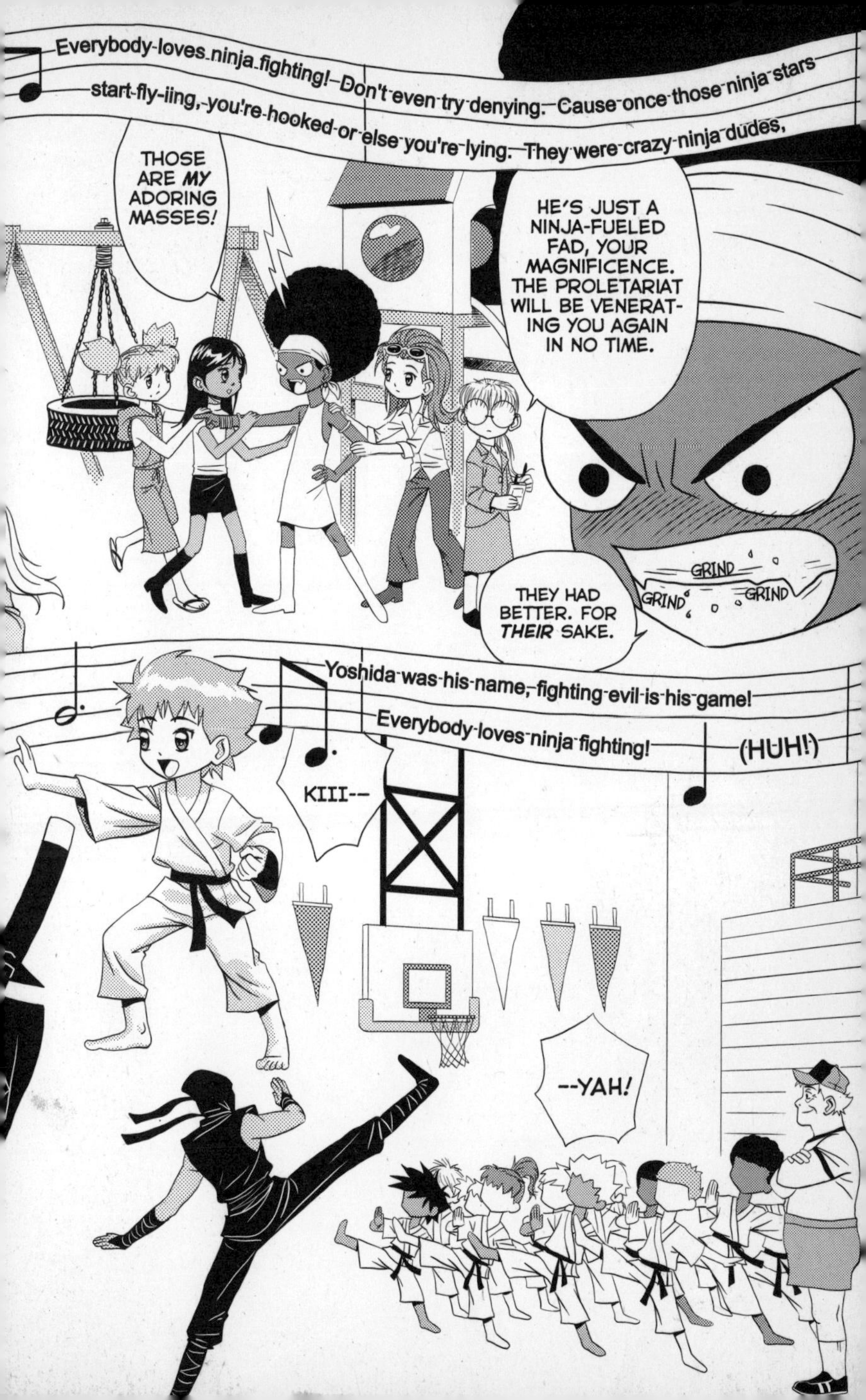
Everybody loves ninja fighting! Don't even try denying. 'Cause once those ninja stars start fly-iing, you're hooked or else you're lying. They were crazy ninja dudes,
THOSE ARE *MY* ADORING MASSES!
HE'S JUST A NINJA-FUELED FAD, YOUR MAGNIFICENCE. THE PROLETARIAT WILL BE VENERAT-ING YOU AGAIN IN NO TIME.
GRIND
GRIND
GRIND
THEY HAD BETTER. FOR ***THEIR*** SAKE.
Yoshida was his name, fighting evil is his game! Everybody loves ninja fighting!
(HUH!)
KIII--
--YAH!

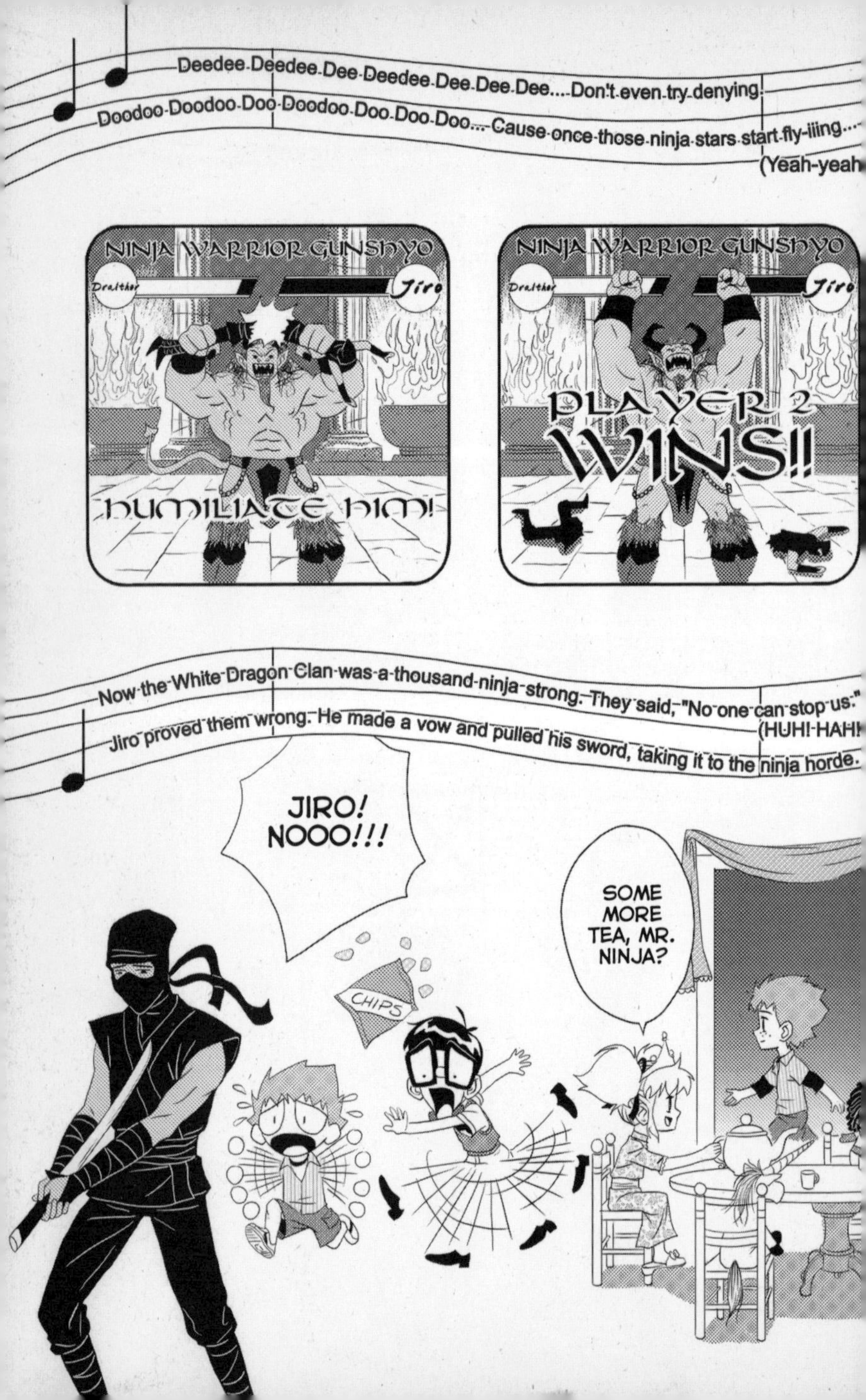
Deedee Deedee Dee Deedee Dee Dee Dee.... Don't even try denying.
Doodoo Doodoo Doo Doodoo Doo Doo Doo.... Cause once those ninja stars start fly-iiing....
(Yeah-yeah
NINJA WARRIOR GUNSHYO
Dralthor
Jiro
HUMILIATE HIM!
NINJA WARRIOR GUNSHYO
Dralthor
Jiro
PLAYER 2 WINS!!
Now the White Dragon Clan was a thousand ninja strong. They said, "No one can stop us."
Jiro proved them wrong. He made a vow and pulled his sword, taking it to the ninja horde.
(HUH! HAH!
JIRO! NOOO!!!
SOME MORE TEA, MR. NINJA?
CHIPS

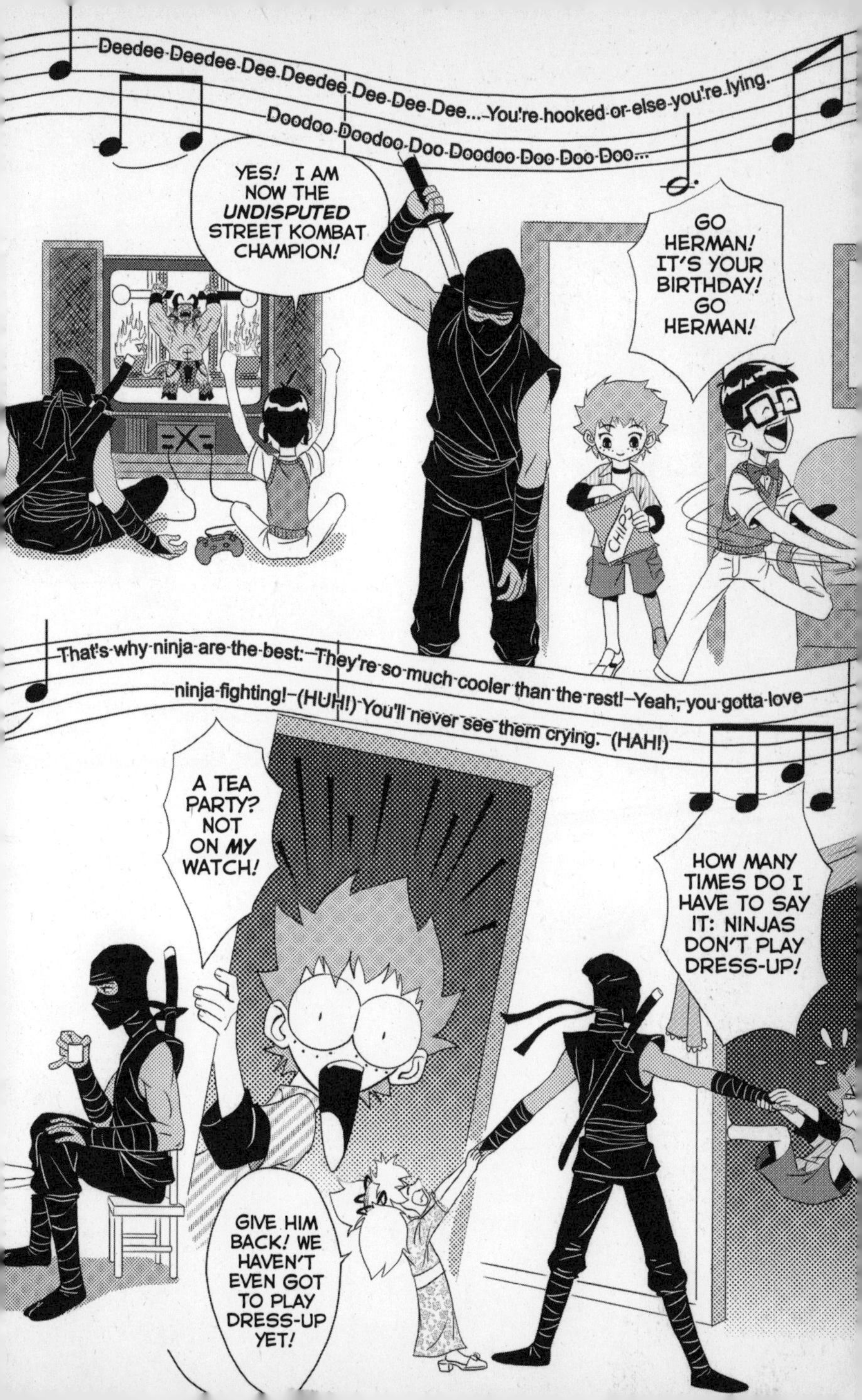
Deedee Deedee Dee Deedee Dee Dee Dee... You're hooked or else you're lying.
Doodoo Doodoo Doo Doodoo Doo Doo Doo...
YES! I AM NOW THE *UNDISPUTED* STREET KOMBAT CHAMPION!
GO HERMAN! IT'S YOUR BIRTHDAY! GO HERMAN!
CHIPS
That's why ninja are the best: They're so much cooler than the rest! Yeah, you gotta love
ninja fighting! (HUH!) You'll never see them crying. (HAH!)
A TEA PARTY? NOT ON *MY* WATCH!
GIVE HIM BACK! WE HAVEN'T EVEN GOT TO PLAY DRESS-UP YET!
HOW MANY TIMES DO I HAVE TO SAY IT: NINJAS DON'T PLAY DRESS-UP!

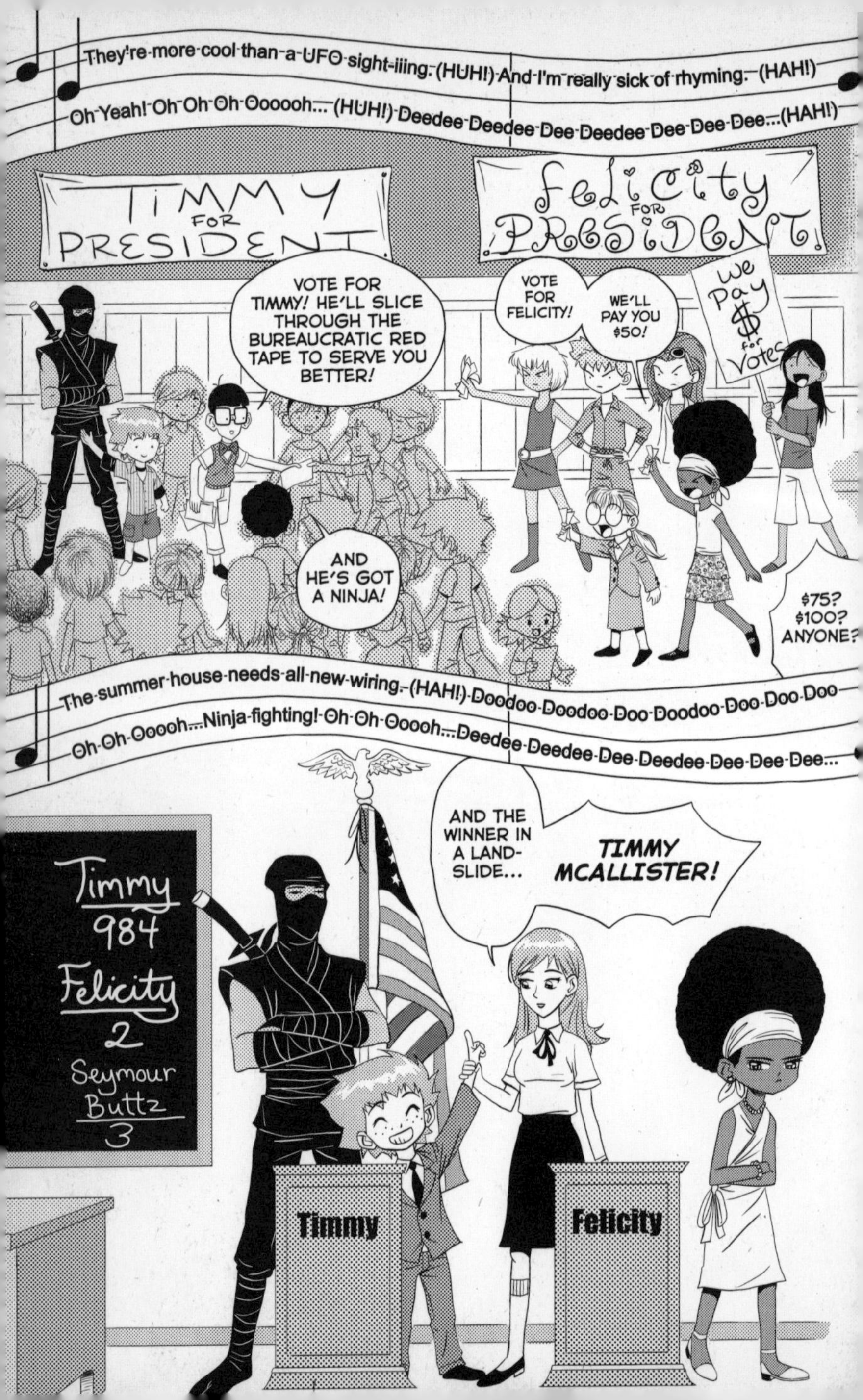
They're-more-cool-than-a-UFO-sight-iiing.-(HUH!)-And-I'm-really-sick-of-rhyming.-(HAH!)
Oh-Yeah!-Oh-Oh-Oh-Oooooh...-(HUH!)-Deedee-Deedee-Dee-Deedee-Dee-Dee-Dee...(HAH!)
TIMMY FOR PRESIDENT
Felicity FOR PRESIDENT
VOTE FOR TIMMY! HE'LL SLICE THROUGH THE BUREAUCRATIC RED TAPE TO SERVE YOU BETTER!
VOTE FOR FELICITY!
WE'LL PAY YOU $50!
We Pay $ for Votes
AND HE'S GOT A NINJA!
$75? $100? ANYONE?
The-summer-house-needs-all-new-wiring.-(HAH!)-Doodoo-Doodoo-Doo-Doodoo-Doo-Doo-Doo
Oh-Oh-Ooooh...Ninja-fighting!-Oh-Oh-Ooooh...Deedee-Deedee-Dee-Deedee-Dee-Dee-Dee...
Timmy 984 Felicity 2 Seymour Buttz 3
AND THE WINNER IN A LAND-SLIDE...
TIMMY MCALLISTER!
Timmy
Felicity

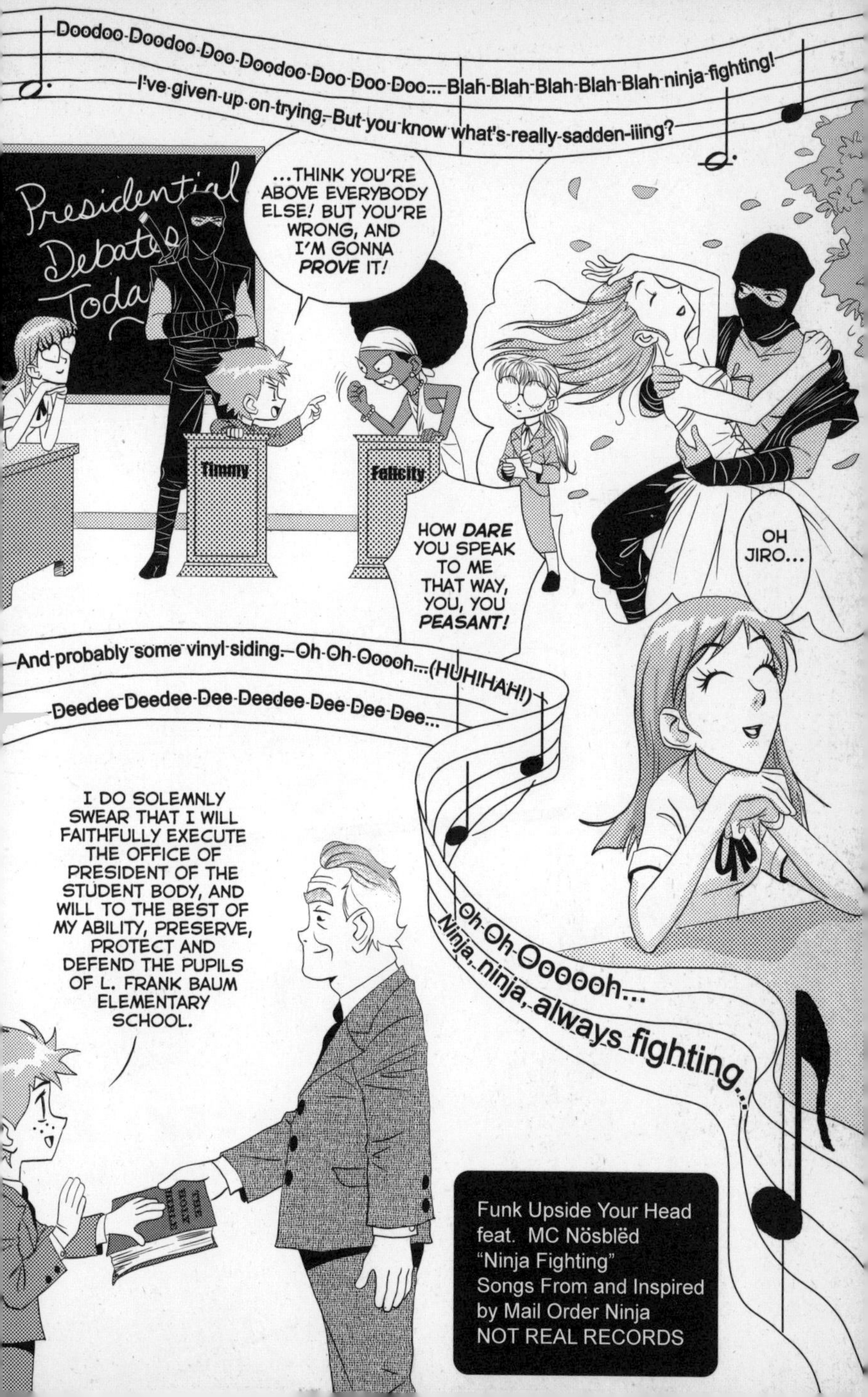
Doodoo-Doodoo-Doo-Doodoo-Doo-Doo-Doo... Blah-Blah-Blah-Blah-Blah-ninja-fighting!
I've-given-up-on-trying.-But-you-know-what's-really-sadden-iiing?
Presidential Debat Toda
...THINK YOU'RE ABOVE EVERYBODY ELSE! BUT YOU'RE WRONG, AND I'M GONNA PROVE IT!
Timmy
Felicity
HOW DARE YOU SPEAK TO ME THAT WAY, YOU, YOU PEASANT!
OH JIRO...
And-probably-some-vinyl-siding.-Oh-Oh-Ooooh...(HUH!HAH!)
Deedee-Deedee-Dee-Deedee-Dee-Dee-Dee...
I DO SOLEMNLY SWEAR THAT I WILL FAITHFULLY EXECUTE THE OFFICE OF PRESIDENT OF THE STUDENT BODY, AND WILL TO THE BEST OF MY ABILITY, PRESERVE, PROTECT AND DEFEND THE PUPILS OF L. FRANK BAUM ELEMENTARY SCHOOL.
Oh-Oh-Oooooh...
Ninja, ninja, always fighting...
Funk Upside Your Head feat. MC Nösblëd "Ninja Fighting" Songs From and Inspired by Mail Order Ninja NOT REAL RECORDS

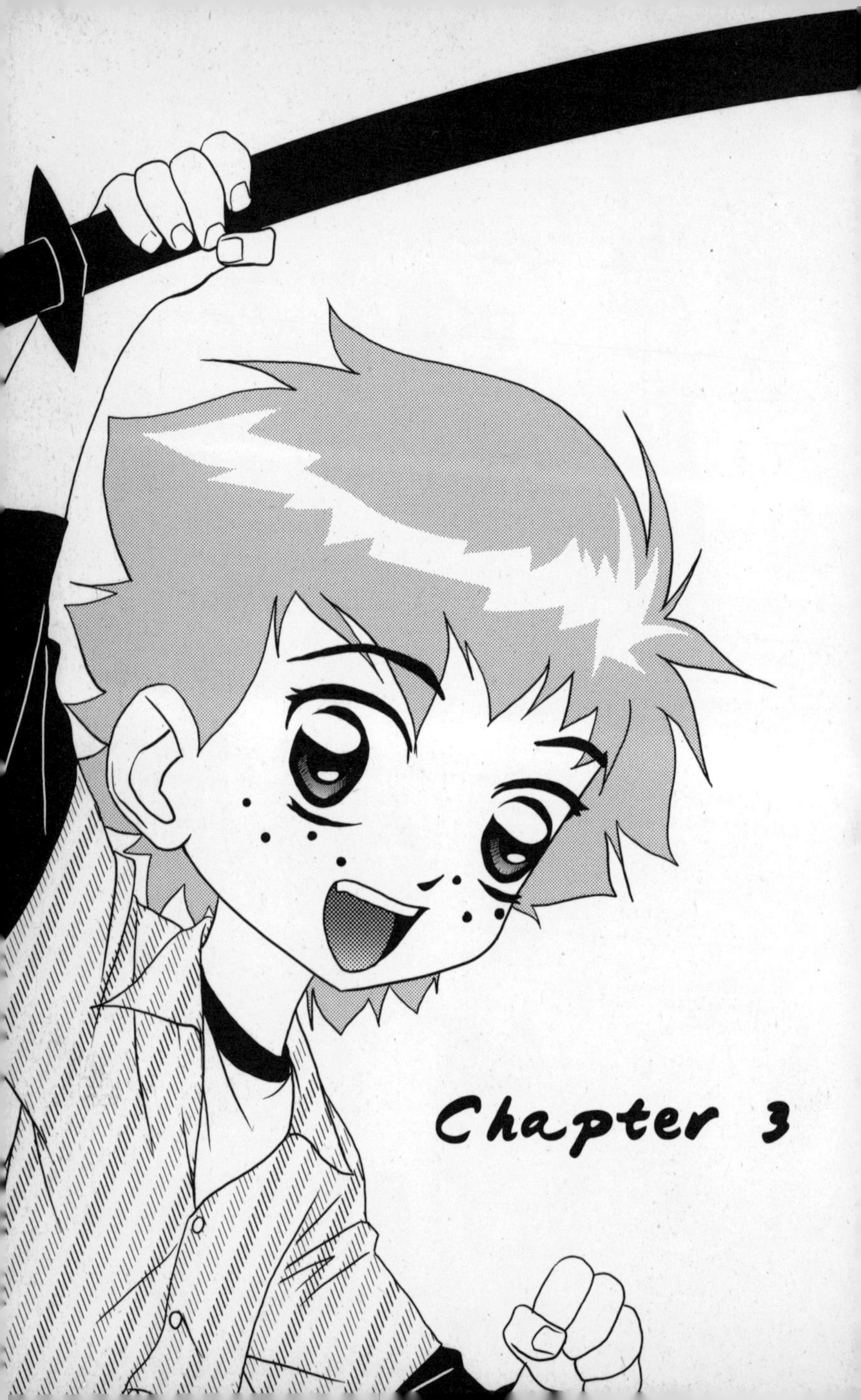

Chapter 3

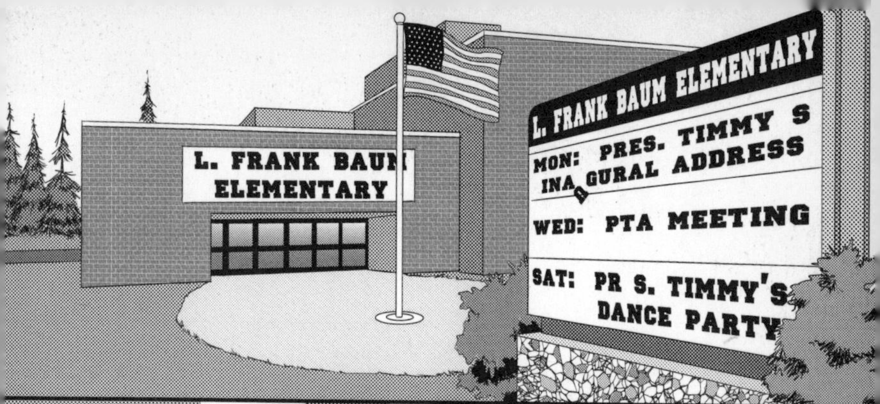
L. FRANK BAUM ELEMENTARY
L. FRANK BAUM ELEMENTARY
MON: PRES. TIMMY S INA U GURAL ADDRESS
WED: PTA MEETING
SAT: PR S. TIMMY'S DANCE PARTY

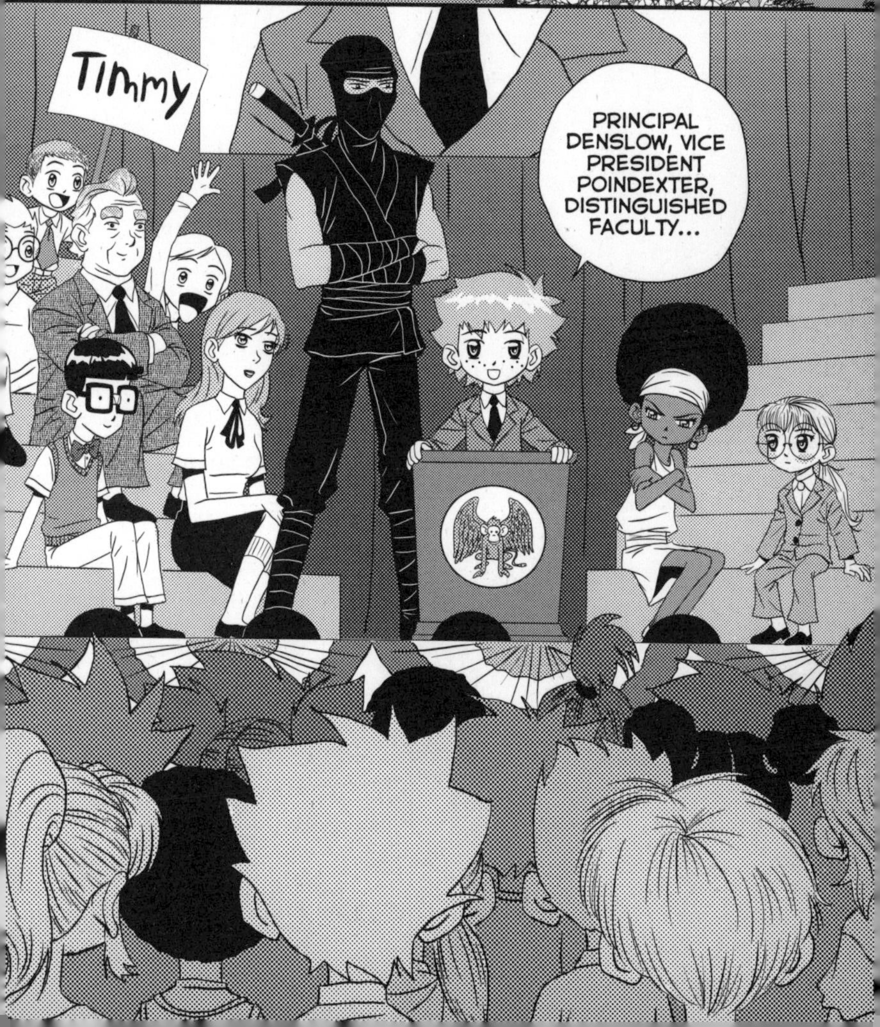
Timmy
PRINCIPAL DENSLOW, VICE PRESIDENT POINDEXTER, DISTINGUISHED FACULTY...

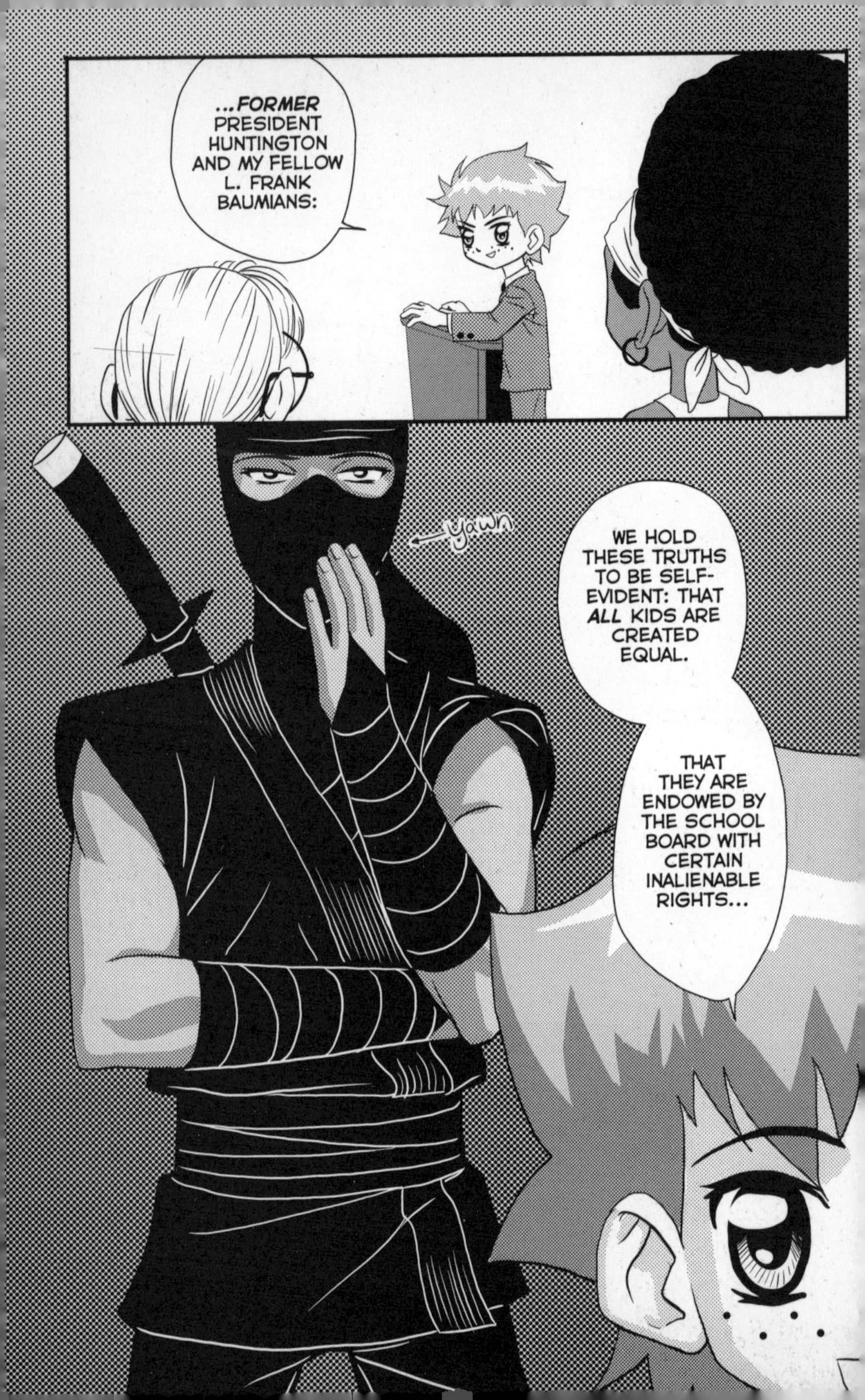
...FORMER PRESIDENT HUNTINGTON AND MY FELLOW L. FRANK BAUMIANS:
YAWN
WE HOLD THESE TRUTHS TO BE SELF-EVIDENT: THAT ALL KIDS ARE CREATED EQUAL.
THAT THEY ARE ENDOWED BY THE SCHOOL BOARD WITH CERTAIN INALIENABLE RIGHTS...

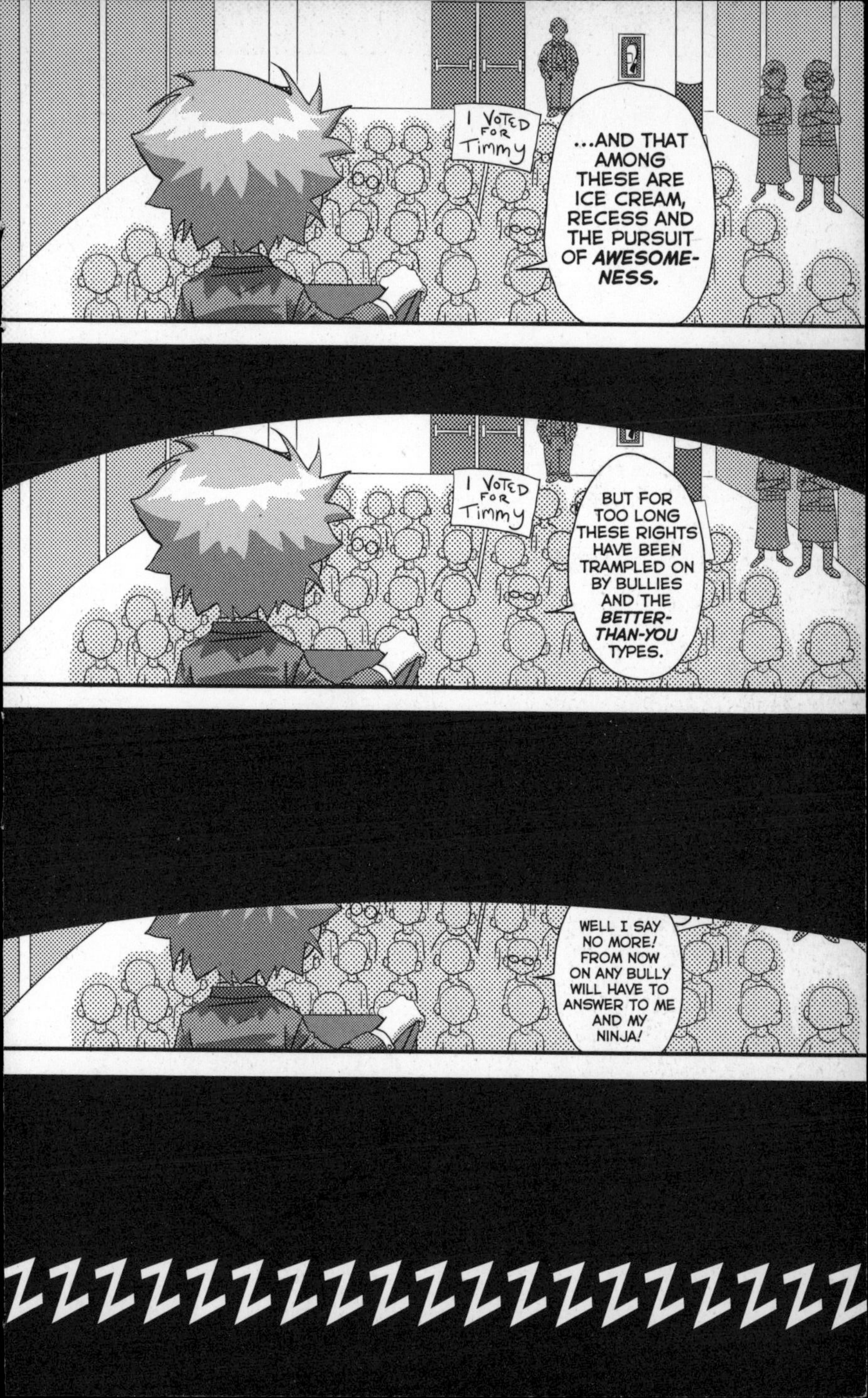
I VOTED FOR Timmy
...AND THAT AMONG THESE ARE ICE CREAM, RECESS AND THE PURSUIT OF AWESOMENESS.
I VOTED FOR Timmy
BUT FOR TOO LONG THESE RIGHTS HAVE BEEN TRAMPLED ON BY BULLIES AND THE BETTER-THAN-YOU TYPES.
WELL I SAY NO MORE! FROM NOW ON ANY BULLY WILL HAVE TO ANSWER TO ME AND MY NINJA!
ZZZZZZZZZZZZZZZZZZZZ

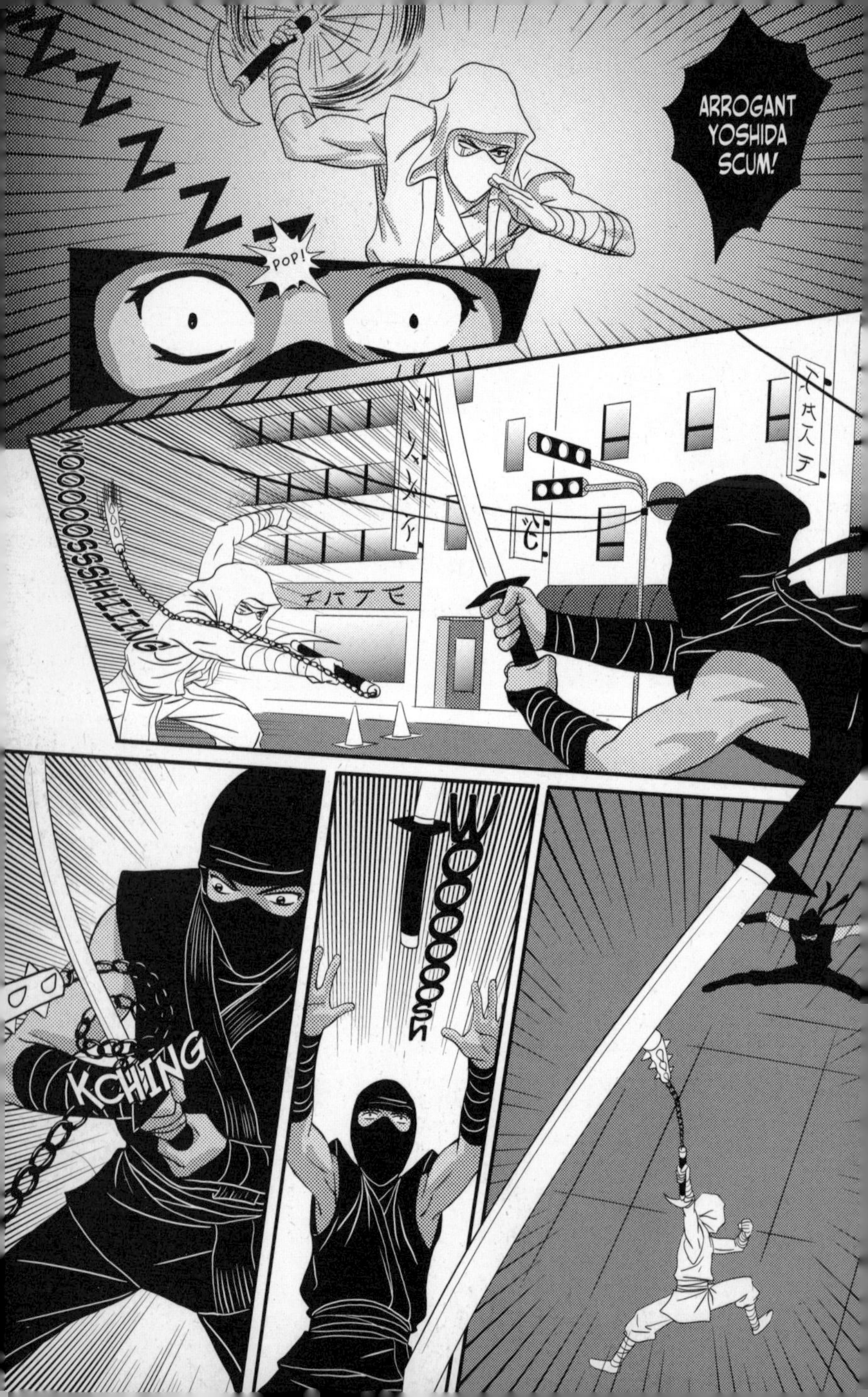
ZZZZZ
POP!
ARROGANT YOSHIDA SCUM!
WOOOOOOSSSHIIING
KCHING
WOOOOOOSH

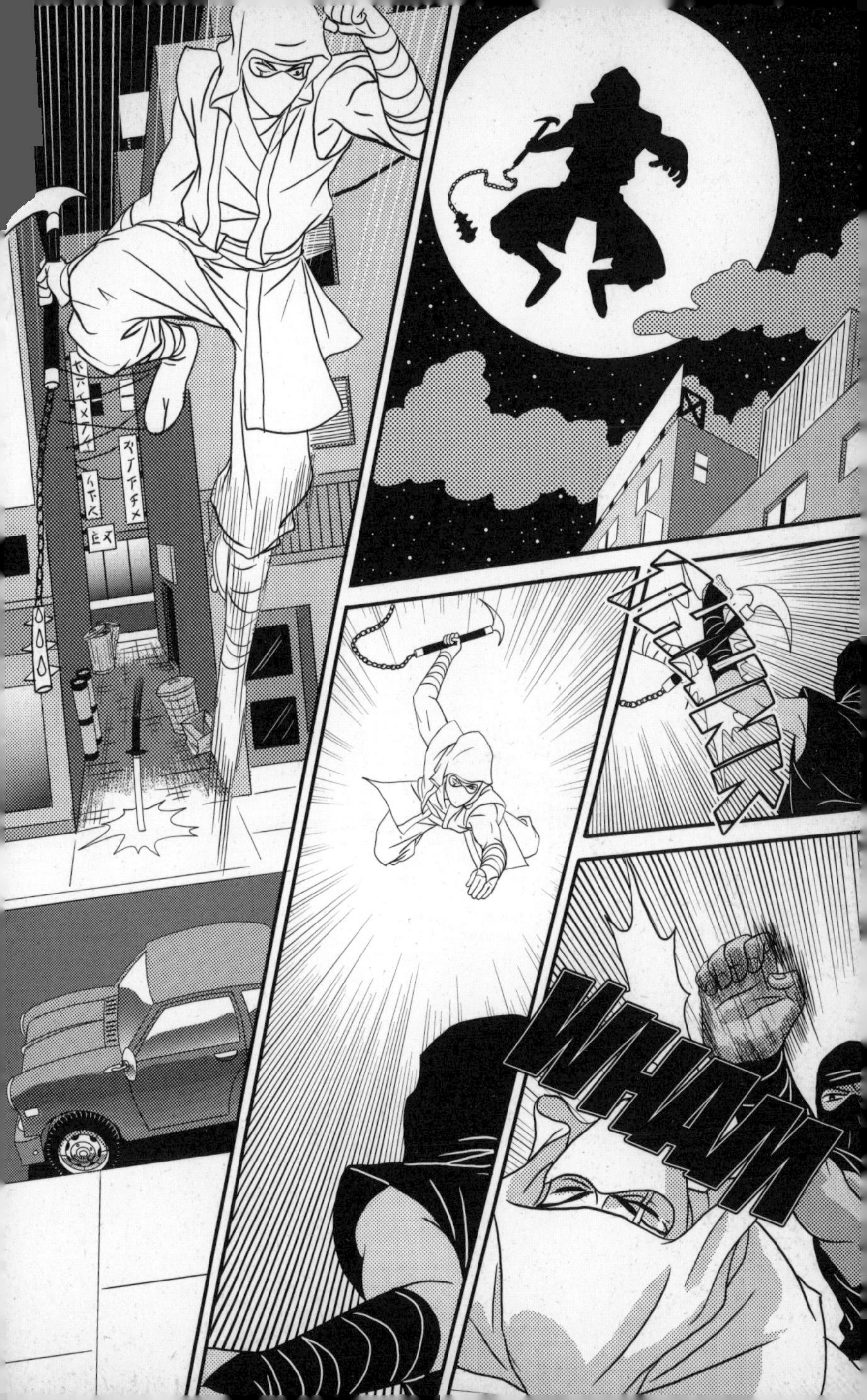
WHAM

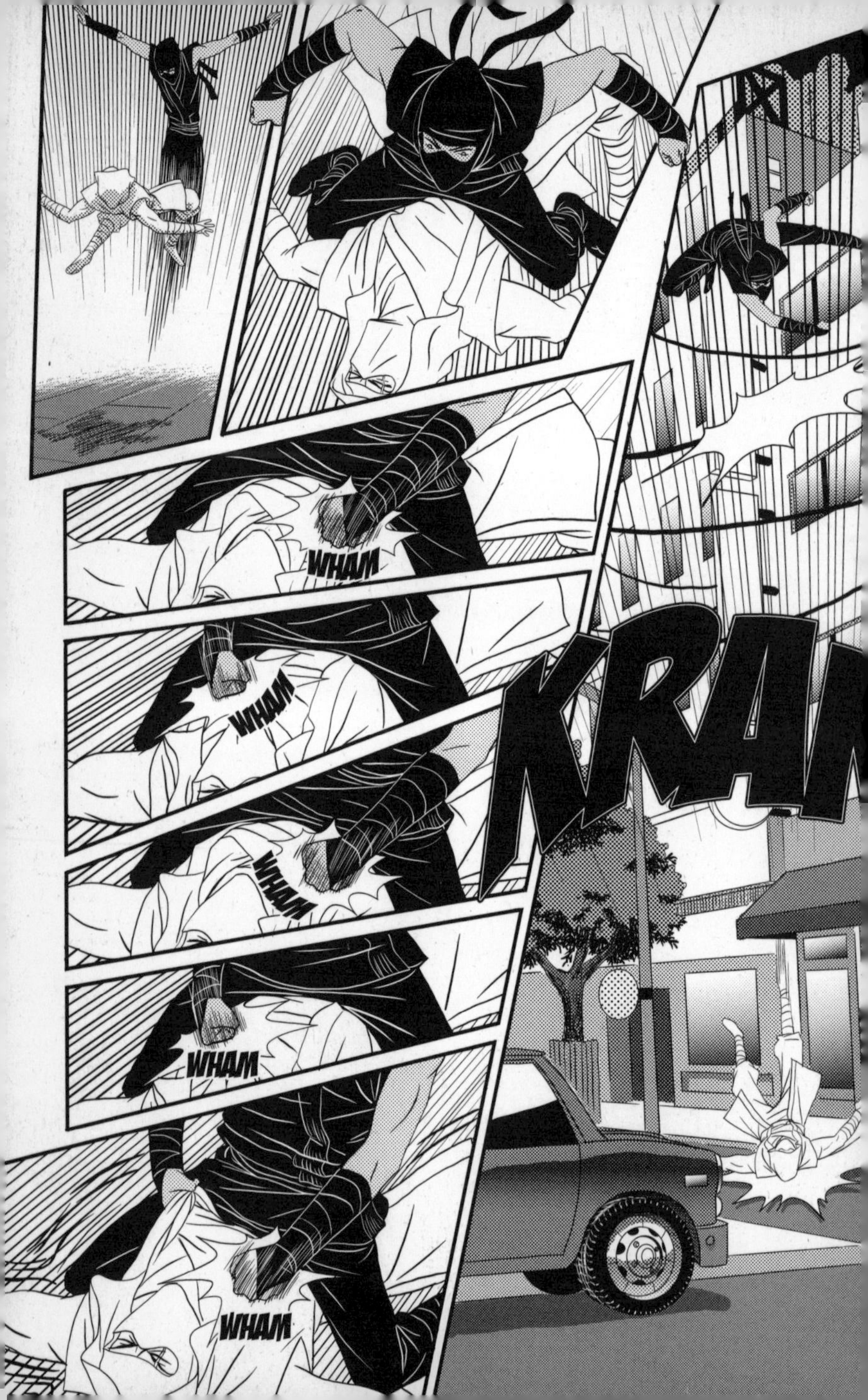
WHAM
WHAM
WHAM
WHAM
WHAM
KRA

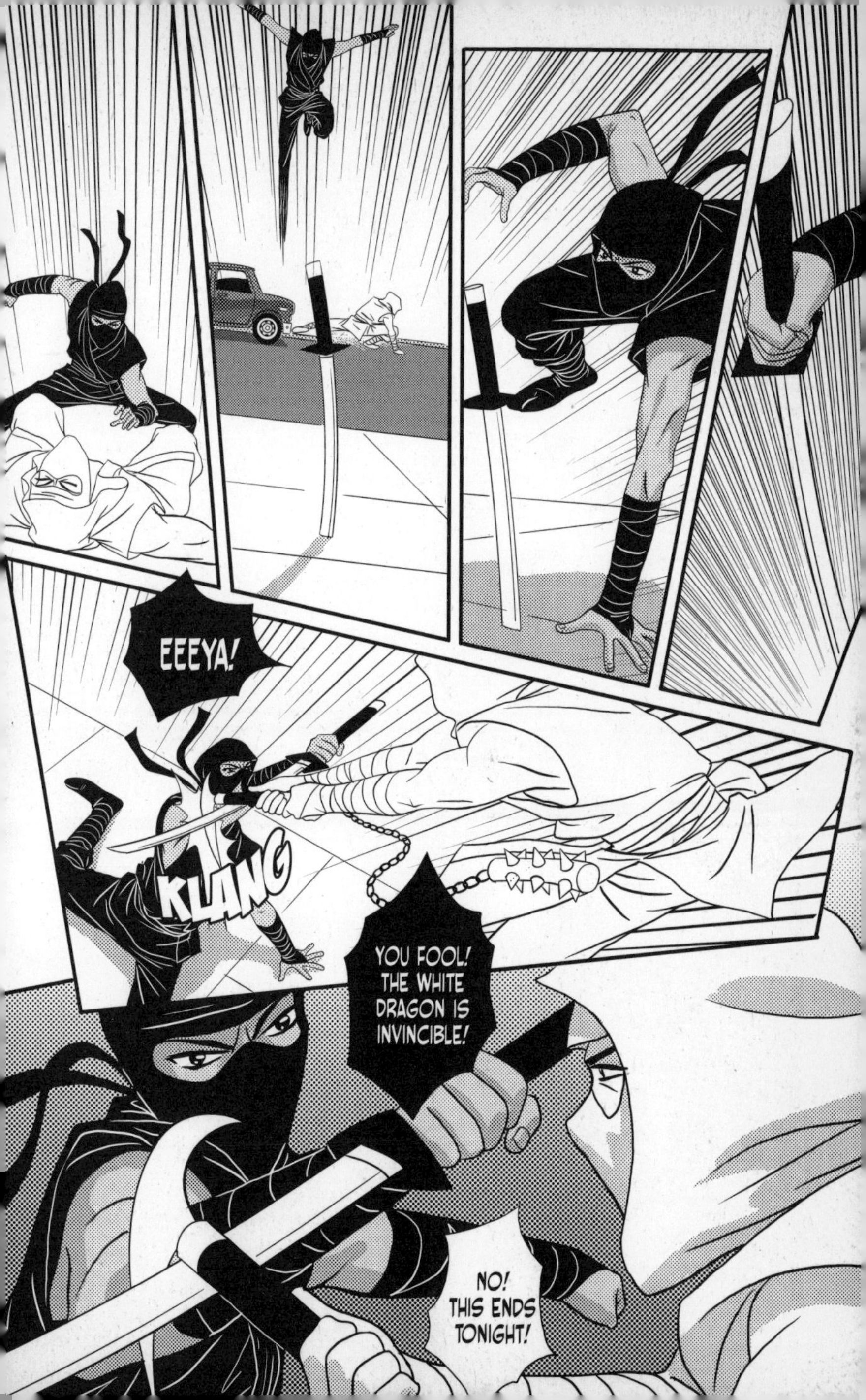
EEEYA!
KLANG
YOU FOOL! THE WHITE DRAGON IS INVINCIBLE!
NO! THIS ENDS TONIGHT!

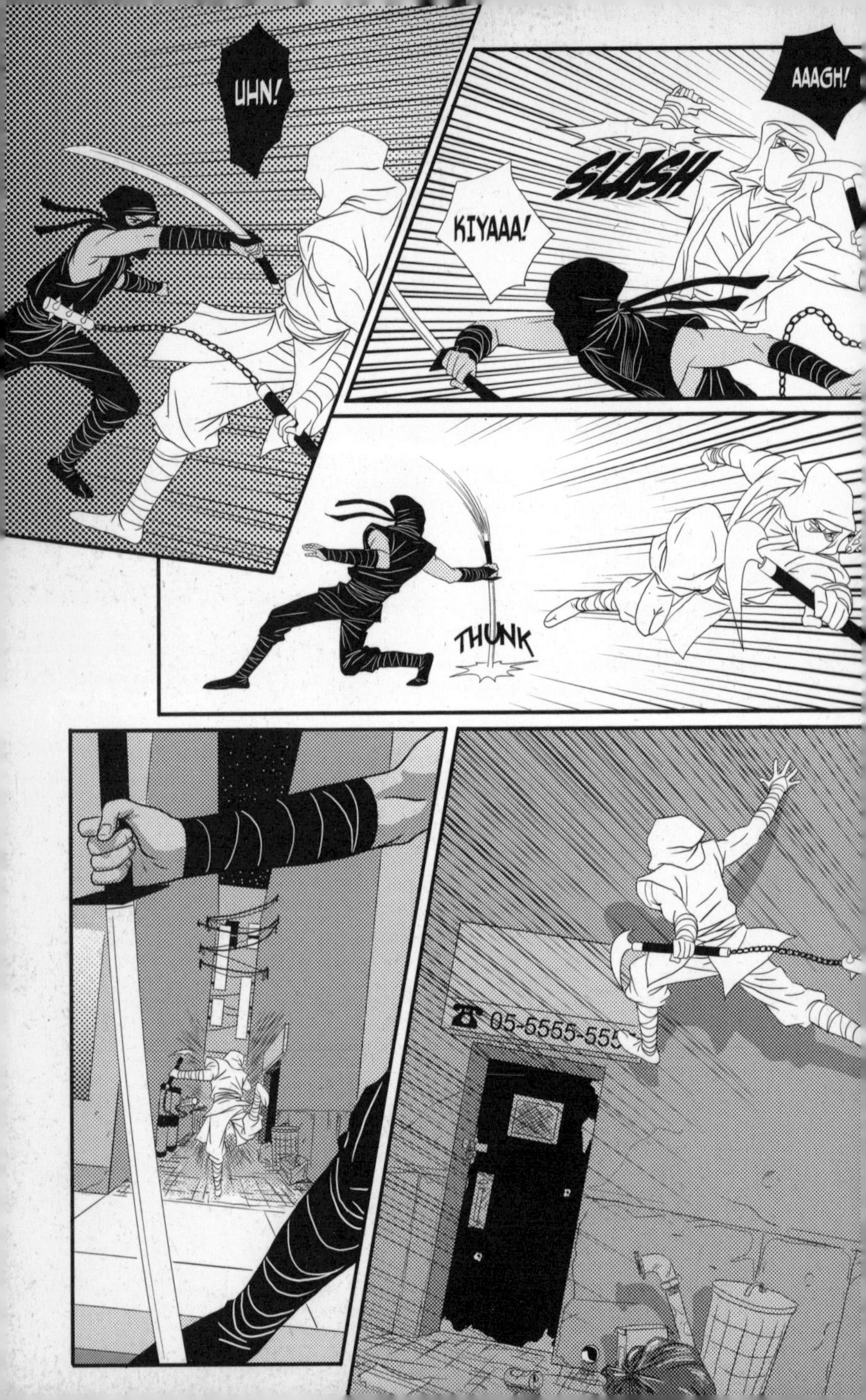
UHN!
AAAGH!
KIYAAA!
SLASH
THUNK
05-5555-555

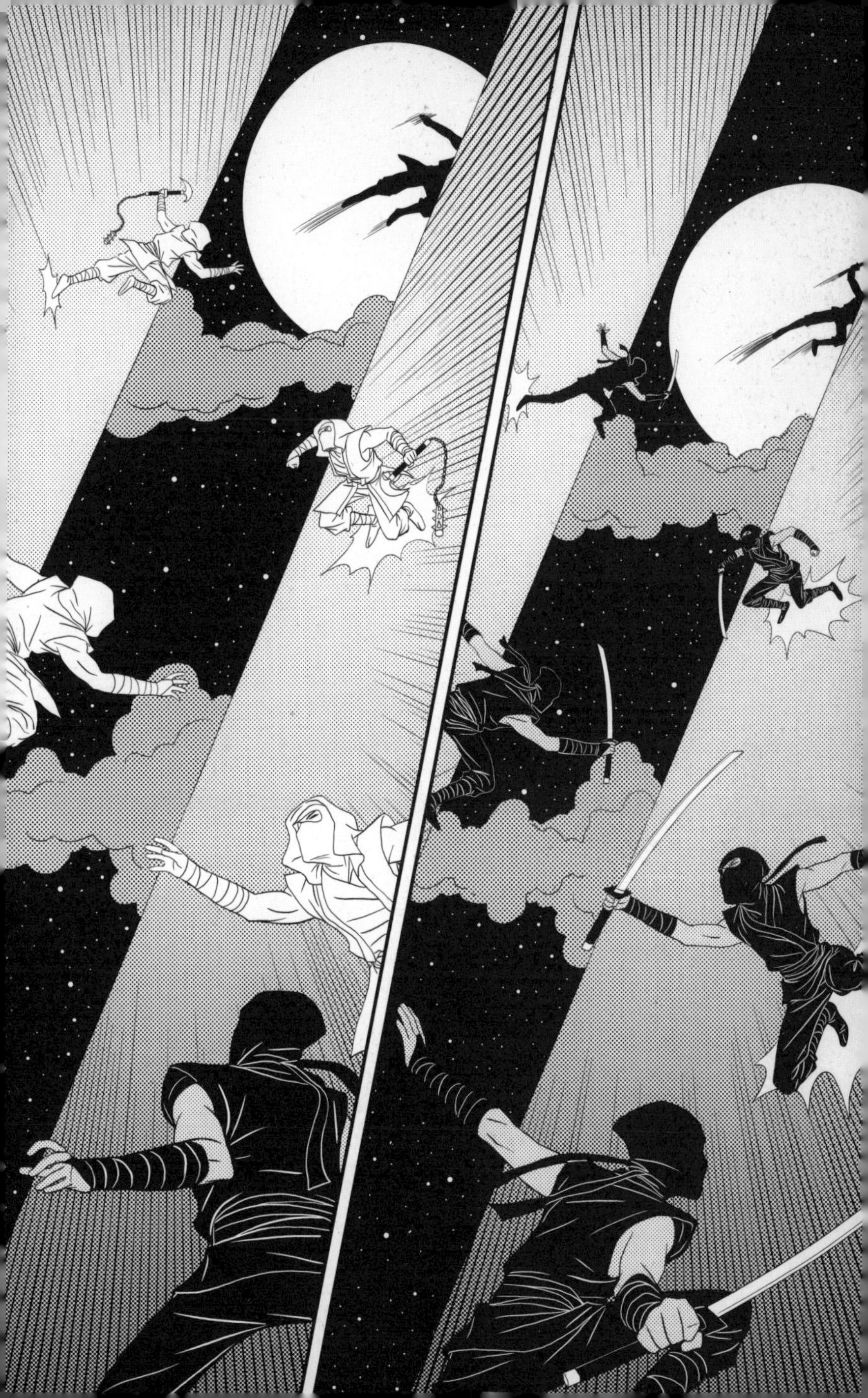

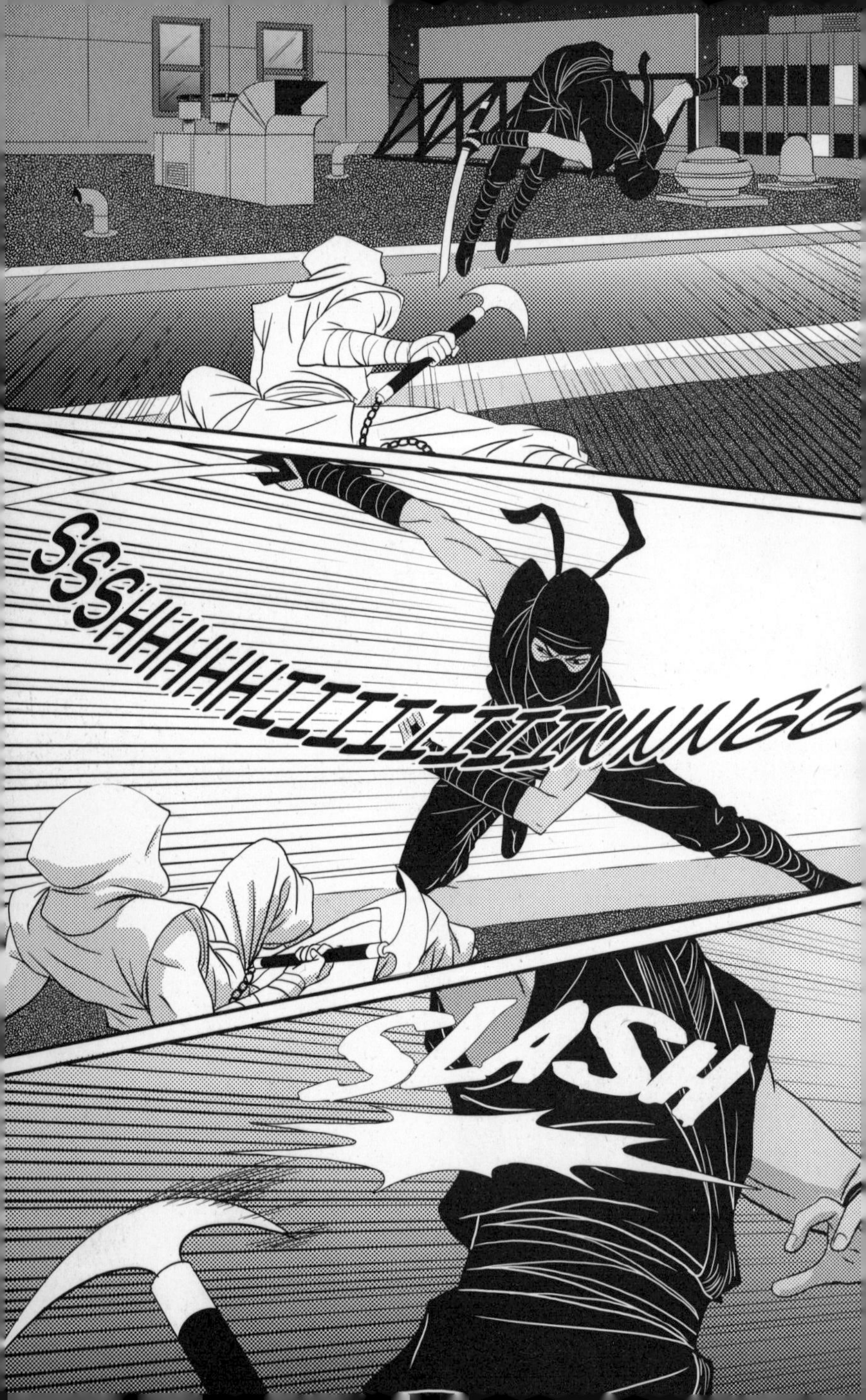
SSSHHHHHIIIIIIIIINNNNGG
SLASH

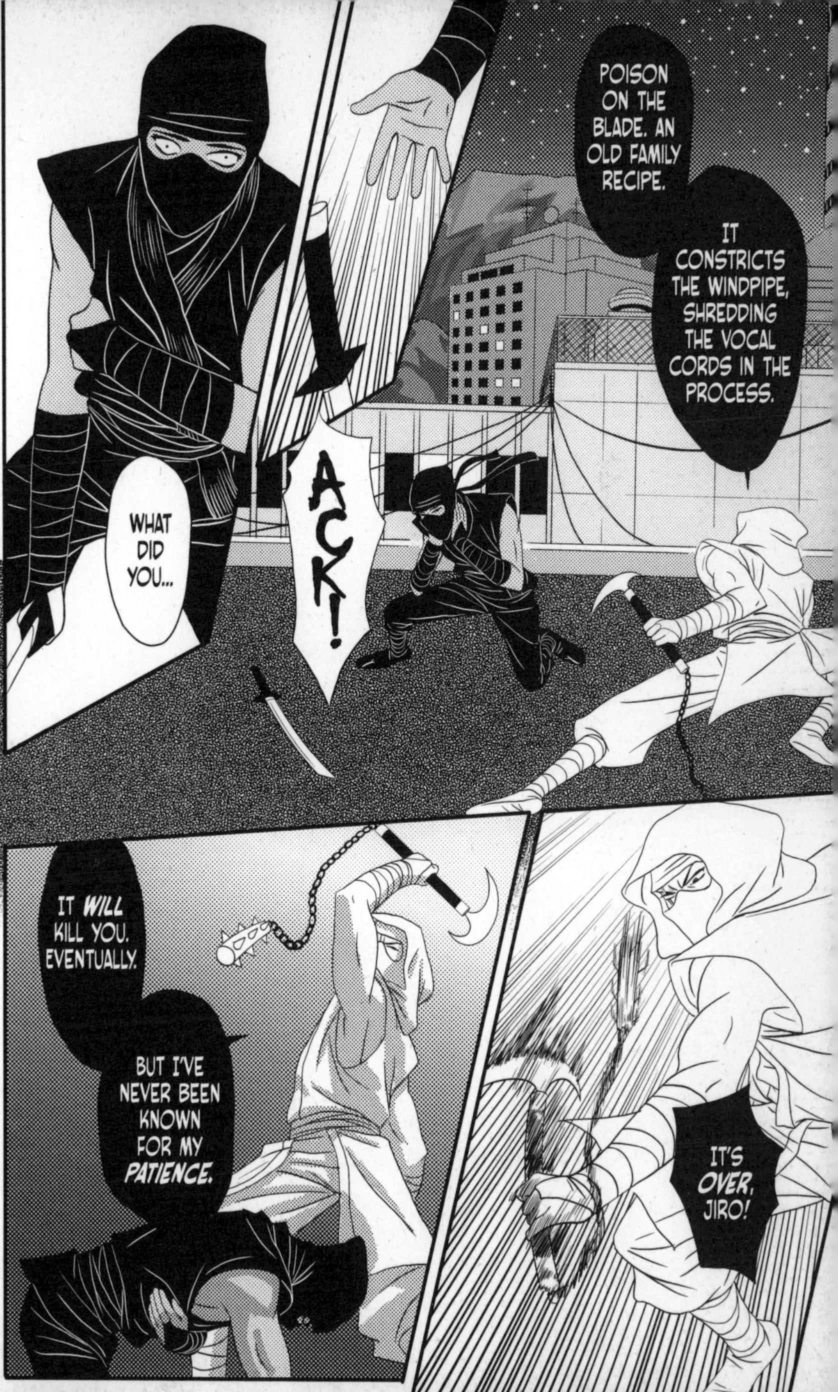
WHAT DID YOU...
ACK!
POISON ON THE BLADE. AN OLD FAMILY RECIPE.
IT CONSTRICTS THE WINDPIPE, SHREDDING THE VOCAL CORDS IN THE PROCESS.
IT *WILL* KILL YOU. EVENTUALLY.
BUT I'VE NEVER BEEN KNOWN FOR MY *PATIENCE.*
IT'S *OVER,* JIRO!

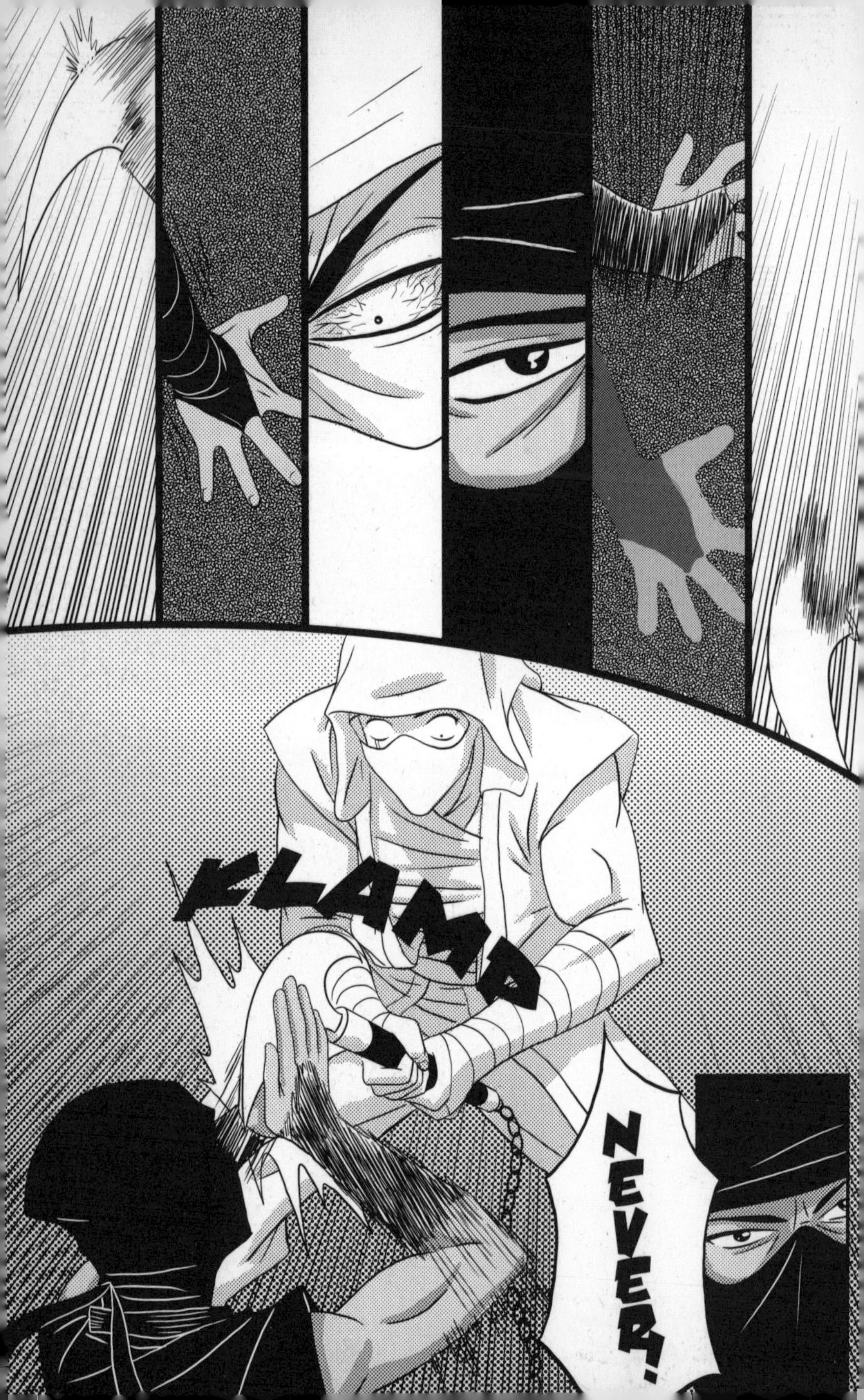
KLAMP
NEVER!

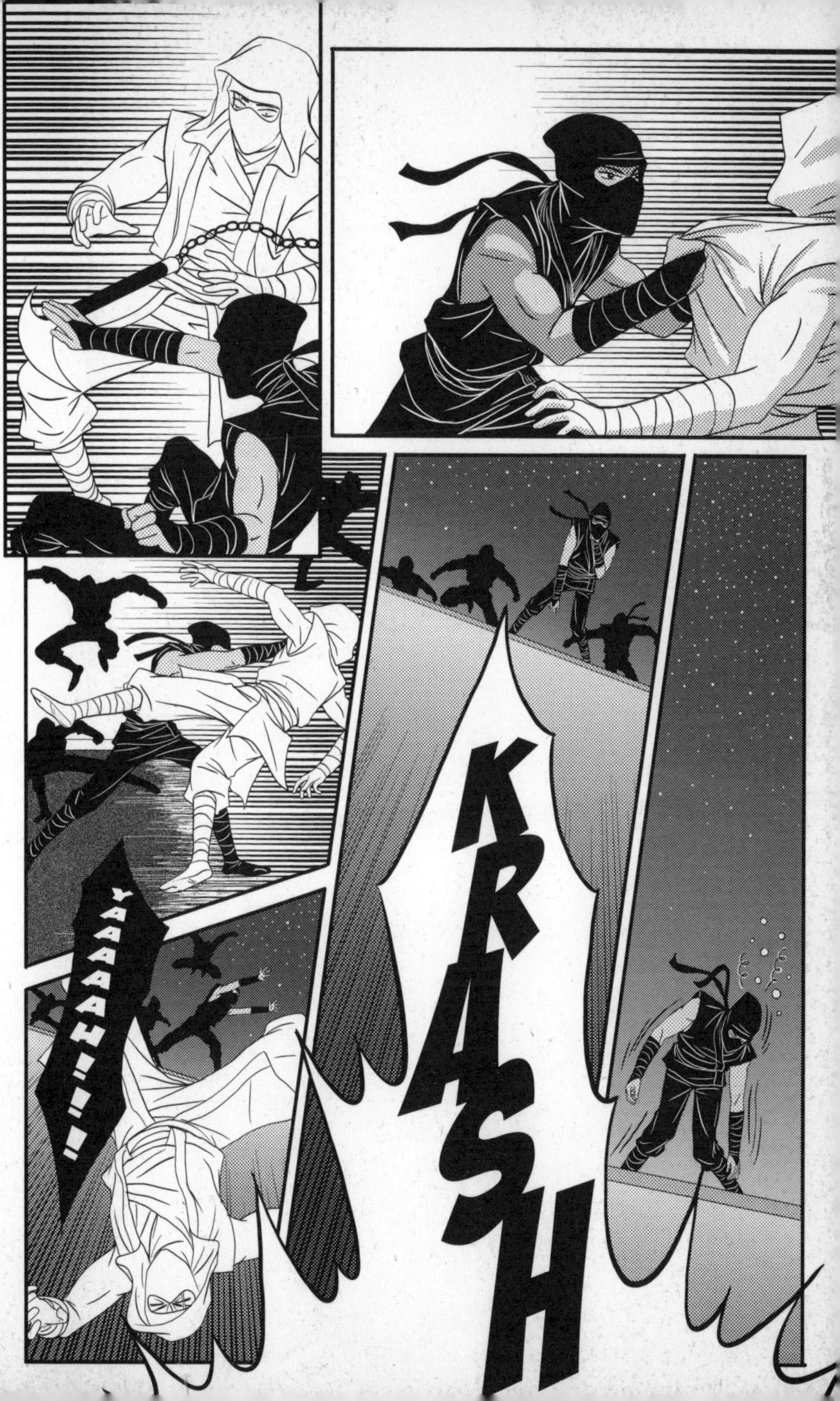
YAAAAAHH!!!!
KRASH

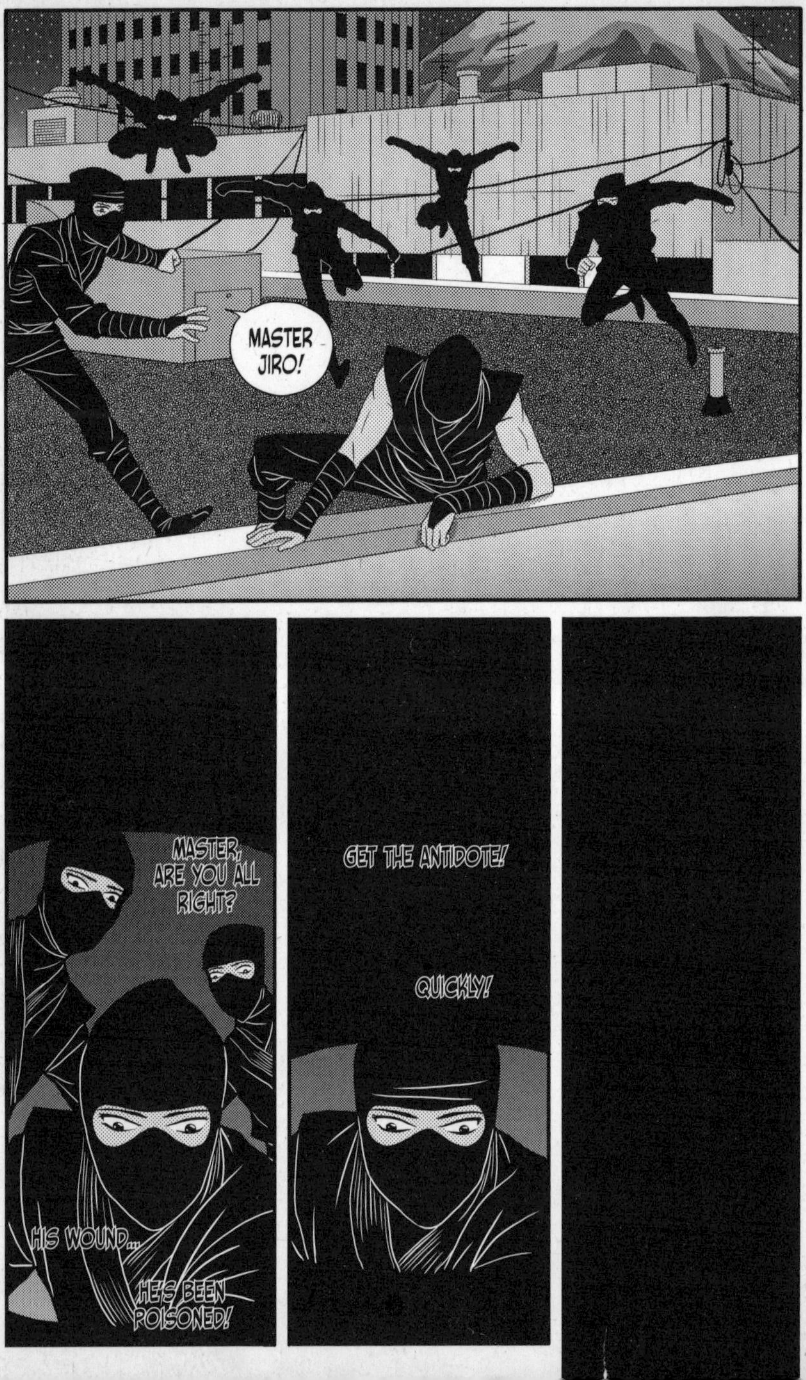
MASTER JIRO!
MASTER, ARE YOU ALL RIGHT?
HIS WOUND...
HE'S BEEN POISONED!
GET THE ANTIDOTE!
QUICKLY!

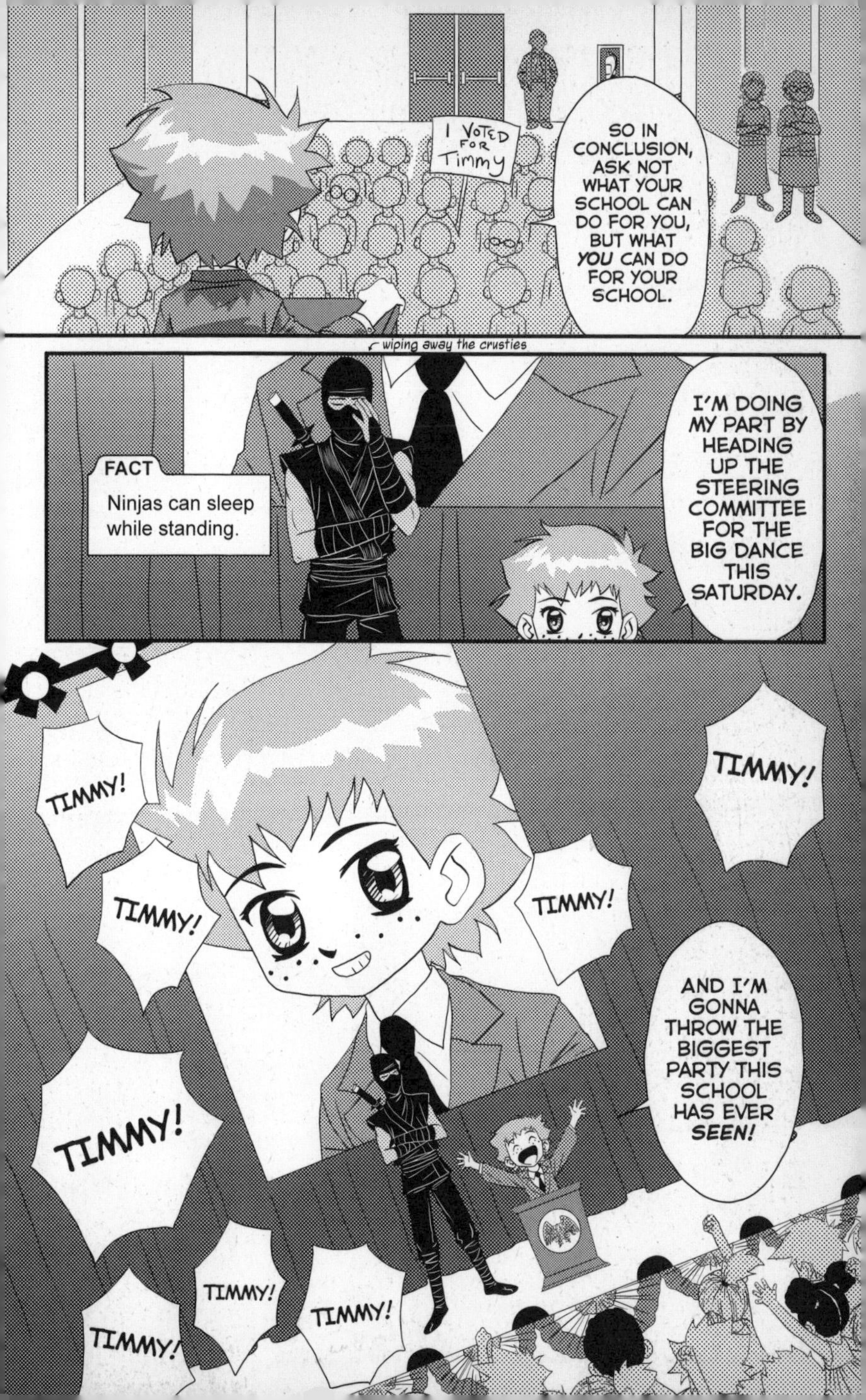
I VOTED FOR Timmy
SO IN CONCLUSION, ASK NOT WHAT YOUR SCHOOL CAN DO FOR YOU, BUT WHAT *YOU* CAN DO FOR YOUR SCHOOL.
wiping away the crusties
FACT
Ninjas can sleep while standing.
I'M DOING MY PART BY HEADING UP THE STEERING COMMITTEE FOR THE BIG DANCE THIS SATURDAY.
TIMMY!
TIMMY!
TIMMY!
TIMMY!
AND I'M GONNA THROW THE BIGGEST PARTY THIS SCHOOL HAS EVER *SEEN!*
TIMMY!
TIMMY!
TIMMY!
TIMMY!

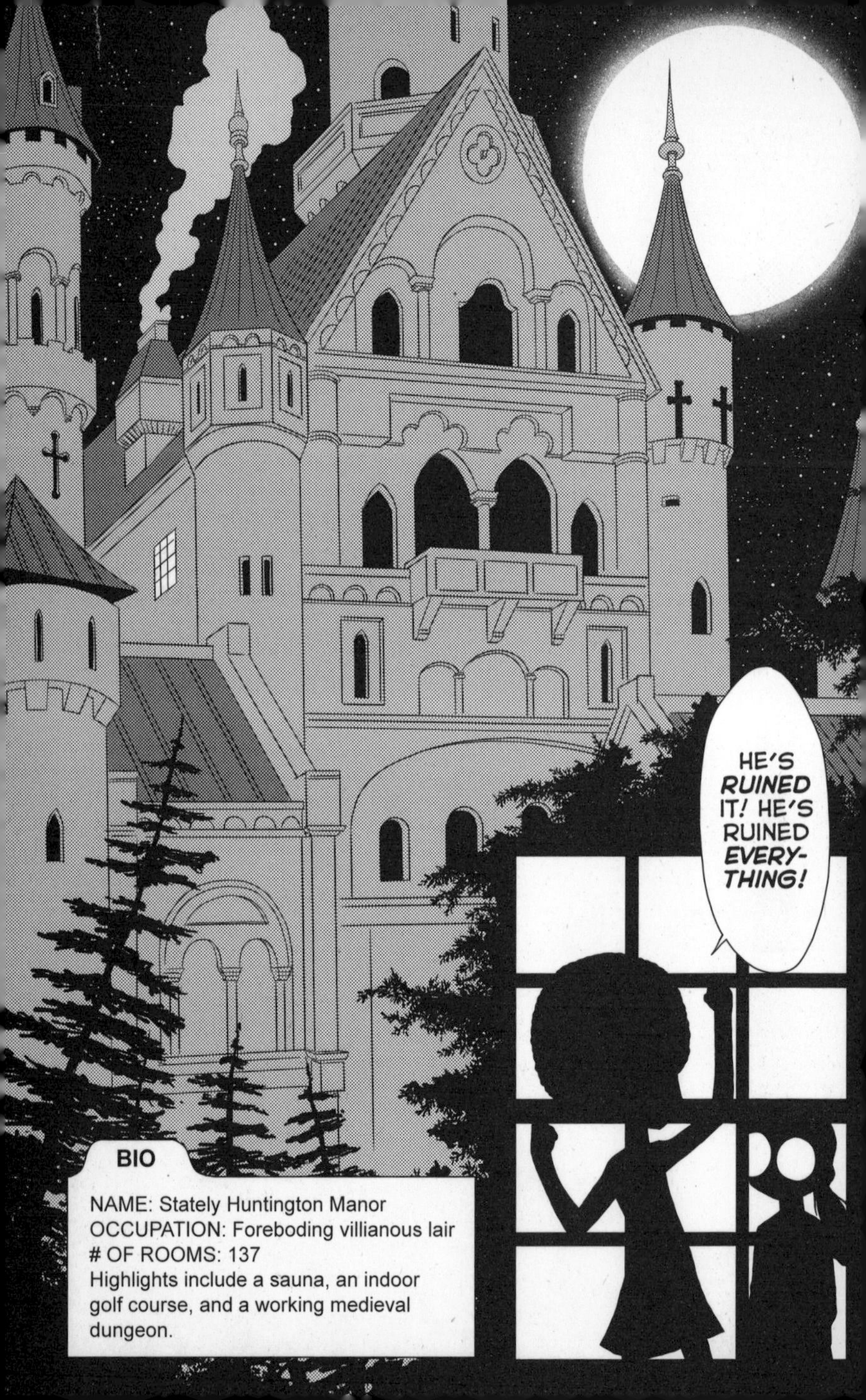
HE'S RUINED IT! HE'S RUINED EVERYTHING!
BIO
NAME: Stately Huntington Manor
OCCUPATION: Foreboding villianous lair
OF ROOMS: 137
Highlights include a sauna, an indoor golf course, and a working medieval dungeon.

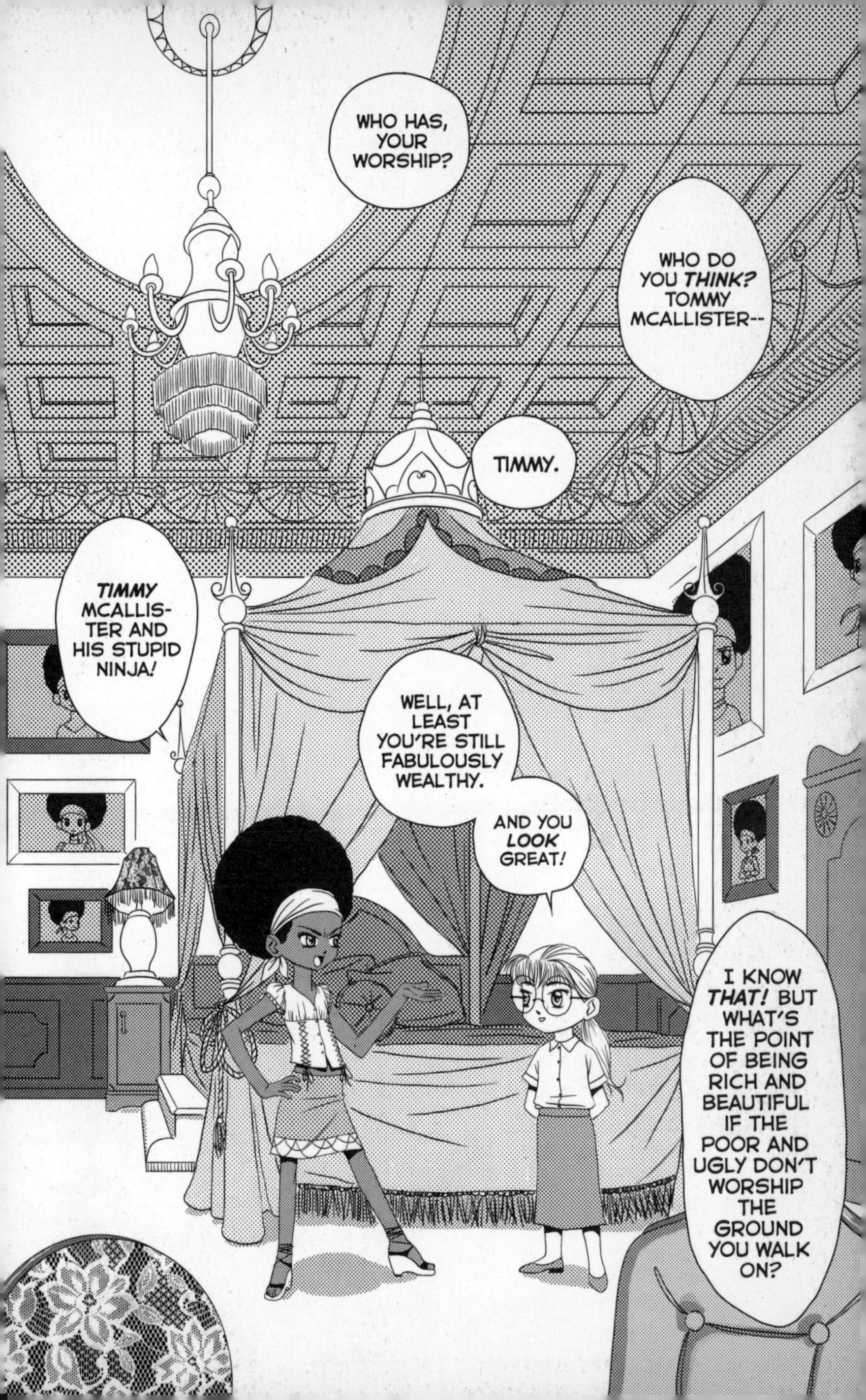
WHO HAS, YOUR WORSHIP?
WHO DO YOU *THINK?* TOMMY MCALLISTER--
TIMMY.
TIMMY MCALLISTER AND HIS STUPID NINJA!
WELL, AT LEAST YOU'RE STILL FABULOUSLY WEALTHY.
AND YOU *LOOK* GREAT!
I KNOW *THAT!* BUT WHAT'S THE POINT OF BEING RICH AND BEAUTIFUL IF THE POOR AND UGLY DON'T WORSHIP THE GROUND YOU WALK ON?

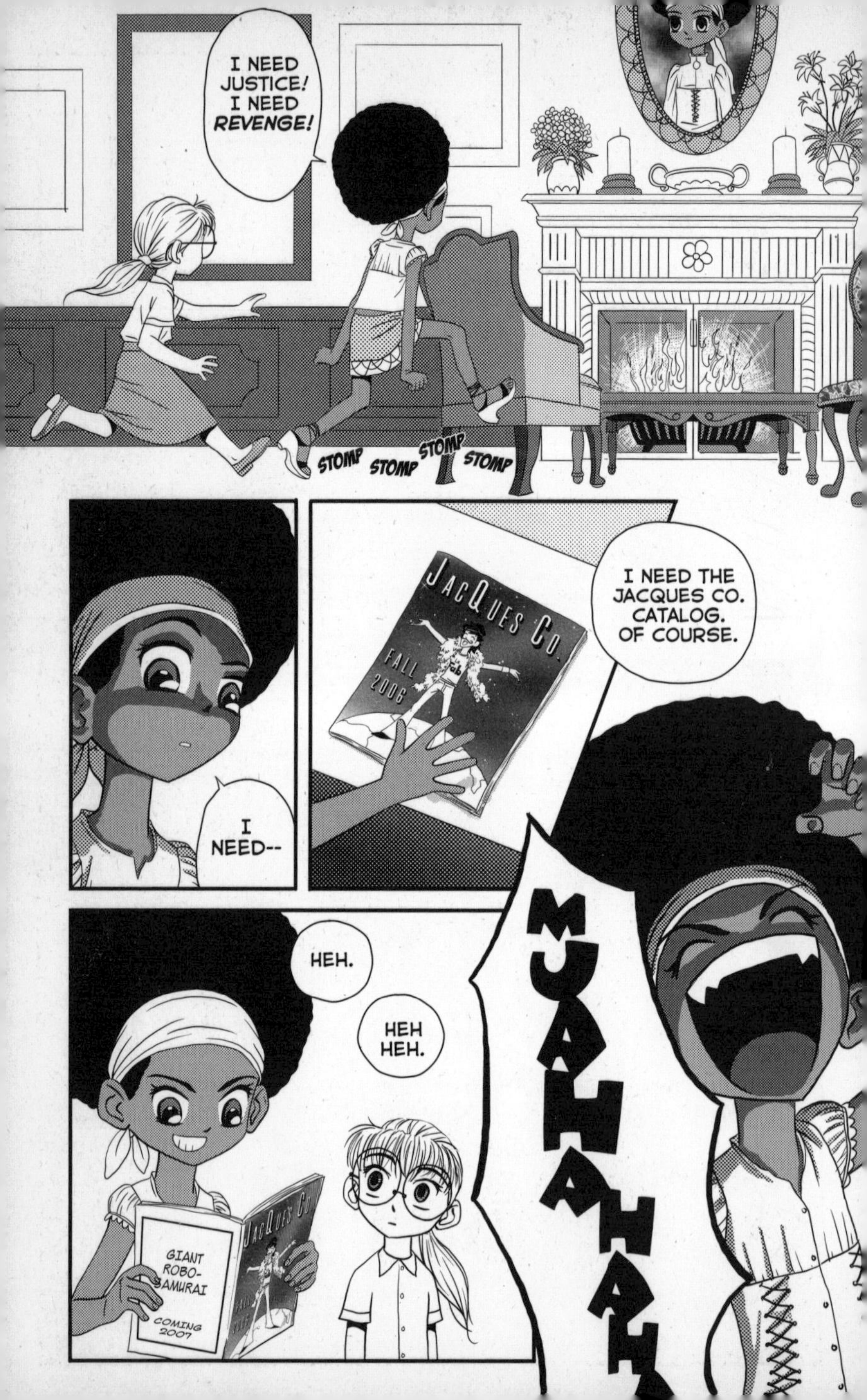
I NEED JUSTICE! I NEED REVENGE!
STOMP STOMP STOMP STOMP
I NEED--
JACQUES CO.
FALL 2006
I NEED THE JACQUES CO. CATALOG. OF COURSE.
HEH.
HEH HEH.
JACQUES CO.
GIANT ROBO-SAMURAI
COMING 2007
MUAHAHAHA

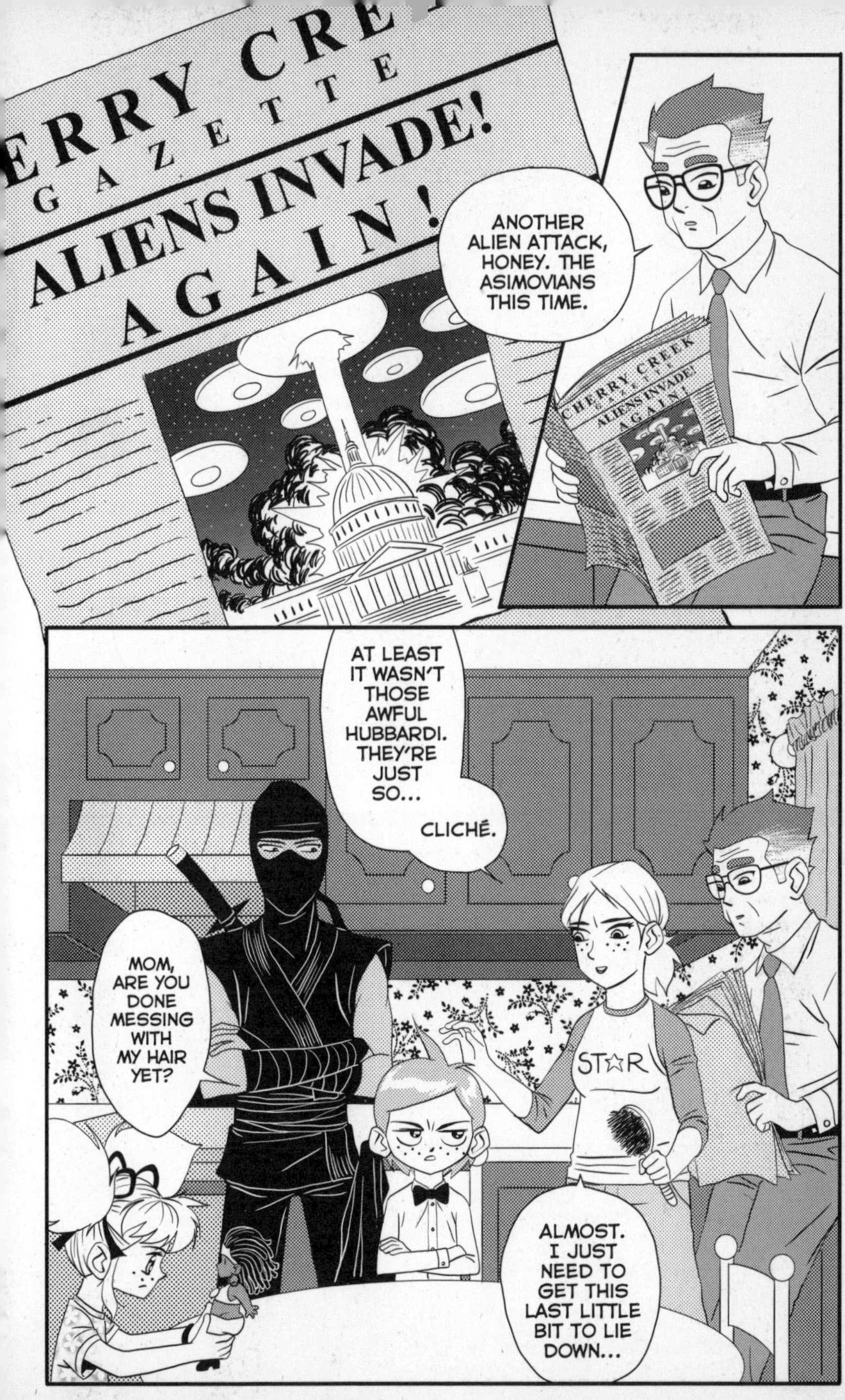
ERRY CRE
GAZETTE
ALIENS INVADE!
AGAIN!
ANOTHER ALIEN ATTACK, HONEY. THE ASIMOVIANS THIS TIME.
AT LEAST IT WASN'T THOSE AWFUL HUBBARDI. THEY'RE JUST SO...
CLICHÉ.
MOM, ARE YOU DONE MESSING WITH MY HAIR YET?
STAR
ALMOST. I JUST NEED TO GET THIS LAST LITTLE BIT TO LIE DOWN...

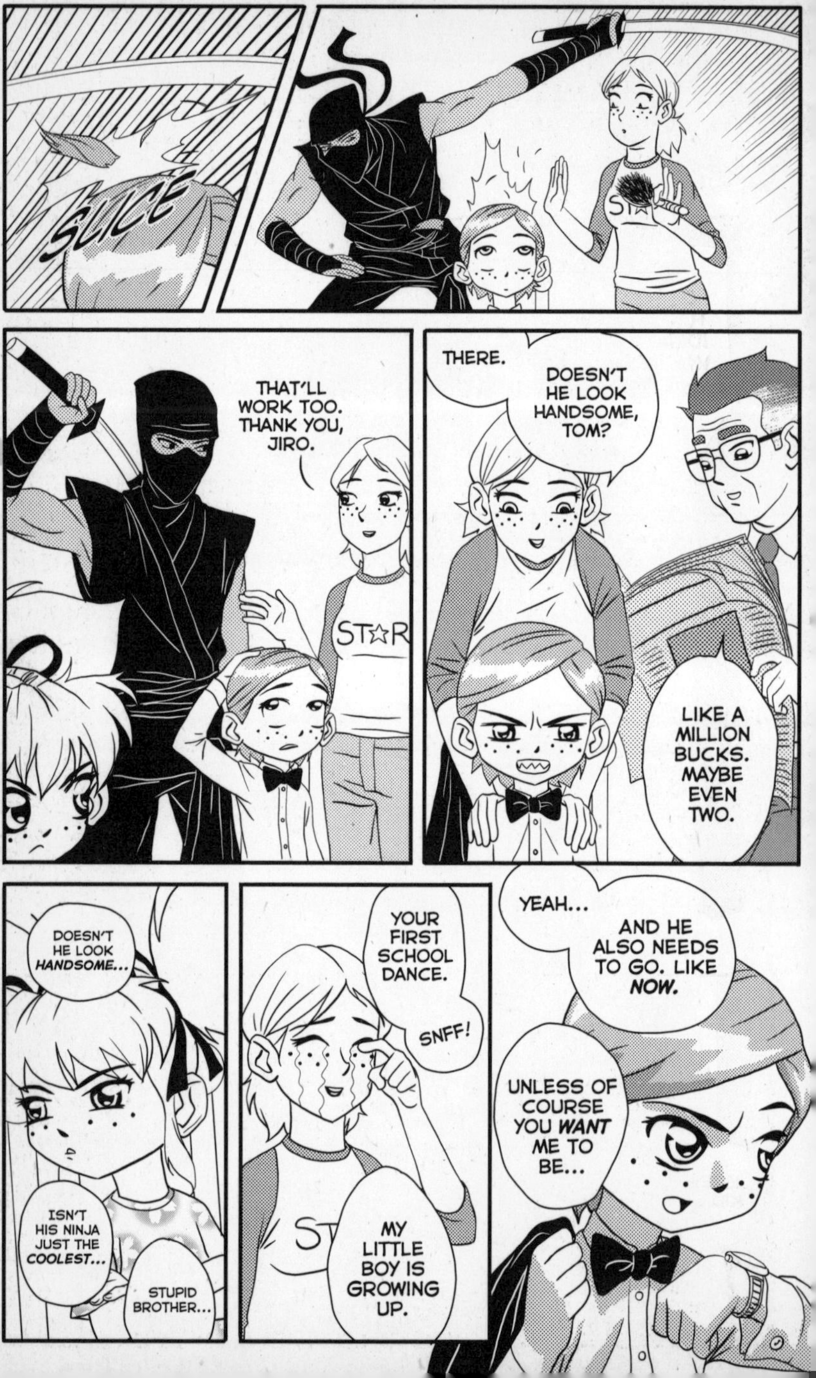
SLICE
THAT'LL WORK TOO. THANK YOU, JIRO.
THERE.
DOESN'T HE LOOK HANDSOME, TOM?
ST☆R
LIKE A MILLION BUCKS. MAYBE EVEN TWO.
DOESN'T HE LOOK *HANDSOME...*
ISN'T HIS NINJA JUST THE *COOLEST...*
STUPID BROTHER...
YOUR FIRST SCHOOL DANCE.
SNFF!
MY LITTLE BOY IS GROWING UP.
YEAH...
AND HE ALSO NEEDS TO GO. LIKE *NOW.*
UNLESS OF COURSE YOU *WANT* ME TO BE...

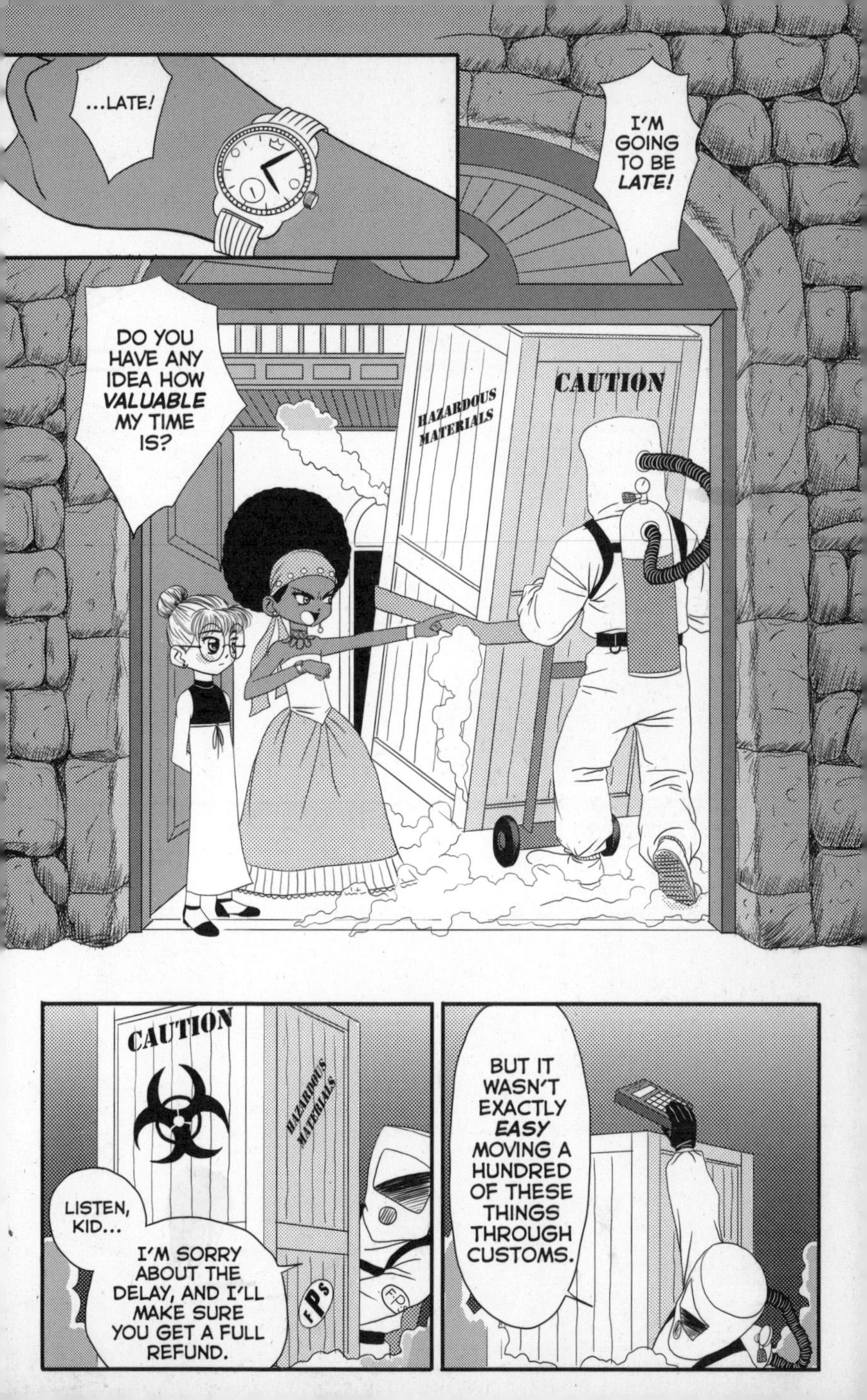
...LATE!
I'M GOING TO BE LATE!
DO YOU HAVE ANY IDEA HOW VALUABLE MY TIME IS?
CAUTION
HAZARDOUS MATERIALS
CAUTION
HAZARDOUS MATERIALS
LISTEN, KID...
I'M SORRY ABOUT THE DELAY, AND I'LL MAKE SURE YOU GET A FULL REFUND.
BUT IT WASN'T EXACTLY EASY MOVING A HUNDRED OF THESE THINGS THROUGH CUSTOMS.

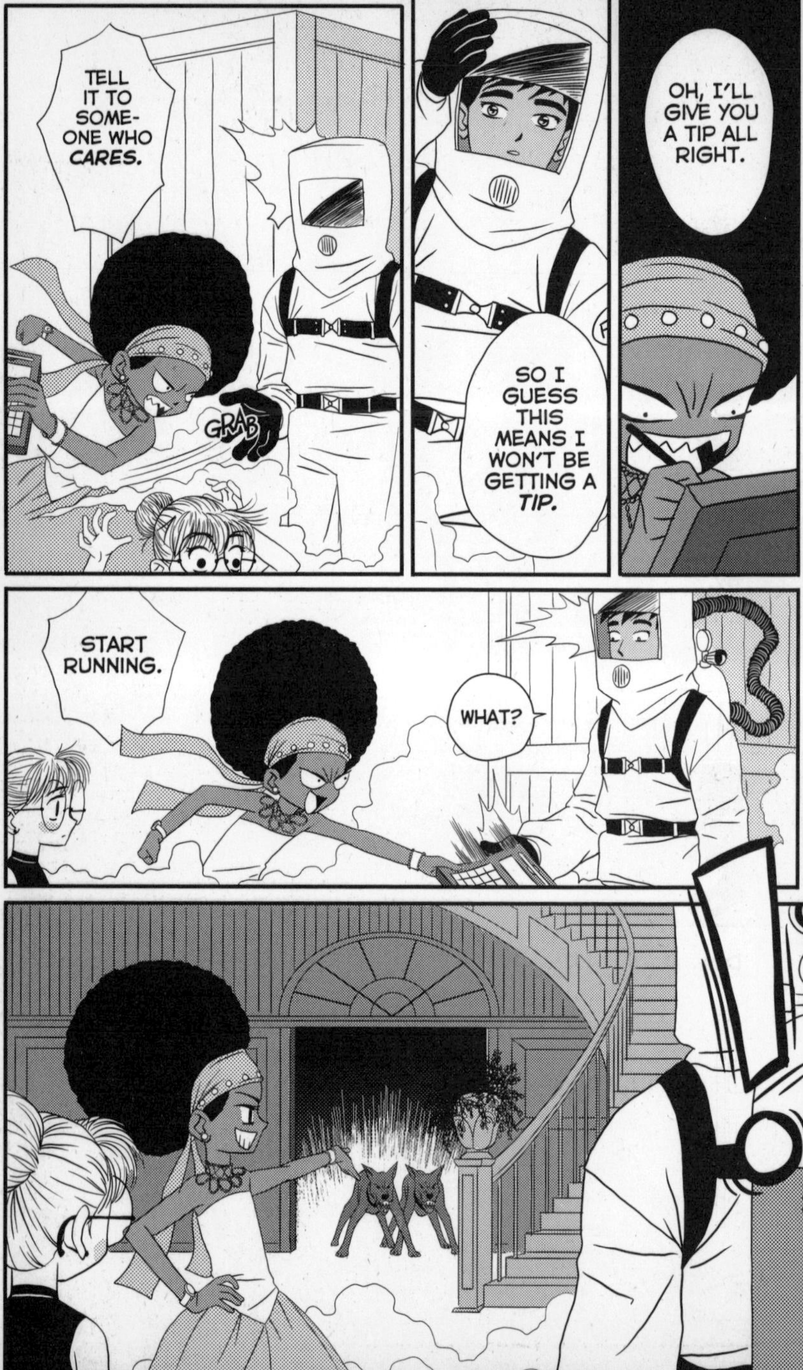
TELL IT TO SOME-ONE WHO CARES.
GRAB
SO I GUESS THIS MEANS I WON'T BE GETTING A TIP.
OH, I'LL GIVE YOU A TIP ALL RIGHT.
START RUNNING.
WHAT?

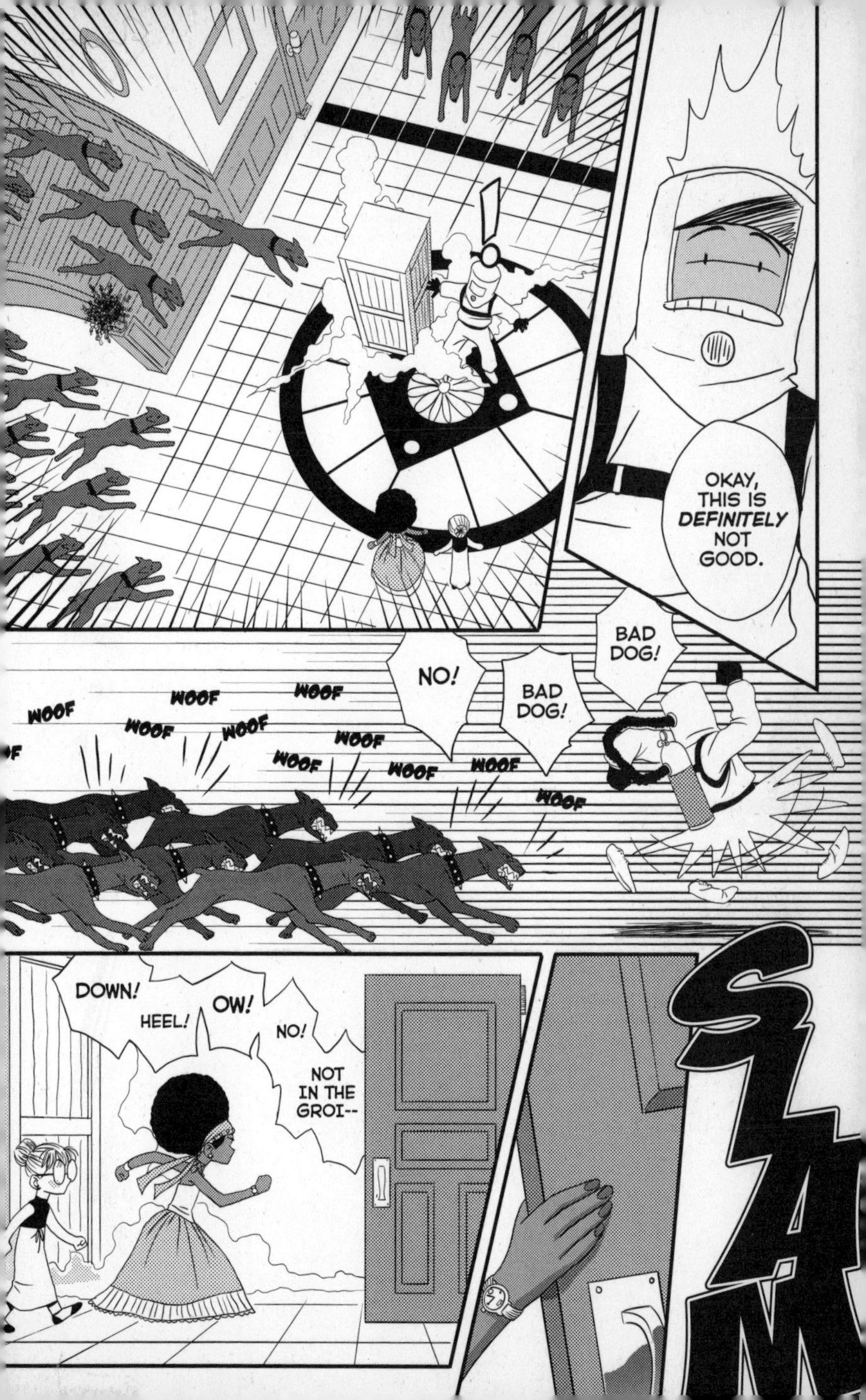
OKAY, THIS IS *DEFINITELY* NOT GOOD.
WOOF
WOOF
WOOF
WOOF
WOOF
WOOF
WOOF
WOOF
WOOF
WOOF
NO!
BAD DOG!
BAD DOG!
DOWN!
HEEL!
OW!
NO!
NOT IN THE GROI--

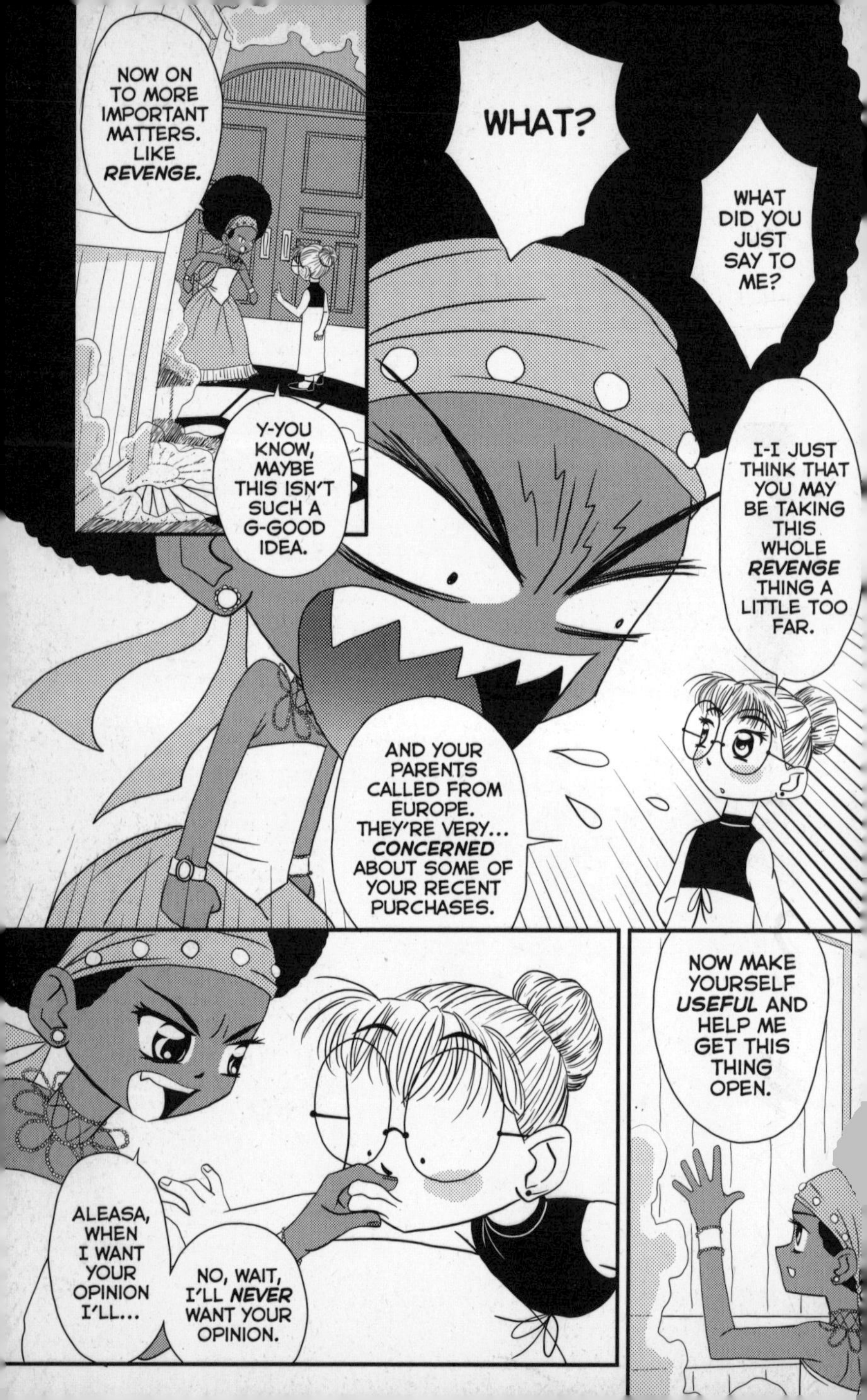
NOW ON TO MORE IMPORTANT MATTERS. LIKE *REVENGE.*
Y-YOU KNOW, MAYBE THIS ISN'T SUCH A G-GOOD IDEA.
WHAT?
WHAT DID YOU JUST SAY TO ME?
I-I JUST THINK THAT YOU MAY BE TAKING THIS WHOLE *REVENGE* THING A LITTLE TOO FAR.
AND YOUR PARENTS CALLED FROM EUROPE. THEY'RE VERY... *CONCERNED* ABOUT SOME OF YOUR RECENT PURCHASES.
ALEASA, WHEN I WANT YOUR OPINION I'LL...
NO, WAIT, I'LL *NEVER* WANT YOUR OPINION.
NOW MAKE YOURSELF *USEFUL* AND HELP ME GET THIS THING OPEN.

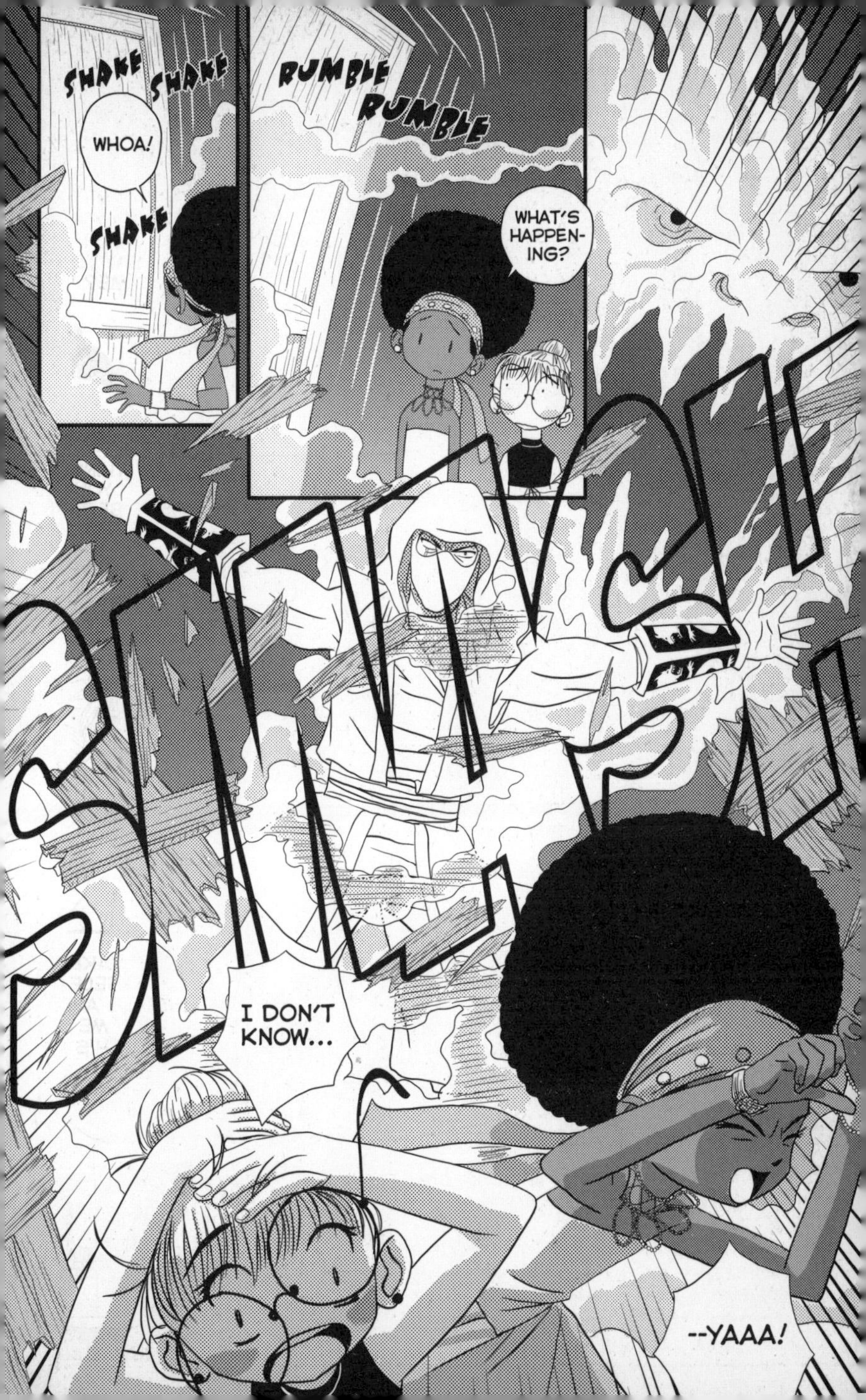
SHAKE SHAKE
WHOA!
SHAKE
RUMBLE RUMBLE
WHAT'S HAPPEN-ING?
SMASH
I DON'T KNOW...
--YAAA!

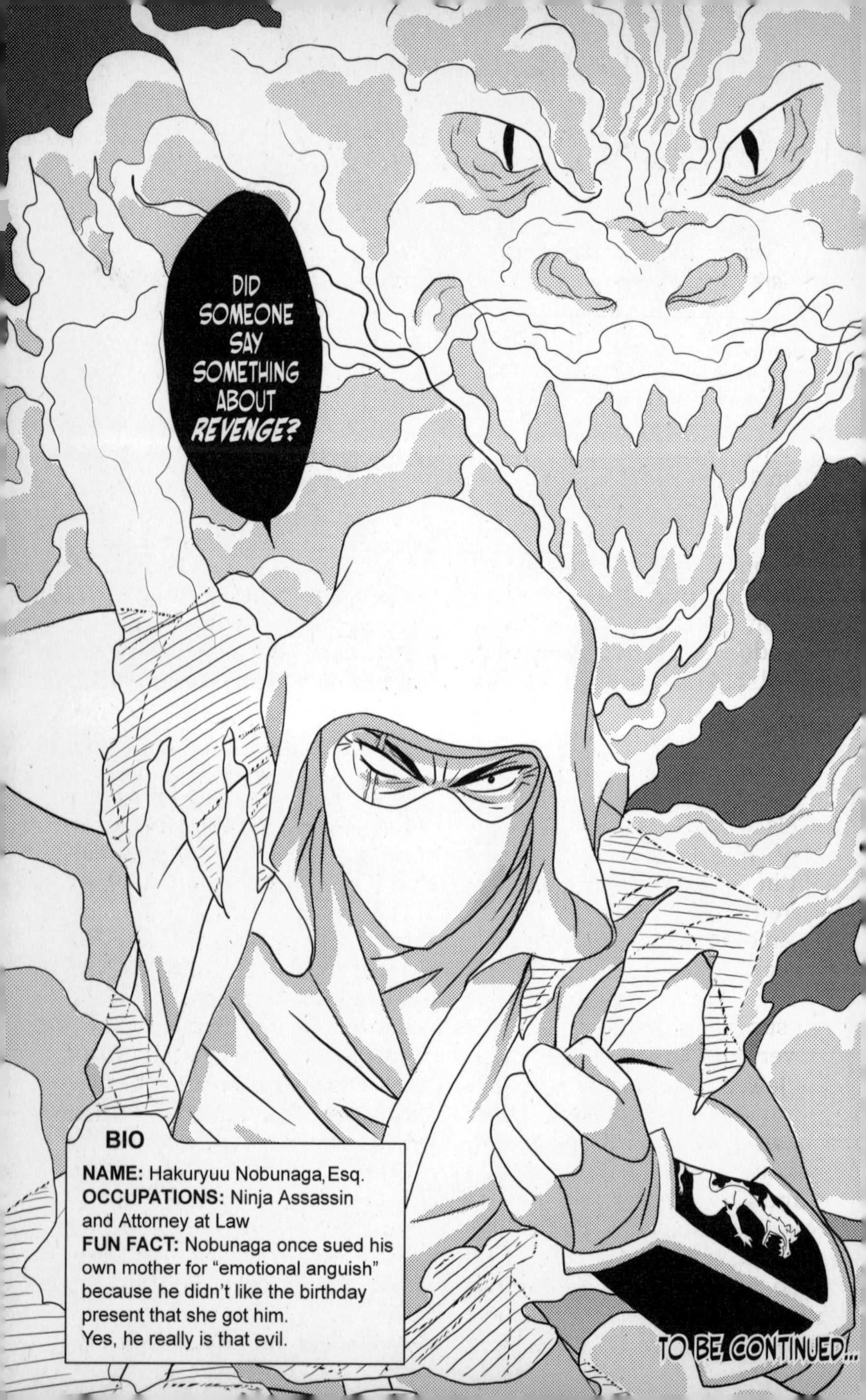
DID SOMEONE SAY SOMETHING ABOUT REVENGE?
BIO
NAME: Hakuryuu Nobunaga, Esq.
OCCUPATIONS: Ninja Assassin and Attorney at Law
FUN FACT: Nobunaga once sued his own mother for "emotional anguish" because he didn't like the birthday present that she got him.
Yes, he really is that evil.
TO BE CONTINUED...

SILENT BUT DEADLY

*Everyone knows that ninja are awesome. But some ninja are
more awesomer than others. And the ninja of Clan Yoshida
are the awesomest of all. This is their story in all its awesomity.*

BY CHARLES EASTMAN-LAIRD

.....

It was a balmy Autumn day in 1974 when I had my first encounter with a ninja. I was a sixth-year student at the Wackford Squeers School for Boys in Sussex, and my class had gone on a field trip to the Tower of London. As fate would have it, the evil shinobi Hakuryuu Katashi chose that same day to attempt a theft of the most valuable collection of shiny trinkets and baubles in existence: the Crown Jewels of England. Which, as every Englishman knows, are kept in the Tower's Jewel House where they're watched over day and night by the ever-vigilant Tower Guard.

Yet such was Katashi's skill at thievery that he was able to nick the Jewels without the guards even noticing they were gone. Disguised as an Arab potentate, Katashi planned to make his escape via the front gate as if he were just another tourist. And he would have gotten away with it too if it weren't for Yoshida Daisuke and his American blood brother Tarantino Jones, who is famous for being the only samurai to ever sport an afro.

The two warriors were in town to play Rosencrantz and Guildenstern in the Royal Shakespeare Company's famous production of *Hamlet* when Daisuke had a fearful premonition that bade him journey to the Tower.

It was there that he found his old enemy Katashi in the midst of an almost-successful getaway. Daisuke's ninja senses allowed him to see through the thieving shinobi's disguise, leaving Katashi no choice but to try and fight his way to freedom. Katashi was the White Dragon Clan's most skilled warrior, but he knew he was no match for both Daisuke and Tarantino. So he did what White Dragon ninja always do: he cheated. At Katashi's command, a dozen Clan Hakuryuu warriors appeared from out of out thin air in their trademark clouds of white smoke. The battle was joined.

Daisuke and Tarantino emerged

NINJA

triumphant, of course. The Crown Jewels were recovered and Katashi fell to his death from the top of London Bridge. Actually, he didn't all-the-way die. He just sort of died and then got better as evil ninja are wont to do. Still, it was a resounding victory for the forces of good, one that I got to witness firsthand. Afterwards, the two victorious heroes signed autographs for me and my classmates and gave us all free passes to their show. It was the greatest day of my young life.

As a rule, ninja don't act this way. They prefer to retreat back into the shadows once their job is done. Not the Yoshida. They may be ninja, but they also know how to party. This dichotomy – silent and serene one minute, fun-loving and flamboyant the next – has made Clan Yoshida the most famous and beloved ninja clan in the world. Though this wasn't always the case.

Long before they were ninja, the revered Yoshida ancestors were simple farmers. Hence the name Yoshida, which literally means "good field." A kindhearted and generous people, the Yoshida lived peaceful lives tucked away in the mountainous Iga province of ancient Japan. They would tend their crops during the day, and at night they would entertain each other through painting, calligraphy, theater, poetry and music. The cultivation of artistic talent has remained a cornerstone of Clan Yoshida training to this day, a way of balancing the scales of karma. For as the old Yoshida proverb says, "History judges a man by what he creates, not by what he destroys. Unless he should also destroy all the historians. Then history won't judge him at all."

Speaking of history, it was nearly 1,000 years ago that the Yoshida Clan made the transition from farmers to ninja warriors. A great army that rode under the banner of a White Dragon was sweeping across the land, destroying all in its path. Its legions numbered in the tens of thousands and its generals wielded powerful magic that made them nigh-invincible on the field of battle. Rather than meet such a formidable enemy head-on, the various tribes and peoples of the Iga province abandoned their villages to hide in the surrounding forest. From there they waged a guerilla campaign against the White Dragon army, but they lacked the skills or the numbers to be anything more than a minor annoyance – the military equivalent of a pebble in one's shoe.

Enter the *tengu,* wily forest spirits that had been driven to near extinction by the White Dragons. They taught the men of Iga the basic principles of what would come to be known as *ninjutsu,* the art of going unseen. With these new skills at their disposal, the men of Iga – led by the warriors of Clan Yoshida – dealt a devastating defeat to the White Dragons. Their power broken, the Dragons had to adopt the methods of their enemies and become a ninja clan in their own right. This led to a lucrative second career for the Dragons as international mercenaries, selling their talents to the highest bidder in order to finance their own plans for world domination. And just like before, the only ones capable of standing in their way were the shinobi of Clan Yoshida.

Thus began an epic blood feud that has lasted the better part of a millennium. Over the centuries the clans have fought on all seven continents, beneath the sea in the lost city of Atlantis, and even on the surface of the moon where a Yoshida ninja prevented the assassination of Neil Armstrong and Buzz Aldrin by a White Dragon agent in the employ of the Soviet Union. Yet for all their sound and fury, the battles signified nothing. The clans were locked in an eternal stalemate – yin forever balanced by yang. A long twilight struggle with no end in sight, etc., etc. Then a new variable was introduced that completely changed the equation: a variable named Yoshida Jiro.

Driven by revenge, Jiro almost single-handedly reduced the entire Hakuryuu organization to a shadow of its former self and then slew the clan *jounin* (literally "high ninja") Nobunaga – who as of this writing remains dead – in single combat. His thirst for vengeance quenched, Jiro soon realized how meaningless his life had become. He had lost everything that he ever truly cared about and had become an empty vessel filled with nothing but rage. He wanted to learn how to love once again – to have fun once again.

So he sold himself into indentured servitude to a random American child as part of a promotional contest for the inaugural issue of the Jacques Co. toy catalog. It was an unorthodox approach to say the least, but that's just how Jiro rolls. For his sake, and for the sake of Clan Yoshida, I pray he succeeds.

ABOUT THE AUTHOR:
Charles Eastman-Laird is a distinguished Professor of Ninjology at Oxford University and the author of *Ninjas: Quite Possibly the Coolest Thing Ever* (Completely Fake Press) from which this article is adapted.

VOL. 2 PREVIEW

NOW THAT FELICITY HAS HER OWN *EVIL* MAIL ORDER NINJA--ACTUALLY, SHE HAS MORE LIKE 100 OF THEM--LIFE IN CHERRY CREEK IS ABOUT TO GET A LOT MORE...INTERESTING. BECAUSE FELICITY DOESN'T JUST WANT REVENGE ON OUR INTREPID HEROES, SHE WANTS TO ENSLAVE THE ENTIRE FREAKIN' TOWN. AND WHEN JIRO FALLS IN BATTLE, TIMMY MUST FIND THE COURAGE TO STAND ALONE AGAINST THE FORCES OF EVIL AND UNCOOLNESS.

SO GET READY FOR A WHOLE NEW LEVEL OF OFF-THE-HOOK NINJA ACTION AND OFF-THE-WALL NINJA COMEDY IN THE NEXT PULSE-POUNDING, SENSES-SHATTERING, SIDE-SPLITTING CHAPTER IN THE *MAIL ORDER NINJA* SAGA...
TIMMY STRIKES BACK!

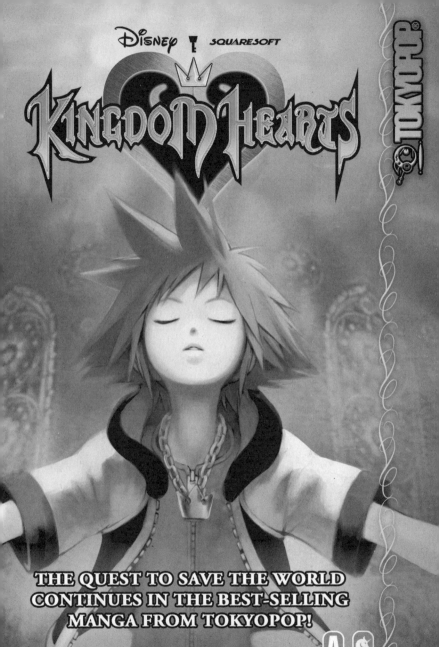

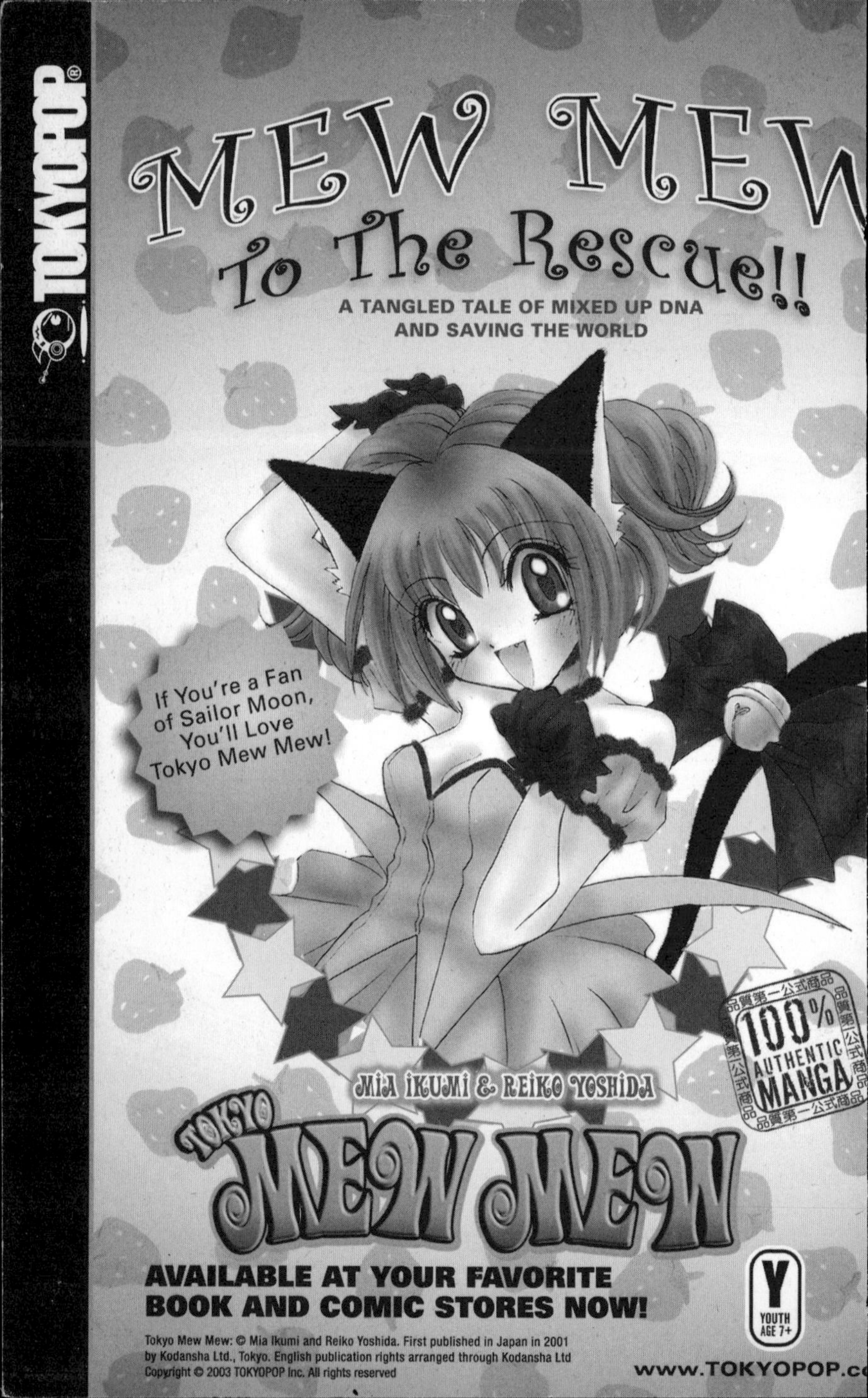

TOKYOPOP
MEW MEW To The Rescue!!
A TANGLED TALE OF MIXED UP DNA AND SAVING THE WORLD
If You're a Fan of Sailor Moon, You'll Love Tokyo Mew Mew!
100% AUTHENTIC MANGA
品質第一公式商品
MIA IKUMI & REIKO YOSHIDA
TOKYO MEW MEW
AVAILABLE AT YOUR FAVORITE BOOK AND COMIC STORES NOW!
Y YOUTH AGE 7+
Tokyo Mew Mew: © Mia Ikumi and Reiko Yoshida. First published in Japan in 2001 by Kodansha Ltd., Tokyo. English publication rights arranged through Kodansha Ltd Copyright © 2003 TOKYOPOP Inc. All rights reserved
www.TOKYOPOP.c